I0626393

## An Important Note

*Mr. Wrong* has been previously published under a different title and author name. I don't kid myself that my books are totally unforgettable, but I'd guess there aren't too many books about a woman pining for an ex-boyfriend while also falling for the soap opera star she's supposed to be spying on. So if that sounds familiar to you, you might have already read this book.

I think this revised version is a million times better than the previous one, but the basic story arc is the same, and if you don't care to repeat the experience, you should definitely return this book. I don't mind, really.

But you also might want to head over to tammilabrecque.com and sign up for my newsletter so I can let you know when the sequel is out.

Tammi
September 2018

# Mr. Wrong

A NEW YORK MINUTE
BOOK 1

## TAMMI LABRECQUE

© 2018 Tammi Labrecque
Happy Ever After, September 2018

*Previously published as Midnight Confessions.*
*Please see "An Important Note" for more details.*

This is a work of fiction. Any resemblance to actual people, places, institutions, websites, or soap opera fanbases is entirely coincidental.

All rights reserved. No part of this book may be reproduced, in any form, by any means electronic or mechanical, including but not limited to photocopying, recording, or any information storage or retrieval system currently in use or yet to be devised.

This ebook is licensed for your personal use and may not be re-sold or given away to others. If you would like to share this book with another person, please purchase a copy for that person. If you did not purchase this book, or it was not purchased for your use, then you have an unauthorized copy. Please go to your favorite ebook retailer and purchase your own copy. Thank you for respecting my hard work and copyright.

ISBN: 978-0-9982127-6-0

*For Jess*
*AAC/WLC/S&C/SFF/MBFan*

# Chapter One

THE ONLY REASON I even agreed to come to Drew's engagement party was so I could see if his fiancée is prettier than me.

This may not paint me in the most flattering light, but I'm not going to start lying this early in my story. Maybe later. I'll be sure to let you know.

At any rate, it's also important to note that Kari talked me into it. She said we'd come have a look and I'd feel better. "Jenna," she said, "you have to face this. You'll feel better."

That's classic Kari. Unlike me, she's fearless.

So we're at Jacks Wild on 5th Street. Kari and I are standing at the bar, and the cool air from the open doorway is a constant reminder that it's not summer anymore. I love fall, but it means winter is closing in. Knowing that Drew will ring in 2005 married to someone else is too depressing for words.

It doesn't help at all that the fiancée *is* prettier than me—gorgeous, in fact. All long legs and milky skin and acres of red hair.

I didn't even know that Drew liked redheads.

The fiancée's name is Gertrude. She goes by Trudi—with

an *i*. The invitation said *Hey! Drew and Trudi are getting married! Come celebrate with us.* I didn't feel much like celebrating when I first saw the invitation, and I still don't.

But here I am. Damn Kari.

"Jenna, there's no way this can last," Kari tells me emphatically. "She's his rebound, you know. Don't worry about it."

"Maybe, maybe not," I say. "This plan of yours doesn't seem to be working. He literally hasn't noticed I'm here."

"That's because he's an idiot," she says—which doesn't even make much sense, but Kari's been pretty hard on Drew this past year.

She pours the rest of her drink down her throat and waves the empty glass at the bartender. He's deep in conversation with some guy in a blue plaid shirt, but he sees her gesture and slides down the bar like Tom Cruise in *Cocktail*, only taller and better looking and Latino—so, not like Tom Cruise at all, really. Anyway, he mixes her another Cosmo, quick and precise in his movements, and lifts an eyebrow at me. I shake my head—I still have half of mine—and he heads back down to the other end of the bar to resume his conversation.

Turning away from Kari, I sip my Cosmo and glare at Gertrude over the rim of my glass. She's wearing a pale green babydoll dress that shows off her fabulous legs. Vera Wang, I'd bet my next paycheck on it. Which, now that I consider, just might cover it.

I own a Vera Wang dress, which I have never worn. I bought it last year on clearance, when it was already a season out of date, but it still cost twice what I have any right to spend on a dress, so I'm afraid to wear it. It just hangs in my closet and taunts me.

Gertrude has *that look* about her; I have a feeling she'll drop hers beside the bed or kick it into a corner when she gets home.

Home. To Drew's apartment. Which used to be *my* apartment, until I asked Drew where our relationship was going and he said (using a good many more words): *Nowhere.*

"Rebound or not," I say, "he's going to marry her."

"He proposed," Kari counters. "That doesn't necessarily make marriage a foregone conclusion." She turns and sneers in Gertrude's direction. "She's in for one hell of a surprise when he decides he's not ready after all."

That's why I love Kari. She's willing to bend the very fabric of reality in order to say something that might make me feel better. She can't stand Drew—since the breakup, he's dead to her—but she also hates the fiancée, because that's what best friends do.

As for Drew not following through on his proposal—well, she doesn't know him very well. Drew is nothing if not decisive. I ought to know, since he was pretty decisive when he told me he wasn't going to marry me.

"We'll see," I say, trying to sound like the whole thing doesn't bother me at all. Kari is the best friend I've ever had, but not even to her can I confide all the doubts and questions inside me. Starting with *Why wasn't I good enough?* "It's none of my business anymore anyway."

She nods and looks proud of me. I put my glass, which has magically become empty again, on the bar.

Immediately, the bartender is there. "Refill?"

I open my mouth to answer, but Kari cuts me off. "Hey," she says, pointing her half-empty Cosmo at the bartender, "do I know you?"

He shakes his head. "I don't think so."

"You look really familiar."

"Familiar how?"

"Have I seen you on TV?" she asks.

He smiles. "Do you watch *Midnight Confessions*?"

Dear God. Why couldn't he have asked any other question?

I adore Kari, but she has this *thing* about soap operas; it's a little abnormal, really. She's obsessed. She's on the internet literally every day discussing and dissecting the entire ABC lineup with other fans—I kid you not. And a couple of times a year she meets up with her online pals and goes on these trips to meet various soap stars. It makes her happy, so I'm careful not to say anything negative, but if I'm not careful she'll talk to me about it for hours.

I love her, but a person can only stand so much, even in the name of friendship.

Anyway, it's too late; Kari is nodding enthusiastically. "I've watched for years!"

"I play a bartender at The Roadhouse sometimes." He has the good grace to look a little embarrassed—if Kari didn't recognize him right away, it must be a pretty small part—but he does look pleased to have been recognized.

Or it may just be that Kari is beautiful and gracefully slender, with huge green eyes, dimples, and black hair in the cutest little pixie-cut you ever saw, so he's glad to have gotten her to notice him for any reason.

Kari just about throws herself over the bar to shake his hand. "I knew you looked familiar! I'm Kari—great to meet you."

"You, too," he says. "I'm Luis." He looks at me. "So, another drink?"

I shake my head. Judging by the way it swims when I do, that's probably for the best. "I'm good."

Kari isn't done, though. "When are you gonna be on again?" she asks. "Have you been taping recently?"

Poor Luis probably thinks she's interested in him, but I've known her long enough to know that he's about to get pumped for info that she can take home and spread around to all her online soap opera pals.

I tug at her sleeve. "C'mon, let's go congratulate Drew and

get out of here." I would rather take the lime wedge off my glass and squeeze it directly into my eyes than go over and tell Drew how absolutely thrilled I am that he found someone better than me, but I can't just leave without talking to them. People would think I was intimidated.

Kari looks at me like I've lost my mind. "I'm not going over to make nice with those two assholes. And anyway, I'm talking to someone."

I roll my eyes, lean in, and whisper, "He's an extra, Kari!"

She's quick to correct me. "He's a *day player*. And everyone's got to start somewhere." She turns back to Luis, smiling her most predatory smile.

I leave her to it and walk away. I'm a big girl; I can do this myself. Time to face down Drew—and Gertrude—and pay my respects so I can get the hell out of here.

The bar is crowded—unpleasantly crowded, actually. Who has an engagement party in a bar? It's ridiculous. I mean, I spend plenty of time in bars, but it's not like I'm hosting parties.

Drew and Gertrude and their crowd of hangers-on are sitting in the six booths farthest back in the bar, and have segregated themselves by pulling two chairs around to block the aisle. I push through, excusing myself as I step on a foot or two.

"Jenna!" Drew calls out, waving amiably.

He's casual in jeans and a black t-shirt, and his bleary smile signals that he's on his fifth or sixth beer—at least, to anyone who knows him as well as I do. As well as I *still* do. It's been just over a year since our breakup and he's just as readable to me as he ever was. Which is irritating, now that he's officially No Longer Available.

Irritating? There's an understatement. Try *devastating*.

I stop when I reach his side, and consider what happens now. Do I shake his hand? Hug him? I settle for kissing the air beside his face. The familiar scent of Old Spice clings to his collar—always the traditionalist, that's Drew.

I blink, pull back, and smile my brightest smile at Gertrude. She smiles back; her wattage exceeds mine. *Damn it.*

She reaches over and delicately but conspicuously removes a long strand of blonde hair from the front of Drew's shirt, lets it fall to the floor beside her chair, then looks at me like I left it there on purpose. Which I didn't, obviously. Okay, I did wear my hair down because Drew loved it that way, but I can't shed at will. And anyway, she doesn't exactly have to worry that the allure of my pale, stick-straight hair is going to outshine her gorgeous tangle of cascading copper. Bitch.

"It was so good of you and Kari to come, Jenna," she says.

Her voice is smooth and cultured, the verbal equivalent of a perfect string of pearls. She looks perfect; she sounds perfect. She has the perfect clothes, the perfect boyfriend.

I know all about this kind of girl, and honestly? I'm not at all surprised that this is who Drew picked. I can tell you right now, thirty seconds after meeting her, that she grew up with money, went to the best schools, dated the captain of the football team. No holes in her shoes for this one. No butter sandwiches in her bag lunch.

"Oh," I say, making very sure that none of my painstakingly eradicated Midwestern accent slips through, "we wouldn't have missed it, Gertrude."

Her smile grows strained, but only at the edges. "Please," she says, with just a trace of grit in those pearly syllables, "call me Trudi. Everyone does."

I nod, not making any promises. Hopefully by the next time we have occasion to speak, I can call her "Gertrude" again without seeming rude, as though her invitation to familiarity slipped my mind. We all have to take our victories, small as they are, wherever the opportunities happen to arise.

Although … while I'm hoping things, I suppose I'll hope that I never have to see or talk to her ever again.

I turn back to Drew. "I'm sorry to cut out so early, but I'm beat. Lots of stuff going on at work." This is a convenient truth; work is hell. We're preparing to launch a new product, and that always means loads of extra hours.

"Where is it that you work, Jenna?" Gertrude asks.

"Home Bank," I tell her. "I'm Director of Marketing."

She's already not listening; instead, she's whispering something to Drew. He smiles at her and I feel a little sick. That smile used to be reserved for me.

"I guess I'm going to take off now," I say, a little too loudly.

Drew nods and continues to flash his blissful drunk grin at Gertrude. "It was great to see you again," he says, but it's hard to take it seriously when he's not even looking at me.

"You, too," I say.

It's true—I mean literally. He's good to look at. His dark hair is cut a little longer on top than on the sides, as always; his eyes are just as blue as ever.

I shake my head. Doesn't matter. Yeah, Drew's handsome, and he takes care of sick animals for a living, which is pretty awesome, and he used to love me—I think—but now it's over. Dwelling on these things doesn't change them, and it certainly doesn't help me feel any better about the situation.

Time to go, before I do or say something embarrassing. I swallow the lump in my throat, nod stupidly at Drew and Gertrude, and turn away, stepping on more feet as I make my escape back to the bar and Kari.

I'm so distracted that I stare at Kari's empty stool for at least half a minute before I realize that she's moved to the far end of the bar. She's sitting with one leg tucked under her, perched on a stool next to the guy that Luis the bartender was talking to earlier—the one in the plaid shirt.

The shirt in question is a shade of blue that's alarmingly close to the color of Drew's eyes, and frankly I'm tired of thinking about Drew and his stupid eyes, and everything else about him, so I take a seat on the stool on the other side of Kari to avoid looking at it.

Kari turns to me and smiles. Her smile is entirely too wide, and I figure I'll be helping her up to her apartment tonight. She doesn't look like she's reached the point where I'll be patting her back while she pukes, but if the night doesn't end soon, I won't be able to rule it out entirely.

"How'd it go?" she asks.

"Just great," I say. "How'd it go over here?"

"It is going *awesome*." She smiles, leans back, and tilts her head at the guy Luis has been talking to all night, the one in the flannel shirt, who's staring down into his pint of beer and doesn't notice us gawking at him. I get my first good look at him, and fail to be impressed. Cowboy boots, of all things. And worn jeans—not artfully worn, but worn *out*. His hair is long, but not in any committed way; it's more like he can't be bothered. It's impressively thick and a wonderful chestnut color, but if he doesn't care, why should I? His jaw is strong, nicely square—very nice, actually—but he hasn't gotten around to shaving for some indeterminate but excessive length of time.

I suppose some women would find him attractive, but I'm not one of them.

"He's no more your type than he is mine," I tell her.

"And that right there is the difference between us, *mon amie*." Her French accent is appalling. "*I* don't have a 'type'— and honestly? Neither do you. You've still got a crush on Cary Elwes, for crying out loud, and he's getting downright saggy. Give me a break."

"He was *Westley*," I say, mortally offended.

"I know." She dismisses me with a wave and hops off her stool, patting her new pal's arm as she does. "Hey, I wanted to introduce you to my friend."

He swings around on his stool and looks at me with eyes

the exact color of coffee with double cream—which, as it happens, is how I like it best. *Yummy.*

"Jenna, this is Mitchell Cole. This is Jenna."

I nod and smile. I figure I'll make nice for a minute, then take off. I kind of need a pair of sweatpants and a chick-flick right now.

Then Mitchell Cole speaks, and time stops.

## Chapter Two

---

"IT'S a real pleasure to meet you, Jenna. And it's Mitch, please."

It's the auditory equivalent of being hit by a crosstown bus. His voice is rich and compelling, and pulls at me like an undercurrent. I catch my breath at the depth and timbre of it, the way the resonance lingers after he's finished speaking. The faintest hint of some kind of accent sneaks into each syllable, rendering every word just the littlest bit alien, and that much more exciting. I'm speechless.

Wow. That's a hell of a voice. A catastrophic, panty-melting, knee-weakening voice. Did *not* expect that.

He offers his hand to me; I take it, my soft palm sliding along his callused one like silk over sandpaper, and raise my eyes to his. His steady gaze is warm and questioning. I'm not sure what exactly the question is, but I'm willing to fudge an answer if only he'll keep looking at me, if only he'll say my name again in that enveloping baritone.

My mouth opens and I cringe inwardly, unsure of what might spill out, but what I say is: "Thanks. You, too."

Kari doesn't seem to notice the way my voice comes out, all strangled and wavering, but I can tell by some subtle shift in the depths of his eyes that Mitch does. He holds onto my hand about fifteen seconds longer than strictly necessary, and then rather than just let it go he places it back in my lap. My breath hitches again. One corner of his mouth tilts up just a little, as though he's amused by me.

"You guys chat," Kari says. "I gotta pee."

She heads off. I watch her go, a little bemused.

Mitch speaks again—Lord have mercy: "Kari says you're here for an engagement party?"

"What? Oh." I come back to my senses. "Yeah. It's my ex getting married, and I'm not exactly celebrating. But good for him. I hope he's happy."

"Your ex invited you to his engagement party?" He sounds incredulous. "That's a pretty insensitive thing to do."

"Well, he didn't invite *me*, exactly," I tell him. "He invited Kari. I'm her plus-one."

"Still. Inviting your best friend? Doesn't sound like a very nice thing to do."

"Well…." I shrug. "We still can't figure out what happened exactly. Gertrude—that's the fiancée. She goes by Trudi. With an *i*. I call her Gertrude."

He smiles. It's easy and natural and his eyes get these crinkles at the corners—I get the feeling he smiles a *lot*. "So would I."

"We figure maybe she just kind of went through Drew's address book and invited everyone who wasn't an ex-girlfriend?"

"Maybe. Still not a great approach."

"I don't know. Maybe she did it on purpose—but whatever the reason, the invitation arrived, and Kari cooked up this plan to doll me up and show Drew what he's missing."

His eyes do a not-at-all-subtle sweep of me, head to toe, then return to mine. "Solid plan," he says.

I feel like squirming in my seat, and I'll be damned if I will. I sit up straighter, shrug like it's no big. "Turns out he's not missing anything."

"Oh, I disagree," he says. "So where is this idiot?"

I wave in the general area of *behind me* without turning around. I don't need to see any more of *that*. "He's over there with his girlfriend—his fiancée—and I *totally* do not care."

Mitch looks across the room, narrows his eyes a bit, then looks back at me. It's disconcerting how he gazes right into my eyes while he speaks to me. Makes me feel a little weird, a little vulnerable. A little like he's rummaging around inside my head—like he can see what I'm thinking.

Which is funny, because even I can't figure that out right now.

"Black t-shirt?" he asks.

I nod.

"You want me to punch him for you?"

I can't help it; I smile a little. "Desperately. But we'd probably get thrown out, and who needs that?"

"No, really," he says. "I know a guy." He raises his voice a little and calls: "Hey, Luis."

But he keeps his eyes on mine.

Luis slides down to our end of the bar. "Yo."

"If I punch a douchebag for being insensitive to a lady's feelings, are you gonna throw me out?"

"Dude, I'll hold your coat," Luis says.

"If you tried to punch all the douchebags here," I say, looking around us, "I think we'd be here till closing."

"Hey," Luis says. "We have a strict no-douchebag policy here."

"At a bar in Alphabet City?" I laugh. "Must be awfully slow in here most nights."

"You insult *Loisaida*, you insult me," Luis says, and looks mock-offended. "She's got a mouth on her, this one."

Mitch, eyes still trained on me, nods almost imperceptibly. "Yeah," he says, "I've been noticing it."

Okay, so I know a come-on when I hear one. And I might even object—not my type, no matter what Kari says, or how much she slanders Cary Elwes—except that the voice gets lower. Deeper.

Let's be honest here. Cowboy boots or no cowboy boots, that voice is ridiculously sexy. I'm starting to think of it as a proper noun: The Voice.

Kari returns and plops back on her stool, coming between Mitch and me. It's a bit of a relief—those eyes were getting to be a bit much. He turns back to Luis, and Kari leans in close to me.

"You are not even gonna believe this shit," she whispers—well, shout-whispers really, because it's a bar. "I'm about to set the online soap opera world on fire."

"That guy?" I nod discreetly toward Luis, who's chatting with Mitch as he pours him another beer.

"No!" she exclaims.

"I guess I'm having trouble keeping up," I say. "Over him already?"

"Well, it's not like I've never met an *MC* actor before. That's no big deal. It films here."

"I know where it films."

Boy, do I ever know. *Midnight Confessions* and *All the World* film right here in New York, and over the course of our friendship I've spent a lot of time sitting around Central Park with a book while Kari paces back and forth on 65th Street, hoping to catch one of the actors leaving the ABC studios. Despite having made brief acquaintance with a couple of minor actors from one or the other of the soaps, she has yet to find her way inside those hallowed halls.

She knows everything about them anyway. Apparently at these fan events there are auctions, and her friends are always winning autographed scripts and phone calls from the stars and, most coveted of all, studio tours.

Kari's never bid on a tour, which is good because she has a hard enough time making ends meet without dropping a couple grand on something like that. I'd have her committed.

But enough of her online friends have been to the studio that she could probably draw an accurate blueprint of the place.

That doesn't stop her desperate desire to get in, though. Like I said, it's abnormal.

So even if it's not a big deal, it's not like her to be so cavalier about a possible *in* at the ABC studios. "So, you didn't try to see if he can get you in, or whatever?"

She shrugs. "He's not filming any time in the next couple of weeks, so I didn't want to push."

This is Kari's way of saying she got bored. Poor Luis. He outlived his usefulness with record speed.

"So how do you plan to set the internet on fire?" I ask, tired of the whole conversation already.

"That guy you were just talking to," she says, tilting her head at Mitch. "Do you know who he is?"

"Of course not," I say. "I never recognize these people. Is he an actor?"

"He used to be on *Doctors and Nurses*!"

I can't stop myself from rolling my eyes. Oh, great. Kari's one regret in life—soap opera regret, anyway—is that she lives in New York instead of Los Angeles. *Midnight Confessions* and *All the World* are just the consolation prizes of the ABC lineup; what Kari and her pals are really obsessed with is *Doctors and Nurses*.

Because it films on the west coast, Kari has only met a few of the actors from "*DN*"—her shorthand, not mine—and always at organized fan events. This doesn't compare to the kind of meeting she sometimes scores with the actors from the New York soaps, where she can press them for info—"scoops" or "spoilers," in the vernacular of her online soap crowd.

"What's he doing in New York?" I ask.

"He left *DN* a couple of months ago and moved to New York. He's been cast on *Midnight Confessions*." It's clear from her tone that this kind of move is a demotion in the soap world. "I can't figure out why I haven't heard about it already.

They must have buttoned it up tight. That's why I went to the bathroom—to call Stace."

What, they have a hotline?

"Call Stace?" I echo.

"Yeah, just to tell her he's been cast on *MC*." Kari is practically vibrating with glee. "I hope I'll have a *ton* of stuff to spill when I get online!"

Hopefully the poor guy won't tell her anything that would get him in trouble. According to Kari, the people that run these shows don't appreciate it when fans know everything that's coming up. Kari and her pals, of course, always know everything that's going to happen weeks before it actually does, in excruciating detail. Somehow, they even find out dialogue and stuff, so they know episodes line-for-line and have already debated and freaked out about them before they air. I don't know why she even bothers to watch.

"That's great, honey." I sigh. "Listen, I think I'm going to head home. You want to get a cab with me?"

She shakes her head and leans in close again. "No way. I'm gonna stick around and … you know. See what happens."

"Kari!" I scowl at her. "You are not going to pick up some random in a bar just to impress your soap pals?"

She has the audacity to look offended. "He's not a *random*, and that would *so* not be the reason." She pauses to consider, then says, "Not the only reason, anyway. Probably only like … sixty percent of the reason. Seventy, tops."

I shake my head and pat her hand where it's resting on the bar. "Okay, you do what you gotta do, you lunatic."

She leans over and kisses my cheek, and I stand up. Mitch swivels on his stool and catches my eye again. I give him a little wave, and he does that up-and-down appraisal again, which gives me a little involuntary shiver. Then he nods, and turns back to Kari. He says something I can't hear and she laughs and puts her hand on his knee as he gestures for another beer.

More power to her; I hope they get married and spend the rest of their lives popping out little soap fans.

And for her sake, I hope he's a nice guy. I really do. But Kari's track record—usually pretty good—has been dismal lately. She's at the tail end of a string of bad relationships—three of them, if I'm counting properly. Each of them turned out to be a bigger creep than the one before.

But right now, Kari's dating woes are not my problem. I've got my own problems.

I take a moment to thank my lucky stars that I didn't move in with Kari when I broke up with Drew. When we first arrived in New York, Kari and I were great roommates, reveling in being single women, congratulating one another over breakfast when the night before had been particularly successful.

Mr. Right Now was plenty good enough for us in those days.

When I was apartment hunting after the breakup, naturally I stayed at Kari's until I found a place. She invited me to live with her, to "revisit the good old days," she said. By which she meant, of course, the good old *nights*.

I almost took her up on it, out of fear of being alone—but now I'm looking for something different. And honestly, I'm glad I didn't. This one-night stand is one I definitely do *not* want to be a party to.

And when my stomach lurches at that thought, I'm quite sure it's just the happy hour food at Jacks coming back to haunt me.

Someone shut the heavy glass door while I was talking to Drew; I wrestle with it for a few seconds, and then I'm outside. The air is crisp and cold, and I wish I'd brought a jacket.

Hell, while I'm wishing things, I wish I hadn't come.

Except as soon as I think that, I get a flash of that moment Mitchell Cole opened his mouth and let loose with that astonishing, unexpected bedroom voice.

Whoa, wait a minute. *Bedroom voice?*

I contemplate this for a moment and, based on the way that my stomach is turning in slow semicircles at the thought of it, conclude that yes, that voice belongs in the bedroom. And then there's that *jaw*. And those eyes.

And my reaction to him—what was that all about? I think about it, but no answer is forthcoming.

So I give up and hail a cab, carefully packing my reaction to that voice away in a little mental box as I head for home and what turns out to be a restless night's sleep.

## Chapter Three

MY CELL PHONE drags me out of a miserable restless slumber the next morning. It's playing *The Battle Hymn of the Republic*, which means it's Kari. She programmed it in herself, and forbids me to change it.

It feels early but, when I open one eye to squint at the clock, it says ten-thirty. My body, on the other hand, says *No way am I getting up right now.* I roll over and pull the blankets over my head until the music stops.

But Kari doesn't give up so easily. Ten seconds later my house phone starts ringing. I resolve to ignore that one, too.

Then Kari's voice, via the answering machine, says, "Bruuu-uunch."

*Oh, yes to brunch.*

I grab my cell phone off the nightstand and call her back, because I'm just that lazy.

"Hey," she says. "Are you still in bed?"

"No."

"Are you lying?"

"Yes."

"Well, get up," she says. "We can meet up and I'll tell you all about striking out last night."

"Did you really?" I ask, more than a little surprised. Kari, as I mentioned, is cute as hell; she doesn't strike out often.

And is it weird that I'm sort of glad to hear it? Probably, since it doesn't have anything to do with me.

"Eh, only a little," she says. "I did some very mild throwing myself at him, and he turned out to be a terrible catcher."

"What is with the baseball analogies? You don't even like baseball."

"Ain't that the truth." Kari's last boyfriend was a baseball fanatic, and I'm sure she hopes she never sees another baseball. "That Luis was cute, though."

"Agreed." And I guess I do agree, but—as Kari would say—*Eh.*

"So, brunch? Dot's?"

Dot's is an authentic old-style New York City diner—with precisely the kind of food and decor that implies—and is located almost exactly halfway between my neighborhood and Kari's. So of course it's one of our favorite places.

"Sure," I say, dragging my sorry self out of bed and over to my dresser. Last night's drinking is wreaking havoc on my head and stomach, and some toast and juice would go a long way toward making me feel human again. "Meet you there."

She hangs up without saying goodbye, which is an irritating habit that I swear she picked up from those damned soap operas. I put the phone down and stare out the window at the flaking paint on the fire escape.

I can't help puzzling over the strike-out. Kari's instincts about guys are pretty much infallible. She wouldn't have made a play for him—great, now *I'm* speaking in sports analogies—if she didn't think he was kind of into her. So what happened between the successful introduction and the derailed pickup?

*Is it that he met me?* I might not have instincts like Kari's, but I think I've got enough mojo to be able to tell when someone is interested in me. Especially when they decide subtlety is not an issue.

No. I'm being ridiculous. I probably misread his signals completely. And it's irrelevant, anyway, as I don't care about him one way or another—except in a *What Not to Wear* kind of way.

For one thing, he was Kari's discovery, so to speak. We've managed for two decades to avoid that unpleasant way women have of stealing their friend's dates or mates—it seems to happen in so many female relationships, and I'm proud that Kari and I have always been supportive of each other's respective love lives.

For another, if he didn't respond to Kari's advances, she's hardly going to be going back for more. So chances are good that neither of us will see him again. Jacks is located a little outside of our normal bar-prowling area, and I could count on one hand the number of times I've been there since the breakup. So it's pointless to be doing all this speculating.

And anyway, totally not my type. I had a lot to drink and overreacted to a very nice voice.

And a great jaw.

*And the eyes…*

But that kind of thing is only to be expected after all that unpleasantness with Drew and Gertrude. Even Mr. Wrong looks good when you're heartbroken, right?

Plus the guy is an actor, even if it is just on a soap. He's trained to have an effect on people. He makes his living being compelling to an audience. It's really that simple.

Glad to have settled that with myself, I pull open my closet and grab a pair of jeans without really looking. This isn't like me, but Kari is notoriously impatient; if she gets there before me she'll order for both of us and I'll end up with sausage or home fries or something similarly stomach-turning. Kari eats the same way whether she has a hangover or not: the more calories the better, and pass the butter please. And even though we're the same height—5'5"—she weighs a good fifteen pounds less than I do. It's grossly unfair.

Jeans on, I hurry into a t-shirt and grab a jacket in case it's colder than it looks. It looks gorgeous, though; it's obviously going to be one of those days when fall forgets what season it is. I twist my hair into a knot and clip it into place, grab my nicest pair of strappy low-heeled sandals—I'm in a rush, but not too much of a rush to pick out good shoes—and run for the elevator.

————

I needn't have rushed. I claim our usual table and nurse a cup of coffee for almost half an hour, enduring the glare of the middle-aged proprietress the entire time. Dot doesn't take kindly to customers taking up tables when they're not ordering food. Actually, from what I've seen over the years, Dot doesn't take kindly to customers at all, and I think it's only the necessity of paying the bills that leads her to even unlock the doors in the morning.

Finally, Kari shows up. She drops into the chair across from me and says, "So this is weird."

"What's weird?"

"Guess who called me?"

"George Clooney."

"Like I'd be here now?" She shuts up as Dot slides a coffee cup onto the table and walks away—friendly as always—then says, "Mitchell Cole."

"Oh, really?"

"Yeah, like … I was heading out to meet you—sorry I'm late—and the phone rang. I grabbed it in case it was you, but it was him—Jenna, that voice. Mother of God, it just stops you in your tracks."

She's not wrong, but I don't say anything.

"Anyway, he makes a little small talk and I'm not sure if

he's ever gonna get to the point—or if he even has a point—so I said I was heading out to meet you for breakfast." She takes a sip of her coffee, sets it back down. "And he asked if he could come, too."

Well, there: I was wrong. He *is* interested in Kari. For whatever reason, he didn't go home with her, but this is probably better. It proves he's not in it for the sex.

Or at least not *just* for the sex.

My God, am I jealous? I take stock and decide that I am. Not of *Kari*, you understand. Just the concept.

"I think I'll probably just be a third wheel," I say. "Plus this whole thing is just weird. Who calls for a breakfast date? This isn't how breakfast dates work."

"What do you mean?"

"Generally when your boyfriends join us for breakfast, they … haven't slept well, shall we say?"

She rolls her eyes and grabs a menu from the tabletop rack. "You have such a low opinion of me."

I roll my eyes right back at her. "Oh, I'm so sorry. You're practically the Virgin Mary, aren't you?"

She scowls, but wisely drops it. She knows that I don't just *know about* the skeletons in her closet; I could, if called upon to do so, *catalog* them. Bone by bone, if you catch my drift.

"Anyway, do you want me to take off?" I ask. I'd be more than thrilled to take off. Delighted, in fact.

"No, not at all," she says. "I'm just curious what he wants."

"Probably to get in your pants," I say, and suppress the pang that accompanies that. *What the hell?* "Kari, I'm not dressed to meet anyone."

I should have taken more time to get ready; no one but Kari ever sees me just thrown together like this. And of course she's radiant in an old pair of Levis and what looks suspiciously like a two-dollar Hanes t-shirt.

I'm not naturally gorgeous; I have to try harder than she does.

"Oh, you look fine," she says, "and you've already *met* him. And no way is he trying to get in my pants. I'm telling you, there was just nothing there."

"Still, I—"

"Plus I told him you'd be here, so you can't leave or he'll think I was making it up, or that I ditched you so we could be alone." She disappears behind the enormous menu. "To hell with it; I'm going to get the Behemoth. It's amazing."

The Behemoth is like a full Irish on steroids: bacon, sausage, eggs, waffles, beans, toast—hell, I don't even know. Everything back there in the kitchen, I guess.

I'm opening my mouth to remind her that it's literally something like six thousand calories, when the door swings open and Mitch strides in, resplendent in faded jeans—with cowboy boots, of course—and yet another plaid shirt. This one isn't flannel, but it makes up for that, saints preserve us, with mother-of-pearl snaps.

Not buttons. Snaps.

"Speaking of amazing," I say, and nod at the door.

Kari turns around and waves Mitch over—unnecessarily, since he's already walking toward our table.

*Walking*, though, doesn't really begin to describe what he's doing. His advance isn't quite a strut, and it isn't quite a swagger. It's somehow both of these and neither of these and something in between. Perfectly, sexily in between.

There's that word again: sexy. It's so incongruous, but good Lord, the voice isn't enough? (*And the eyes*, I can't help thinking. *And the jaw.*) Does he have to exude overwhelming masculinity and raw pheromones with every step as well? It's insane. I can't look away.

I'm not too caught up in watching his progress to note, however, that every other woman in the diner—even Dot—has stopped what she's doing to watch him make his way across the floor.

Finally, validation! I'm not imagining things.

While this is a relief, it doesn't speak well for the taste of the women in the diner—myself included. I mean, really. Mother-of-pearl snaps?

He stops when he reaches our table, and favors each of us with a smile. I stare at him, bemused. That smile is as much a killer as the voice and the eyes, exposing perfect straight white teeth even as it shows off those eye crinkles I noticed last night. *And* it shows off his dimples, which I did not have the privilege of seeing last night.

Great. Dimples, too. I wonder what other surprises he has in store for me.

Our usual table against the wall normally seats two, but he snags a chair from the next table over, turns it around and—of course!—straddles it, crossing his arms over the back. He doesn't seem to notice that his knee is now resting against mine, though I can't seem to notice anything else.

Actually, that isn't true. I'm also spending a lot of time noticing the way his jeans stretch over his thighs.

"Good morning," he says. "Have you ladies ordered yet?"

Did I actually think I remembered what that voice was like? If so, I was wrong; memory can only capture a pale shadow of that voice. It coats the words like warm maple syrup, rendering me speechless from the joy of listening to it. It's outright stupid that anyone can sound like that.

I appraise the snaps again.

They're still there.

"We haven't had a chance yet," Kari says. "I just got here myself."

"Are you feeling better this morning?" he asks, and when Kari doesn't answer I realize he must be talking to me.

I look up, and find he's giving me that intent stare again. "Fantastic," I say. "Never better."

"You seemed like you might be a little down. The ex, and all that."

"Not a bit. I'm great—I'm awesome—and Drew and Gertrude can seriously fuck off directly into the sun."

He goggles at me a little bit, and I wonder if I've gone too far.

Kari pipes up. "Dot's going to kill you for sitting on that chair like that."

I don't think Dot is going to do any such thing, and Mitch doesn't look terribly concerned either. Probably doesn't find himself on the receiving end of too many stern lectures from the fairer sex, and Dot is still one of us, after all.

"I'm sure she'll forgive me." He leans precariously backward to try and steal a menu from the next table over. "I'll order a ton of food."

Kari holds her own menu out. "Here, take mine."

It's a good thing his back is now turned to the rest of the place, because the smile he flashes her would make Dot—and every other woman there—relive their first orgasm. I want to kick myself. My immediate reaction is to wonder why I didn't give him *my* menu; then he would have smiled at *me*.

My next reaction is to remind myself that I'm really not attracted to him.

"What's good here?" he asks, and there's a long pause before I realize that since Kari isn't answering, he must be talking to me again. I look up and catch the full brunt of those eyes.

Kari kicks me under the table and when I look at her she's giving me the raised eyebrows. I know Kari pretty well, but I'm not quite sure what those eyebrows mean.

"I'm not hungry," I blurt, hoping the eyebrows were the *Get the hell out of here and leave me alone with the hottie* signal.

Kari shakes her head so subtly no one who didn't know her would notice. Okay, I read the eyebrows wrong.

"I am," Mitch says. His voice is lower, almost a rumble, and I just about fall off my chair. He's doing it again! I swallow hard, and his lips twitch. Is he holding back a smile? Is that *supposed* to be a double entendre? And does it even matter, when he's wearing cowboy boots and mother-of-pearl snaps?

*When he's got those eyes, and those dimples? And a voice like butter melting on toast?*

I try to come up with a snappy reply, and come up utterly blank. I've lost my composure, which is unusual—and unwelcome—and this guy has me completely tongue-tied. It's a bit embarrassing; I have to bail. How am I going to sit here and eat toast or whatever, when he's sitting there being … *appealing.*

"You know," I choke out, "now that I think about it, I'm *really* not hungry. Would you guys mind if I bowed out of breakfast and left you to your own devices?"

Kari gives me a little eyebrow thing and tilts her head subtly toward Mitch. "Of course not, but—"

"Great! Awesome." I stand up and sling my purse over my shoulder.

Mitch turns a little to look up at me; his knee grazes along the front of mine and comes to rest against it, so that I'm almost straddling his leg. He doesn't even seem to notice.

I notice it—so much noticing right now—and my hands are shaking a bit as I fumble some crumpled ones out of my pocket, to pay for my coffee.

Before I can put them on the table, Mitch catches my wrist. "It's okay, I'm sure we can cover it."

There's a tremendous crash and the sound of breaking glass from the kitchen. Whatever it was, it sounded like there was an awful lot of it hitting the floor. Dot flies through the double doors and out of sight, and starts screaming at some poor soul. Across the table, Kari turns and cranes her neck to see through the crack between the doors.

Now would be a great time to make a graceful exit, except that Mitch hasn't let go of my wrist. Kari's still trying to see into the kitchen and hasn't noticed this odd business. I look down at his hand rather pointedly, and when I look back up he's got that lip-twitching thing going on again.

I'm trying to decide whether or not to pull away—I don't want to make some kind of silly scene—when I feel his grip loosen. He runs the ball of his thumb over my wrist just hard enough to send a jolt of something like electricity through my whole body; I jump a little, and he lets go and rests his hand casually on his own thigh like he never dreamed of doing such a thing, and squints up at me.

Even his squint is sexy, and those crinkly corners of his eyes that showed up when he smiled are even more devastating.

Dimples. Eye-crinkles. That smile. The voice. That *walk*.

*Just kill me, already.*

"I hope to see you again, real soon," he says softly, and I can only nod stupidly as I back away a few steps and then turn to go.

Kari shouts after me. "Call me later!"

I wave over my shoulder without looking back, and practically bolt for the door.

## Chapter Four

MONDAY MORNING. It's only nine o'clock and I'm already thinking about tearing my hair out when Ryan, my admin, pokes his head in the door. His office is between mine and the hallway, like a little antechamber you might find in a pyramid.

I guess I'm a Pharaoh in this scenario. Fanciful!

Anyway, because you can't get to my office without going through his, he's excellent at preventing interruptions. Actually, I'm surprised to see him interrupting me himself, especially when I'm on the phone.

Then he hands me a yellow message slip, and everything makes perfect sense. Apparently my boss, Ben, just called to set up a meeting with me before lunch. As if I'll have time to see him this *month*, let alone today. I'll have to see him and then work through lunch to catch up. I hate my job.

No, I don't. I love my job. But right now I'm on semi-permanent hold for Aiyana, our Creative Director, and I've got three new pieces of collateral material to review. Also, I've had to pee for twenty minutes.

I nod and wave Ryan away. He gives me a thumbs-up and disappears back into his office.

Aiyana finally comes on the line. "Jenna!" she says. "I'm

sorry you had to wait. I was getting the same old song and dance from Web Development."

I laugh. Aiyana and I have been working together two years now, which is a long time when you consider how fast people in marketing burn out. It helps that we both have the same intense attitude, and we're both good at seeing the big picture *and* the little details.

"I assume you told them no frills?"

"Yeah," she says, "but they actually made a compelling case for a more sophisticated design. We're talking about college kids here; they're pretty internet-savvy. So I'm letting them dummy up some stuff for me and we'll go from there. How's your end?"

"I've got Ben having eight heart attacks a day because I don't have a working brochure yet. I'm running a little behind on that now, and I have to have the design so we can see what kind of space we'll have for text. When can you send it up?"

She pauses. "I sent that up a week ago."

That can't be right. "I don't have it."

"I gave it to … what's her name? Melanie?"

"Melody?"

"Yeah, her."

Now I *know* this can't be right. Melody, who is technically a *Marketing Associate* but is in reality kind of a glorified intern, has only been with us a few months, but she's already become my right-hand man—woman—and she never misplaces or forgets anything.

"I definitely didn't get it," I say. "Can you send another copy?"

"Of course I can. I'll send someone up."

"Thanks a bunch. I'll be looking for it." I hang up and look at the phone for a minute, then pick it up and dial Melody's extension.

She picks up on the first ring. "Melody here."

"Mel, did Aiyana give you the mock-up for our in-lobby brochure?"

"Sure," she says cheerfully. "Last week, sometime." I can hear her flipping through her planner. "Monday."

"Well, what did you do with it?" I ask.

She pauses long enough for me to realize my tone is more than a little testy, then says, "I gave it to you to approve, and you said you'd give it back to me this week."

Now why the hell would I have said that? Giving it back *this week* puts me a full week behind schedule. Okaying the brochure design should have taken about twelve seconds, at which point it should have been in the hands of the copywriters. "I don't have it. I had to ask Aiyana to send up a new one. Will you be on the lookout for it?"

"Sure thing."

"Thanks." I hang up, perturbed. It's not like me to misplace something. I have systems, and schedules, and lists—*so* many lists. I don't screw up. Ever.

But then I think back to last week, most of which was consumed with thoughts of the upcoming party, and how Drew would look, and how I would look, and how Gertrude might look. I was completely preoccupied. I'll be lucky if I didn't overlook ten other important details.

I pick up the phone to try to postpone my meeting with Ben, but before I can finish dialing, Ryan pokes his head in again. "Kari's on line three."

I consider for about a nanosecond. Ben's not going anywhere, and I probably shouldn't try to put the meeting off anyway. Hopefully I'll have the dummy brochure in hand before it's time to talk to him.

So I pick up line three, which is what I wanted to do anyway. "Hey, lady! How's it going?" I gave myself a stern talking-to last night, and now I'm rooting for her and Mitch. Or trying to. "How was the rest of your day?"

"I seriously can't even believe we're about to have this

conversation," she says, and I can hear the laughter in her voice.

"Hey, if this is going to be one of those grossly detailed TMI kind of things, feel free to skip it." There's only so much my newfound resolve can take. "I've got plenty of disasters here to occupy me, Lord knows."

"What's going on?"

"The usual. I supervise; my minions work … until I do something dumb like lose an important item that's central to the whole campaign." I sigh, turning in my chair to look out my office window. "I was really distracted last week, and it's showing."

"I'm sorry, honey."

"Never mind. I'm sick of thinking about it, and I'm sure you didn't call to talk about me."

This time, she actually does laugh. "As a matter of fact, I did."

"What does that mean?"

"Well, after you beat feet out of Dot's like your ass was on fire, Mitch and I had a very pleasant breakfast."

"I fail to see how this is about me, but okay."

"I'm getting to that," she says. "And over said breakfast, what do you suppose we talked about?"

Well, that's an easy one. "Probably *Midnight Confessions*."

"Okay, I'll give you that. I did bring it up a few times. And he shot me down every time. The guy's buttoned up like … something with buttons. I don't know. A coat. Whatever." She laughs again. "What we talked about, my dearest BFF, was *you*."

I marvel at—and then ruthlessly squash—the tiny thrill of excitement this brings. "About me?"

"About you."

"What—" Where is this going? "What about me?"

"Oh, you know. Had I known you long. Oh, how interesting that we grew up together. When did we move to the city. How long have you been broken up with Drew." She pauses. "Are you currently single."

This is so unexpected that my mouth literally hangs open for a second. I'm quite sure I misheard her. "I'm sorry, what?"

"He asked me if you were seeing anyone right now."

"Why on earth would he ask you that?"

"He said he was normally the sort to ask directly, but you keep running off."

I do keep running off, that's true. If he didn't make me get all flustered like a teenage girl, maybe I wouldn't have to.

"I don't know what to say," I tell her.

"I told him that yes, you were single, if that helps."

That most decidedly does *not* help. "Kari!"

"Well, you are."

"Why would you do that?" I ask. "I thought you liked him."

"Well, I'd *like* him to give me some goddamn spoilers, but beyond that? Seriously, you can have him."

"You liked him first," I say. "You take him."

"That ship has sailed, pal. We had our chance, and then you came over and ruined everything."

"Are you—"

"If you actually ask me if I'm serious," she says, "I'm going to come over there and slap your lips off your face. Of course I'm not serious. I gave him your number. I think you should go out with him."

"But I don't want to go out with him." *Much.*

"Because…?"

Lord have mercy. I would do just about anything to stop having this stupid circular conversation. "I *told* you. Not my type."

"And I told you, shut up with that. You and your issues."

"I just like a certain type of guy."

"You like Alan Rickman, for God's sake."

"He was Colonel Brandon!"

"Listen to me," she says. "The guy is *objectively* hot. I mean, smoking hot. You had your eyes all full of Drew and whatsherface, so maybe you didn't get a good look."

Oh, I got a plenty good look. And then another one yesterday morning. But I'm trying not to think about that. "I saw plenty. Kari—"

"And," she says, "I confess, it's not entirely altruistic."

"What does that mean, exactly?"

"I was just figuring, if you went out with him, maybe he would spill some interesting tidbits. About work."

There I go, hanging my jaw open again. "You want me to go out with some random guy so that you can get *soap opera scoops*?"

"You don't have to make it sound so awful. I'm sure you'll like him. You might want to date him more, even."

"And pass on even *more* scoops?"

Apparently she misses the sarcasm dripping from every word because she says, a little too eagerly, "Well, only if you wanted to."

"You've lost your mind," I say. "If you want some kind of insider info, get it yourself."

"Oh, like I haven't tried. He's not spilling anything because he knows I watch the show—but you don't. I bet he'd talk to you. You're my *in*."

"I am not your *in*. I'm your best friend." This is an enormous tactical error, and I know it as soon as the words leave my mouth.

"*Exactly*," she says. "You're my best friend, and if you can't ask your best friend for a favor, who can you ask?"

"This is a pretty big favor, Kari."

"Oh, yeah, do your friend a favor and spend lots of time with a hot guy." I can practically hear her rolling her eyes on the other end of the phone. "My heart just bleeds for you. So will you do it or not?"

I sigh again. Kari's done a lot for me since we were kids—

lots of big stuff but lots of little stuff too, the stuff that really makes a friendship. And even though I've already established he's not my type, he *is* kind of electrifying to be around.

This is insane.

"Okay, fine," I say, and even as I say it I can't believe the words are coming out of my mouth. "I'll do it."

She squeals in glee. "Thank you, thank you! I will never be able to repay you for this."

"Settle down a minute," I say. "I have some conditions."

"Anything."

"Okay, I'm only going out with him the one time, I swear. That's going to have to be enough."

"Oh, that," she says breezily. "I'm sure he'll be so charming you'll want to date him lots of times."

"I'm serious. And I'm *not* going to sneak around trying to trick him into spilling secrets. If he lets something slip, it's all yours, but I'm not some kind of soap opera Mata Hari. And anyway, I wouldn't even know what to ask."

"I'll tell you what to ask."

"No, you're not listening. I'm not kidding. I'll pass along anything he *happens* to mention, but that's it."

"My pals are gonna die."

Thinking about her online soap friends raises another question for me. "Is this going to get him in trouble? I don't want anyone in trouble."

"Oh, goodness no," she says. "Leaks are all over the place, and any info you get is pretty much something that a *lot* of people know—all the actors plus the crew plus the soap magazines. And we'll be careful."

"You didn't know he was going to be working at *Midnight Confessions*, remember?"

"Yeah, every once in a while they really lock something down. That was top-secret stuff. I think they honestly didn't want anyone to know until he showed up one day." She laughs. "Of course, everyone knows *now*. The message boards are freaking out."

"So he must be a pretty big deal then?"

"Seriously, Jenna—getting him is a *huge* deal for *MC*. His *DN* character was supposed to be a bad guy for a six-week arc, and he turned it into eighteen months of some of the best work I've seen in daytime. He is just phenomenal."

Lord, she's going to start waxing eloquent. He's a soap actor, for crying out loud. I head her off at the pass. "So you already gave him my number?"

"Yeah, just your work number though. I knew you'd have my back. You're such a good friend."

"Thanks. I think."

"Don't mention it," she says. "Let me know when he calls." Then—of course—she hangs up without saying goodbye.

## Chapter Five

LATE TUESDAY MORNING finds me on the phone again with Aiyana. This time I've got an email from the copywriters—there are three of them but I tend to think of them as one amorphous mass of brains, and they seem to see themselves the same way, frankly—saying that there's not enough room on the inside flap of the dummy brochure to allow them to list out the five things I targeted as our main selling points.

We're already behind on this, thanks to me losing the first brochure, but they pulled some pretty impressive copy out of their asses, on a tight turn-around time. I'm not sending it back to them for more revisions.

"There's plenty of room for five lines," Aiyana says. "I don't see what the problem is."

"The problem is that five *items* doesn't necessarily translate to five *lines*. You know that."

She doesn't answer right away, because of course she knows that. "Can't they, I don't know, condense it a little?"

"It's marketing copy for a financial product. It's already so condensed I'm thinking about slapping a Campbell's soup label on it." I sigh. "Which, come to think of it, that would probably be a more effective approach than the one we've got right now."

"Redesigning is going to put me way behind, Jenna." Unspoken is the fact that she was already behind, because of me.

"You and me both, but if the selling points aren't on the brochure then what the hell is the brochure for?"

I understand that she's not being obstinate on purpose, that she has deadlines to meet just like I do. But if there isn't enough space then there isn't enough space. That's not going to change no matter how much she and I click our heels together and wish it would.

"Hang on a sec, Jenna, let me check something." She puts me on hold. Great.

Ryan comes in with a message slip. Unless a message is important or personal, he generally gives me all my messages in a batch two or three times a day, so I put my hand over the mouthpiece of the phone. "I'm on hold. What's up?"

"Some guy called, said it was personal." He gestures with the slip of paper. "Mitch."

*Oh, Lord.* I feel myself go pale. I didn't think he'd call so soon.

"Mitch who?" I ask, as though I know a hundred Mitches, a *legion* of them, and can't begin to imagine which of them has graced me with a phone call.

Ryan shrugs. "I don't know. He didn't seem to think he needed to leave a last name. You want the number?" He holds out the message slip.

"No!" I say without thinking.

Ryan stares at me. He's too polite to say anything, but I can read him like a book. He thinks I've lost it.

He may be right.

"I mean, not right now—" I begin, but then Aiyana comes back on the line. I hold up a finger and turn my back on Ryan so I won't have to decide what to do about the piece of paper with Mitch's number on it. "What did you find out?"

"What if we swapped the colors?" she asks.

"I don't know." I close my eyes and try to picture it in my head. It might work. Or it might look like complete crap. I sigh. "Why don't you try it, just for the hell of it, and we'll see how it looks. I don't have any better ideas."

We both make polite goodbyes and hang up. She's probably totally pissed at me. Just what I need: her mad at me for bossing her around. I'm technically her superior, but I'm not the sort of person that goes around lording it over people.

Ryan must have taken the message slip with him, because it's not on my desk. I buzz him.

"Yeah?" he says.

I gnaw at my lip for a second. Why can't things be easy?

"Jenna?" Ryan *has* to think I'm losing my mind. Most people are happy to receive phone calls. Especially personal phone calls, at work. Especially from men—well, if they're women. Or gay, I suppose. And I would think especially from men who sound like Mitch.

In fact, if Ryan had to deal with that voice, he probably can't understand why I didn't hang up on Aiyana immediately and return Mitch's call.

Ryan is right. I *am* losing my mind.

"Do you still have that message?" I ask.

"Of course," he says cautiously.

"You can throw it out." I'm not going to do it. I can't go through with it. It's too weird.

"Are you sure?"

"Yes," I say. "No."

*Oh, God.*

Ryan doesn't say anything.

I relent. "Oh, give me the number."

"Okay," he says slowly. "Got a pen?"

"No," I say. "Never mind. I don't want it." I hang up.

I pick up the phone and dial Kari's work number. I get her voice mail.

"Kari, it's Jenna. Please call me. I need to talk to you." I hang up and think about it. If I don't go through with it, she's going to kill me.

I think about *that* for a minute and then buzz Ryan again, but instead of answering, he opens my door.

"I think I'd like that number after all," I tell him.

He crosses the office and puts the message slip on my desk. "Why don't I just leave this here," he suggests carefully, "and you can decide what to do from there."

I nod. "Good plan."

He turns to leave, then turns back. "You know I'm not gay, right?"

"Of course!" What an odd thing to say. I met Ryan's girlfriend at the Christmas party and she is *gorgeous*. And anyway, why would I care if he was?

"I've never regretted it, until I talked to that guy." He winks at me and I laugh, feeling just a little bit less like throwing myself out my office window. Not that it opens. "You should call him," he tells me, and leaves.

I really shouldn't. But I do. I dial each number very carefully, knowing I'll only dare to do this once.

He answers on the first ring. "Hello?"

Good Lord, he can't even say hello without making my knees weak. This is impossible.

"It's Jenna," I say. "From the bar the other night?" *And the hot breakfast date the other morning?*

"I'm so glad you called." His voice softens, gets deeper. Is there no end to the subtle variations of that voice? This is the first time I've heard this one. It would melt rocks.

"So am I." I realize I'm breathless and—more importantly—I'm telling the truth. That freaks me out a little, and I decide

I'd better keep this short. "I'm sorry, but I only have a few minutes."

"That's all right. I'm sure you're busy."

"I am," I say. "I've got this new product and we're not even half ready—I don't know if you know what I do—"

"Kari told me," he says. "Well, I asked."

"As you can maybe imagine, it's been a hard week."

"But it's only Tuesday."

I laugh. "You're right. God, I can't wait for Friday."

"Actually," he says, "that's why I called."

I appraise this conversational gambit with admiration. It's obvious what he's about to do, and of course I would have to say *yes* no matter how clumsy he was, but I can't help but admire his approach. He is *smooth*.

"Is it?" I ask.

"Yes. I was wondering if you'd like to have dinner, maybe tell me what it is about your job that's putting that frown in your voice."

This is crazy. I can't do this. I open my mouth to say *No, thank you*, but nothing comes out.

I should have thought about this more carefully before I called. On the one hand, there is an actual ethical issue here, dating him to get soap opera scoops for my friend. On the other, Kari is my very best friend and it means a lot to her.

On the other hand—I guess I have three hands now—I'd get to listen to him talk some more. I can't say I wouldn't appreciate that. Not that I'm interested, or anything. But I can still *enjoy* him.

One way or the other, I should probably give him an answer before he thinks I hung up or something.

Mitch is clearly a master at this. Where another guy might be intimidated by my silence and press too hard, he's just waiting for my answer.

Caught between *yes* and *no*, I go with: "I probably won't be fit company by the end of the week. Work is really killing me."

"Why don't you let me worry about whether or not I enjoy your company, and you just be ready at six."

Wow, he's good.

"I guess I could do that," I say slowly.

Apparently that's all he needs. "Fantastic. Give me your address and number."

I do, and he repeats it back to make sure he's got it right. He gets it right the first time, of course. I won't have to worry about him getting the directions wrong and being late. I'm starting to have a feeling I won't have to worry about him doing *anything* wrong. Apparently the big cosmic joke is that this guy who is totally Mr. Wrong is, so far at least, doing everything exactly right.

"Anywhere in particular you want to have dinner?" he asks. "I have a place in mind but if you want to choose—"

"Oh, no, that's fine," I say. "Whatever you like. Just tell me how to dress."

"Dress to kill," he says—no, that's not right. He *growls*.

It's a good thing I'm sitting down, because my legs get a little wobbly. I hope we get to know each other well enough that I can ask him to tone it down with the voice. It's really too much sometimes.

"I will," I say, though I don't really know what that means. Dress super-fancy, because we're going to Per Se? *Not likely*, I think. Literally dress to kill, because there could be a rumble at the Taco Loco?

"Excellent." There's some shouting in the background and he says, "I'm sorry, I gotta go."

"Okay. I'll see you Friday." I'm surprised to find that I wish he didn't have to get off the phone. I could listen to him all day. Well, I'll be able to listen to him all night Friday.

All *evening*, rather; not all night. I will not be having an all-night date.

"You sure will," Mitch says, and for an awful second I think that I've spoken aloud. Then I realize he's just agreeing that I'll see him Friday. "Can't wait." And he hangs up without saying goodbye.

Damned soap opera people. I *know* that's where Kari gets it.

*Kari.* Damn it. I got a little … carried away with setting up our date-that's-not-a-date, and kind of forgot about Kari there for a minute. *Oops.*

As if thinking about her has conjured her up, Ryan buzzes to tell me she's on line two.

"You called?" she says, when I pick up.

"The eagle has landed," I intone solemnly.

"The red fox runs at night," she replies, and we both bust out giggling.

"Okay," I say. "So he called."

"Score! What did he say?"

I fill her in on the details.

"Awesome," she says. "I bet you'll have a great time."

"Well, at least I'll have dinner."

"Don't be ridiculous. I had tons of fun talking to him on Sunday."

"You had a lot to talk about," I remind her, "what with trying to ferret out all the details about his job."

"Speaking of which," she says, "get a pen and a piece of paper."

"What for?"

"I'm going to explain all the storylines on *MC* for you."

"Kari, I'm not comfortable pumping him for information."

"*Pumping*," she says, and does her little Beavis and Butthead laugh. It's a pretty good impression, actually.

"Kari!"

"Okay, seriously, you don't have to pump him"—she does the laugh again—"for anything. I just want you to have *context*, in case anything slips."

I half-listen as she drones on, and make encouraging noises like I'm writing this down. As if.

"Okay," she says, finally. "Have fun! And you have to tell me every salacious detail."

Why do I have the distinct feeling that she isn't listening to me at all?

## Chapter Six

FRIDAY TAKES *FOREVER* TO ARRIVE. If it's true that time flies when you're having fun, this makes sense, because this has been a miserable, wretched week. *Fun* has been permanently stricken from my work vocabulary. In fact, I can't remember under what circumstances it ever *was* in my work vocabulary.

One thing I *do* know: I do not get paid enough. Not nearly enough.

But somehow Friday has finally gotten here, and I left work at three o'clock despite still having a desk full of problems. Oh, well. If anyone doesn't like it, too bad. A girl needs a good chunk of quality time to get ready for her first date in a year.

Yes, it's true. I haven't been on a date since Drew and I broke up. By accident, not by design. Maybe Kari's right and I'm just putting out some kind of anti-relationship vibe—at least, that's what she's been telling me for the past year—but whatever the reason, the unpleasant truth is that no one has asked.

I *really* wish she was here now to help me get ready, but she wouldn't come; she said if Mitch saw her he might catch on to our little plan.

I didn't have any trouble dealing with the makeup and

underwear issues; I'm a minimalist as far as cosmetics go, and I wouldn't even go as far as the laundry room in the basement of my building without my Wonderbra.

Okay, well, maybe there, because how else would I wash my Wonderbra? But I certainly wouldn't go *out*.

But now, with the easy stuff completed, I'm standing in front of my closet, scowling ferociously at my clothes. I have a sinking feeling that my clothes aren't intimidated.

It's not that I don't have anything to wear. It's that I have too much to wear, and no idea which thing is right.

*Okay, start with what you do know*, I tell myself.

One thing I know for sure is that I'm not wearing the Vera Wang. No food or drinks.

I think about it some more and realize that's pretty much the only thing I *am* sure of.

The problem with making a decision is that I don't know where we're going. Uptown or down? The Village? Harlem?

If I had to guess, I'd say I shouldn't wear jeans. That's not normally in anyone's definition of "dress to kill." But both times I've seen Mitch he's been in jeans. Maybe he only frequents jeans and t-shirt type establishments. Maybe "dress to kill," in this case, means "wear a clean shirt."

But he's seen me twice, and I was only wearing jeans the one time. So if he was paying attention he knows that—in my extremely fashionable opinion—jeans are for hung-over morning-after breakfasts at greasy-spoon diners, and nights out call for something a little nicer.

What did I wear to the engagement party? I check out the pile of clothes in the corner. Oh, yeah. Basic black sheath. I remember now; I was trying to look as if I hadn't spent much time getting ready. It always takes so long to look as though you just threw something on.

Anyway, he's seen me in my best *Oh, this old thing?* dress. So I should maybe go with medium-expensive but casual? I wonder if pants are okay.

This is ridiculous. It's not even like it's a real date, at least not in the sense of him being anyone I could possibly get involved with. It doesn't matter what I wear.

But I can't just put on any damn thing. I'm not going out looking like a slob, even if he shows up in mother-of-pearl snaps.

Oh God, he's not going to show up in mother-of-pearl snaps, is he?

It's not completely out of the question.

And it's quarter of six, and I still haven't picked out an outfit.

For lack of any better ideas, I finally settle on a pretty floral D&G tank with halter straps. It's one of my favorite tops—sweet and feminine, flattering without being *too* sexy. And I got it on mega-super-crazy clearance so if the absolute worst happens and I spill something on it, it's not a tragedy. After dithering for a while about my bottom half, I go with a pair of wide-legged black slacks with a high waist. Not gonna lie: I got them at H&M.

But they don't look cheap, and I spent like a quarter of a week's salary on the shirt; I'm calling it fair.

I glance regretfully at my favorite boots and tell myself to forget it—they cost literally twice as much as the rest of my outfit put together, and I'm *not* going to chance them when I don't know what kind of dive I might wind up in. What if the floor is sticky? What if someone spills something on me? Instead, I retrieve my strappy black sandals from the corner of the living room, where I kicked them when I got home from the diner on Sunday.

Thinking about Sunday reminds me of that quick, subtle caress Mitch gave me right before I left. Even five days later, it gives me a little shiver to think of it.

Probably better, then, not to think of it.

Someone buzzes to be let in from downstairs, and I thumb

the intercom button. I don't bother with the camera button, which hasn't worked since I moved in. "Yes?"

"It's me," Mitch says, and—no real surprise—even over the cheap, tinny-sounding intercom his voice is much as always. Which is to say, exhilarating.

"Come on up." I push the button to unlock the inner door, and hear him push it open. The intercom crackles and cuts out briefly, and I sigh. I don't know how much longer it's going to last, and then what are people supposed to do? Throw rocks at my window?

I open my apartment door and pop the deadbolt out, then let the door swing shut. The deadbolt catches on the inside of the doorframe and stops the door from shutting all the way—what my mom calls "leaving it on the latch." She calls it this when she's warning me that my habit of doing it will get me raped and murdered. My mom is really quite sure that it's only a matter of time before one of the countless rapist-murderers in New York finally gets me, and she refuses to visit to see how—relatively— safe it is. This is why it's always up to me to go visit her, which is something she's been nagging me about quite a bit recently.

But, back to the point: my building has the slowest elevator on the entire island of Manhattan, and I don't have time to sit around waiting for people to knock, so I leave it on the latch for Mitch while I make sure the place is presentable.

I cross back through the living room—all eight by ten feet of it—and peek into the bathroom to make sure I didn't leave anything embarrassing laying around in there. All clear. I shut the door anyway. No one wants to see my toilet.

It occurs to me that my bedroom is a pigsty and I should shut that door, too—but when I turn to do so the front door is open and Mitch is standing there. I scream a little, sort of by reflex, even as I realize it's him.

He's at my side in an instant, rubbing my shoulder. "I'm *so* sorry," he says. "The door was open and—"

"No, *I'm* sorry," I say, trying to focus my thoughts. It's hard. A second ago he was over there, and now he's right here —wow, he's tall—and he smells *fantastic* and his hand is really warm and squeezing my shoulder just enough to feel great but not enough to hurt. I bet he gives a hell of a massage.

My heart is racing. From being startled, of course. Plus he is *totally* in my personal space.

"Still sorry," he says.

"It's really okay. The door was open because I wanted you to feel free to come on in. I just didn't hear the elevator."

"I took the stairs."

"Why?" I never take the stairs. There's an excellent reason for this: I live on the fourth floor, and I'm lazy.

"There was an old woman with a walker in the vestibule, and she said the elevator was slow." He smiles at me—eye crinkles, dimples, and all. "I was in a hurry to see you."

Dear God. What am I supposed to do with *that*?

"That was Mrs. Corinthos," I say. "She's just down the hall from me."

"They should put her on a lower floor," he says absently, letting go of my shoulder and looking around the apartment.

That's actually really thoughtful and sweet. Who the hell is this guy?

"This is nice," he says, and to his credit he sounds like he means it.

I look around to see if maybe my place got more sophisticated when I wasn't looking, but it's the same as ever. There's a small kitchen area with a high table and two barstool-type chairs. Just beyond the table, the linoleum floor ends and carpet begins; that's how you know you're in the "living room" area. Almost half the floor space there is taken up by an enormous cranberry-colored chaise, threadbare and half-covered with a blue throw and a battalion of pillows—I like to be comfortable while I watch TV. There's a tiny coffee table, at which I usually eat my dinner, and the TV, on its somewhat wobbly shelving unit. And a door to my bedroom and a door to the bathroom. That's it.

I live here because it's what I could afford in the neighborhood I wanted. It's not what I'd call *nice*.

"Thanks," I say. "It's kind of small, but it's home."

"That's all that matters." He flashes that sexy grin that makes me forget he's the kind of guy who wears mother-of-pearl snaps.

He's not wearing any tonight, though. He's still in jeans, and he's still in cowboy boots, but he's wearing a gorgeous lightweight sweater that's almost exactly the same caramel color as his eyes. I love caramel. Not that that has anything to do with anything; I'm just saying.

Of course, he's still got the hair and the scruff, but it looks like he's made some attempt to tame everything into some semblance of order, and he's shaved at least some of his face, so I guess some of that scruff is on purpose. Not everyone can pull that off, but he looks good. *Not* my type, but really good. Objectively, I mean—Kari was right about that. Broad shoulders, enough bulk under that sweater that I can tell he works out. Thick, strong-looking thighs, and his jeans, as usual, stretch over them in a really flattering way. It's almost enough to make a girl want to get him out of them.

Not *me*. I mean some *hypothetical* girl who is definitely not me.

Okay, enough of that.

"Is what I'm wearing all right?" I ask.

"You look gorgeous," he says appreciatively, looking me up and down very slowly.

I blush, both from his frank appraisal and because I'm afraid he'll think I was fishing for compliments and I didn't even tell him he looks nice first. And I can't tell him *now*; it will look like I only said it because I didn't want to be rude. "No, I mean, am I dressed-up enough?"

"You look gorgeous," he says again, and favors me with another of those mouth-watering smiles.

*Lord have mercy.*

"I just don't want to look out of place. Where are we going?"

"SoHo," he says, as though this tells me what I need to know.

"Where in SoHo?" I ask.

"Nowhere you know."

This isn't helping at all. Dinner in SoHo could be anything from a falafel stand to a three-star restaurant. Why is he making this so difficult?

Exasperated, I say, "Look, basically what I'm trying to find out here is what am I going to pay for an entrée?" I don't actually care—I can afford whatever—but this is the best question to ask if you want to know what to wear.

He looks at me like I've lost my mind. "*I* asked *you* out, remember? I'm paying."

"That's not why I—" I stop short, a little surprised. That wasn't why I was asking, but I had sort of planned to pay for myself—which is not how people go on dates. It's just that I haven't been on one in so long, I honestly kind of forgot.

Once Drew and I moved in together, he stopped paying for me when we went out. He explained it as a natural progression in our relationship. We weren't wooing one another anymore, and he wasn't in a place to support anyone. I told him I totally understood. I'm not some kind of gold-digger, after all. So we split the rent and bills right down the middle, and we always went Dutch. It's funny how things become a habit.

I think about it for a second and decide it will be nice to have someone else buy me dinner. But I still need the answer to the question. I decide what the hell, honesty is the best policy. "Mostly I was asking because I just want to make sure I'm dressed appropriately."

His eyes do that up-and-down-slowly thing again and I get tingly in a lot of places where I am not supposed to be getting tingly. But when his eyes meet mine again, I kind of forget what I'm *supposed* to be doing.

"Yes," he says. "It's upscale, but not pretentious. And you look perfect."

Okay, that's good. "You wouldn't lie just to flatter me, would you?" I ask, and if I'm flirting just a little bit, well who could blame me?

He shakes his head slowly—and yeah, he's flirting back. "What kind of a guy do you think I am?"

I wish I knew. That's exactly the problem, I guess: I thought he was one kind of guy, but sometimes he seems like another, and I don't know where the lines are anymore. I don't know what the rules are. And I don't know how to reconcile this guy, who seems to be making up his own rules and appears to be totally comfortable with that, with the kind of guys I'm used to, who follow the rules I understand and behave in predictable and familiar ways.

"I don't know," I say feebly. "What kind of guy *are* you?"

"The guy of your dreams." He grins and offers me his arm. "You ready?"

I grab my purse, tuck my arm in his, and let him escort me to the door. But when I stop to fix the deadbolt, something occurs to me. "Wait here one sec," I say, and hurry into my bedroom.

I kick off my sandals and pull my boots on. They're soft black leather with stack heels, and they make me four inches taller as well as making my ass look fantastic. And all this without throwing my back out or pinching my feet. Thank God they go with virtually everything. That's why I chose these instead of the red ones I *really* wanted—so that I could get as much use out of them as possible.

Taller, and with at least a fifty percent improvement in my ass, I rejoin Mitch at the door.

"Hey," he says. "You changed your shoes."

I can't believe he noticed. "I did," I admit, locking up. "It's probably silly, but I decided I like these better."

"I totally understand." He looks down at his feet fondly. "I wouldn't feel right without my boots."

I laugh, delighted. "Let's go," I say. "I'm starving."

## Chapter Seven

THE CAB RIDE PASSES QUICKLY, with Mitch and me making small talk until it drops us off on Mulberry Street. I know I said I can afford whatever, but now I'm glad I don't have to. Wherever we're going, it would have made a pretty serious dent in my bank account.

Mitch pays the driver, then takes my hand—oh, my—and leads me down the street until we come upon a line of people waiting at a nondescript door below street level. The building is an old one with a cast-iron facade, carefully restored. I really love this neighborhood, actually, and wish I could afford to live here.

"Here we are," he says, and I realize there's a menu display box beside the door. This is our restaurant? It doesn't even have a sign. And there's a line! I can't wait in line; didn't I just say I was starving?

But Mitch pulls me past all the people waiting and walks down the short flight of stairs. He opens the door and gestures for me to go in. I look at him with eyebrows raised—a silent *What are you doing?*—but he just smiles at me and waits for me to precede him through the door.

I'm starting to think he flashes those hundred-gigawatt grins on purpose, to shut people up. If so, it's working—at least on me.

Inside, the restaurant is only about twice the size of my apartment, with ten tables, all of them empty. There's candlelight, soft music—perfect first-date ambience. I hope he's not planning to make another pass at me.

I *hope* that I hope he's not planning to make another pass at me.

He steps in beside me and guides me forward with a hand on the small of my back, and I hope—

Never mind.

An absolutely perfect-looking woman with amazing curves, olive skin, and masses of waist-length jet-black hair detaches from the shadows in the far corner and crosses the room. Mitch steps forward and she takes both of his hands in hers.

I hang back, feeling distinctly outclassed.

"*Mi caro*," she says. "I was wondering when you would show your gorgeous face."

He raises both of her hands to his mouth and kisses them. "Angela. How could I stay away?"

She practically purrs. My God, am I jealous?

But I only have a second to fret about it before he lets go of her and turns to slide his arm around my waist, pulling me forward and against his side at the same time. It does not escape me that Angela's eyes flash in a way that's not exactly friendly when he does so.

It also does not escape me that my body fits perfectly against his, which is weird because he's got to be seven or eight inches taller than I am. But we just sort of fit together, like puzzle pieces.

Which is literally the worst analogy I could have come up with, because now I'm thinking—

"Jenna, this is Angela," Mitch says.

"Pleased to meet you," I say.

"Very pleased," she replies, nodding regally at me.

She's frosty, but not rude. I can live with that. I can live with a lot, if he's going to hold me all pressed up against him like this. He smells very, *very* good. Like something spicy, but with an undertone of clean.

Angela gestures to the empty room. "Wherever you like," she tells him. "We do not open until seven."

I look at Mitch again, and this time he answers my unspoken question. "For me, she opens early."

Angela's gaze sweeps him from head to toe, lingering on the good parts. "Yes," she says. "For you, I am always open."

*I just bet.* I have to resist the urge to spit and hiss. What is *wrong* with me?

Mitch leads me to a table in the back and pulls out a chair. I sit, and he helps me push my chair in, then takes a seat across from me.

"Do you want a cocktail or something?" he asks. "Or should I order wine?"

"I'd prefer wine," I say. "Your choice."

"Okay," he says. "For dinner—allergies? Anything you hate?"

"What are we eating?" I ask. I don't have a menu, so I'm at a bit of a disadvantage when it comes to deciding about dinner.

He smiles again. "Let me take care of that. Since I don't want to kill you, allergies?"

I laugh. "No. And I like pretty much anything."

He gestures to Angela and she comes over; they put their heads together and have a brief discussion. I don't hear what they're saying; I'm far too busy watching to make sure Angela's hands aren't doing anything they shouldn't be. They're not, exactly, but I'm not thrilled about them either.

And even once she's hurried off to order the food or whatever, and Mitch and I are making small talk, she keeps stopping by the table to ask one thing or another, and on each visit she finds a reason to smooth down a stray lock of Mitch's hair, or brush imaginary lint off his shoulder.

It's not that I'm jealous or anything; it's just that it's rude. He's obviously on a date with *me*. I mean, not a real date, but *she* doesn't know that.

The crazy part is, he doesn't even seem to notice. I mean, he notices—obviously you notice when someone is touching you—but he just doesn't really have much of a reaction. It's like he doesn't even consider that it's … whatever it is. I guess I don't know what it is. I don't know what's between them—now or in the past.

But now I'm starting to wonder why he sat all the way over there instead of over here next to me. Maybe he doesn't want her to think that we're together? I mean, obviously we're together, but maybe he doesn't want her to think that we're *together* together?

Why does that thought make me so mad? After all, we're *not*. But still.

Our appetizers arrive and they're delicious—some kind of cheese torte and crab cakes. I'd do just about anything for crab cakes; it's a damned good thing they're legal. These ones have some kind of spicy red pepper coulis or something on them, and I don't know if I've ever tasted anything this good. It's all I can do to put my fork down between bites.

"Good?" he asks, wiping his mouth. He must have to be really vigilant about napkins, I think, with all that facial hair.

"Beyond good," I take a sip of my wine, which is also delicious. The guy sure knows how to pick a restaurant.

The doors have finally opened, and other diners are starting to trickle in. I notice that *they* all get menus when they sit down.

"Ready for more?" he asks.

I polish off the last bite of my crab cake. "Absolutely."

He beckons to Angela; she comes over immediately and starts smoothing invisible wrinkles out of his sweater. It's obviously just an excuse to put her hands all over his broad shoulders, but he either doesn't know that or doesn't care. They have another confab—I stifle another stab of jealousy—and apparently whatever he says meets with her satisfaction, because she graces him with a beatific smile and bustles back off to the kitchen.

"What am I getting?" I ask.

"The best dinner of your life," he assures me.

I suppose he's probably right—he's been right about so many other things. I decide to just sit back and let him take charge. He certainly didn't steer me wrong with the crab cakes.

"So," he says, "let's talk about this engagement-party-slash-ex-boyfriend thing."

"It's not a particularly enjoyable topic for me," I say.

"I'm sorry—"

"No, I wasn't saying we couldn't talk about it." Now that I think about it, it's probably best if we do. That way he can understand about the kind of guys I date, understand why things between us really can't get serious. "It's really okay. I just wanted you to know if I was testy about it or whatever, it wasn't because of anything you did. It's just a touchy subject."

"I understand."

I give him a quick rundown to start. "Drew and I met when I was in my last year of my Master's. I was getting my MBA and he was just finishing up his internship—he's a veterinarian. A friend asked me to go with her when she took her dog to be put down, and Drew was working that day. He was so kind, so incredibly gentle, both with my friend and the dog. I think I fell a little bit in love with him right there."

Mitch doesn't say anything at all, and I take a nervous sip of my wine before picking the story back up.

"But the thing about Drew is, he's much better with

animals than he is with people. And the short version of our relationship—which was actually pretty long—basically goes like this: I wanted a lot more commitment than he did, and when I pushed him for it, he … oh, I don't know. He pushed back. And I got mad and left."

"What do you mean, *pushed back*?" he asks. "Did he do something to you?"

"Oh, good God, no," I say, astonished at how steely and angry he sounds. "Drew would never—no. He just…." I don't want to think about it anymore. I have tried not to think about any of it since the night it happened, and I'm not about to start thinking about it now. We both said a lot of things that we should have thought better of. "He basically told me that I wasn't the girl for him, that's all."

"Sounds like you're better off."

"But the point—at least for me—is that Drew is *exactly* the kind of guy I should be with. So it hurt to hear that he didn't want me."

"The kind of guy you *should* be with?" Mitch sounds … skeptical, I guess. "What kind is that?"

"Perfect in almost every way."

"What ways would those be?"

"He's … he's Mr. Right, you know? Handsome, accomplished, well-educated." I tick them off on my fingers. "He's from a good family, he has a great job, he has plenty of money—should I go on?"

"No, I get it," he says. "Sounds like some kind of checklist."

I'm a little taken aback by that. It *does* sound like a checklist, and I've never thought of it that way. "Yes, I suppose it does," I say. "But it's irrelevant because he's marrying someone else now. So it really doesn't matter how good a catch he is. And anyway, I said it *did* hurt. It's ancient history. I'm *so* over it."

Mitch looks pretty unconvinced, but he lets it lie, which is good. Real date or not, it's rude to talk about your ex the whole time.

"So tell me about your folks," he says. "What do they do for work?"

"Oh, my mom stays home. She always did, first to take care of me, and then just because she could, I guess. My dad's a janitor. I didn't see him much."

"That's too bad."

I shake my head. "No, I totally understand it. He had to have his priorities, you know? He had a kid to take care of, and we didn't have much money."

He thinks about it for a second. "Still, it's a shame."

"I don't really look at it that way," I protest. "He just had things he had to do."

He drinks his wine, seems to think about it some more. "You seem like a very forgiving person."

"It's not that, really." I shrug. "I don't talk about it much, but things were pretty difficult and he didn't have much choice."

"You don't have to tell me about it, but I'm interested."

And, oddly, I find myself telling him. "It's not that he didn't want to be with us more often. He was just really busy, trying to keep us afloat. My parents are reasonably comfortable now—they don't have a kid to support anymore, and Dad's union got him some wage increases. But when I was a kid my dad never just had *a* job—he always had a day job and a night job, so my mom could stay home. We lived in a broken-down old house in a town that didn't have many of those, because the schools were better there, and it was all my parents could do to pay the mortgage. So it was tough, that's all."

He nods. His face is serious—probably more serious than it needs to be, because it's honestly not a big deal. My dad wanted me to have every opportunity, and he worked like a dog to see that I had a chance. He was so proud when I went off to college in New York City, of all places. He doesn't even give me too much trouble about not coming home enough, and when he does it always seems to be on my mother's behalf.

And yeah, this informs the way I feel about who I should date, and who I should settle down with—not because I need a man to take care of me, I can take care of myself—but because I need so badly to make good on everything my parents sacrificed for me.

But I don't know how to say these things to someone who's obviously feeling bad for me when I don't feel bad for myself.

Well, not on this topic, anyway.

There's a long silence—so different from our ease in the cab —and I sneak a look at my nail polish, which I should really have redone before going out in public.

"So," he says.

I look up to find his eyes on me. It's discomfiting to have someone just look right *at* you like that.

I can't help it; I have to know. "So how do you know Angela?"

"I knew her in LA; she used to be on *DN*. She's the one who got me my audition, actually."

"Were you, like, a thing? She seems very … comfortable with you."

He grins at me. "Angela's *comfortable* with everyone," he says. "That's just sort of how she is."

I don't know what to say to that, exactly, so I decide maybe I should get down to business. "So, speaking of *Doctors and Nurses*, are you excited about the move, or…?"

"I am. It'll be cool to play something different."

A waiter appears beside us with two plates full of something that smells exquisite, and in this moment I could not possibly care less about Angela or *Doctors and Nurses* or anything but this food. I take stock: there are huge scallops, blistered grape tomatoes, and asparagus, plated on an absolutely decadent-looking cream sauce that somehow also smells of citrus. Mitch's dinner appears to be the same thing.

"Dear God," I say. "I don't even dare to eat this; I'll gain twenty pounds."

"I had Angela take the calories out," he counters.

I laugh and try a bite. It tastes even better than it looks.

"By the way," he says, "speaking of calories—"

"Oh, no. I don't want to hear it."

He flashes that marvelous grin at me again, and his shaggy hair falls forward onto his forehead. I'm so drunk on delicious food that I forget to think he's anything but astonishingly sexy. "I just wanted to remind you to save room for dessert."

I groan. "You're kidding, right?"

He shakes his head; he's really not.

I dig in with gusto, forgoing conversation in the interest of overeating. It's a nice silence, though, not awkward like the one earlier. I feel really at ease with him. It's wonderful to stop being uptight and just have a good time.

It's not long before I'm so full that I have to slow down—I would say I regret the crab cakes, but it would be a dirty lie—so my food is barely half gone when Mitch and Angela start conferring about dessert. Soon after, the waiter spirits our dinner away—I'm very sad to see it go—and replaces it with an enormous dish of crème brulée and an even bigger piece of tiramisu.

"I can't eat even one bite of this," I protest. "I have nowhere to put it."

He laughs. "Sure you can." He stands up and moves to the chair on my left, then scoops up a spoonful of crème brulée and holds it out. "Just try it."

I hesitate, then lean forward and let him feed it to me. I know right away that I'm in trouble. I'm going to snatch it away from him and eat the whole thing, and I'll never fit into my black sheath dress again. "Oh. My. God. That is not normal."

He takes a bite for himself. "That *is* good."

"I know." I try the tiramisu, and it's everything I could have wanted and more. I offer him the plate; he takes a forkful, and I laugh because he's got mascarpone cheese on his upper lip now. I lean forward without thinking and wipe it off with my napkin.

"Hey, thanks!" he says.

I laugh again at his genuine surprise and gratitude. "No problem."

"Man, this stuff is great," he says, shoveling in another spoonful of crème brulée. He's becoming steadily less eloquent as the food gets progressively better.

"It's heavenly." I fork up another bite of the tiramisu before pushing the plate away. "I can't eat one more bite."

"Okay with me." He gives Angela a little wave, and she heads toward us. "The camera adds ten pounds and all that."

"Is that true?" I ask.

"I don't know." He shrugs. "I never watch myself."

I ponder that while he deals with the check. If I were an actress I would watch myself obsessively, I think. I'd probably TiVo it and watch it over and over, finding some new fault with every viewing. I've been known to be hard on myself. I'm amazed all over again at how totally confident and comfortable with himself he is.

"Okay," he says, standing and pulling me to my feet. "Where to?"

"What did you have in mind?"

"There's a cool-looking indie film playing a few blocks over, or we can go to Jacks, play some pool. Let Luis give us free drinks." He smiles. "I'm happy with whatever."

I realize I have yet to ask him even one of the questions Kari gave me. "Let's go to Jacks," I say. "I don't know how to play pool, but we can sit and chat instead of being quiet at the movies."

"Sounds great."

We head back out to the street, where the line has, if anything, gotten longer. I catch a couple of women looking at me with open envy. Is it the dinner, or my date?

Except this isn't a *real* date.

And I kind of wish—just a little—that it was.

## Chapter Eight

JACKS IS CROWDED. The jukebox is loud and apparently someone is having an 80s flashback, because Bon Jovi is playing when we come in. We slide into the last two seats at the bar, and while Luis pours us Guinness drafts I get down to business and start asking questions.

I find out that Mitch started filming this past Monday. His character, Blake Ratcliffe, is the recently-discovered long-lost son of the show's matriarch, Lucille, a formidable woman both in and out of her role. Mitch speaks of her with enormous respect, and insists she's very well-liked by everyone.

I file that away for Kari but I know that's not going to hold her. I try another tack. "So, if you're so long-lost and everything, does that mean they didn't know you existed at all?"

He shakes his head. "They had no idea. Grown children you never knew you had are a soap staple. I get to be the black sheep and shock everyone in my very proper family, especially my mother, with my wild ways and womanizing."

"Womanizing?" I echo.

"Yeah, they're hooking me up with this character named Cassie—she's Lucille's husband's daughter."

I think about that for a moment and say, "Wouldn't that make her your sister?" Kari will love this.

"*Step*sister," he corrects me. "But yes, it's terribly scandalous. Apparently I'm the sort that doesn't care what other people think."

"Typecasting?"

"Damn straight," he says. "I can't remember the last time I cared what anyone thought about me."

*Must be nice*, I think.

Luis drops off our beers, and I take a sip, flipping through my mental rolodex of *Midnight Confessions* questions. What should I ask next?

He heads me off, though, by saying, "So tell me about this project at work that's got you so frazzled."

And to my surprise, once again it seems like the most natural thing in the world to talk to him.

"We're launching this new savings and investment product. My boss wants to call it *Grow*; hopefully I can talk him out of it, but only if I can get my people to come up with something better. The idea is to market it to college students, who are kind of an untapped market in that they're not generally looking to save or invest anything; they're too busy taking out student loans."

"So," he says, "the problem is, how do you get someone who's so broke that he's borrowing for school to make a long-term investment decision that won't show any results for years?"

"Exactly. The plan is to offer some very good opportunities for a much lower initial investment, and to give preferential rates to people who have other accounts with us."

He smiles broadly. "Including student loans?"

"*Especially* student loans." Man, he's quick. I can't help but slip into my marketing persona, and sell it to him like I would anyone else I was trying to convince. "The basic rationale is that kids that choose to go to college are going to go on to get good jobs where their investment potential is much greater. And these kids are already predisposed to understanding the value of saving and long-term investment, by virtue of the fact that they've decided to pursue a higher education in hopes of a better job—and, one can reason, enough money to prepare adequately for retirement."

"So you want to get eighteen-year-olds thinking about retirement."

"I didn't say it was going to be easy. But I'm really excited about it, and I think that if we market it the right way it could work. Spectacularly."

"And that's where you come in," he says.

"That's where I come in. If we're going to sell it, it's going to be because of me. Or because of my department, which for all intents and purposes is the same thing."

"That's a lot to take on one set of shoulders."

"It's just the way it is," I say. "I'm the head of the department, so Creative and Copywriting and Web Development and all of that falls under my umbrella. This is why the whole thing is making me a nervous wreck. If it fails, it's on me."

"And if it succeeds?" he asks.

"Then I might get a raise. And a big success under my belt should I need leverage later on."

"Leverage for what?"

"Who can say? But this is the corporate world; it always pays to have an ace up your sleeve."

"Office politics," he says with distaste. "Sounds too stressful for me. I don't do stress."

"*Doing* stress isn't really a choice, is it? I mean, I would think no matter where you are, stress is going to find you. Surely your job gets stressful."

"I enjoy my job enough that the normal stress of it doesn't bother me at all," he says. "And if the stress gets to be too much … well, I can just move east and find a new soap, right?"

He smiles at me again, but for the first time I don't see his eyes backing it up.

"Is that what happened?" I ask quietly.

"I don't really want to talk about it." He doesn't sound angry, but he also doesn't sound like he's going to budge on that, so I leave it alone.

Before I can think of what to say next, Mitch switches the conversation back to me, asking me questions about where I grew up and stuff. I find myself telling him all sorts of things that I generally keep to myself. We both have a good laugh over the story about the year my dad walked in on my birthday party and didn't remember it was my birthday. It's one of my favorites—I mean, it sucks that my dad forgot my birthday, but it really *is* a funny story. Especially the way I tell it.

"And he goes 'What the hell is the cake for?'" I say, laughing.

"Seriously?" Mitch shakes his head like he can't even believe it.

"It's true, cross my heart. And so cranky, like it was a huge inconvenience to come home and find all these kids in the house." I take a big gulp of beer and smile, remembering his face.

Mitch just shakes his head again, but he's laughing a little, too. "You're really tough, to be able to laugh that off."

"Seriously, it wasn't a big deal. Still isn't. He loved me like crazy." I'm still giggling when I realize he's not laughing anymore. I turn to look at him and he's staring at me, his eyes hooded and undecipherable. The color looks different in this light, darker. "Mitch—"

"Don't say anything," he says, and I hush up obediently. "I know we don't know each other well, and this is our first date."

"Yes."

He reaches out and cups my face in his hands, strokes my

cheek with his thumb, slides his hands down to cup the curves of my shoulders. "But you look really beautiful when you're being brave, and I've decided that I'm going to kiss you."

*Uh-oh.*

I start to say something—what?—but before I can get a word out he's leaning half out of his seat and pulling me halfway out of mine to meet him. I put my hands on his knees to balance myself and then, as promised, he kisses me.

*Oh, my.*

It's a soft kiss, not much more than a shared, lingering breath. It's not at all like I thought it would be.

*Wait a minute*, I think, *does that mean I've been thinking about what it would be like to kiss him?*

Well, maybe a little.

His teeth tease at my lower lip, then his tongue flickers out and traces along the path where his teeth were. His lips are perfect, and he's kissing me quite expertly, with just the right amount of pressure. I part my lips almost involuntarily and he gently meets my tongue with his.

What is going on? How is this happening? How much have I had to drink? My God, is anyone watching?

These questions flit in and out of my mind, but I can't seem to concentrate on them. I can't seem to do much of anything, really, except kiss him back. So I do that, moving to meet his tongue with my own, learning the taste and feel of his mouth.

His hands leave my shoulders and trail down my arms, and as the kiss deepens and gets more intense I feel his hands slipping under my shirt. His fingers brush across my back, just above the waistline of my pants. His skin is rough against mine; frankly, it's sexy as hell.

But it's also one hell of a wake-up call. What am I doing? Kari sent me on a mission; she didn't send me out here to get kissed.

I break off the kiss and pull away, and he backs off immediately. He moves his hands and rests them on the curve of my hips—in a position that, to be honest, isn't any less indecent. But at least my pants are between us this way. I take my hands off his knees and fold them in my lap to hide their trembling. My God, he smells so good.

He doesn't say anything; he just looks at me.

"I'm sorry," I say. "I should never have agreed to this. This is awful."

He looks mildly offended. "I didn't think it was that bad."

"That's not what I mean." I fumble for the words. "I like you very much."

"Good—"

"You don't understand. I don't like you *that* way."

"You were doing fine just now," he says, but he takes his hands off my hips and reaches for his beer.

I resist the urge to tell him that he wasn't too shabby himself. Not to mention the urge to reach out and stroke that gorgeous jawline until he stops frowning at me like he's doing now.

I keep my thoughts—and my hands—to myself. There's no sense in encouraging him any more than I already have.

The thing is—and it makes me sound shallow, but it's not that—there's a very specific sort of guy that, for me, is the end goal. And it's not about money, it's not about his job exactly, or any one thing I can put my finger on. I just know what Mr. Right is supposed to be like, and this isn't it.

A few years ago? Mitch would have made a spectacular Mr. Right Now. But that's not where I'm at anymore. And he can call it a checklist if he wants to, but I'm not ashamed of wanting very specific things in my life—and I don't need some sexy dude swaggering in and upending my ideas about what I need. I know what I need.

But *oh Lord*, what I need and what I want are *not* the same thing right now.

"It's not that I didn't want to kiss you just then"—Lord, it sure isn't—"but there are so many reasons why we really should keep this strictly just friends."

"Give me *one*," he challenges.

I rack my brain, trying to remember all the good reasons I had. "You're just not my type, Mitch," I say lamely.

He shakes his head. "That's a stupid reason. I don't think that even *qualifies* as a reason."

"It's not stupid. Everyone's got a type—a Mr. Right."

"Like Drew."

I nod. "Well, yeah."

"And I'm Mr. Wrong."

I shake my head. "I'm not saying that. It's just … people are attracted to a specific kind of person, you know?"

"So you don't find me attractive?" He sounds like he doesn't believe that for a second. Does he have to be so unshakeable, so supremely self-confident?

"No, it's not that—of course you're—I mean—" This isn't working out how I'd hoped. "Whether or not someone is attractive isn't the only thing that matters."

"So what *does* matter?" he asks. "What is it about me that you don't like?"

Huh. I'll be damned—I can't think of a single thing.

"You don't understand," I say again. This is, apparently, the best I can do.

"I understand more than you think," he says. "I understand that if you stopped worrying about Mr. Right, you might find that things aren't as cut and dried as you think. You might find that people don't fit into those neat boxes you want to put them in."

I don't know what to say to that. Do I put people in boxes? I certainly don't mean to. "All I'm saying is, I think you're a really nice guy, and I would like us to be friends."

"Friends," he says.

"Yes, I've enjoyed talking with you and I would like to do more of it." I try on a smile. After all, it's the unvarnished truth. The *whole* truth. Just friends. Whatever just happened here was an anomaly.

After a moment, he nods. "Friends it is, then. That's probably for the best, all things considered."

What's *that* supposed to mean? Oh, wait, isn't that pretty much what *I* said to *him*? Somehow it sounds different when he says it. Plus, why did he give in so easily?

"So ... *friend*," he says, "let's go find a cab and take you home." He stands up and offers me his arm again.

He's not very good at this *friends* thing. Kari never escorts me around with our arms wound together.

"I can just take the train, really," I say.

"Friends or no friends, I'm not letting you wander off on our first—and only—date. I'll see you home."

And how is a girl supposed to say no to something like *that*?

## Chapter Nine

KARI LETS me sleep until eight o'clock on Saturday. Then she starts calling—first my house phone, then my cell. I ignore each of them twice, then finally drag myself out to the kitchen to answer the phone there when it starts ringing again.

"Hi, Kari." I open the cupboard above the coffee machine only to discover that I have no coffee. I meant to stop on the way home from my date. My *not*-date. My *evening*.

"How'd you know it was me?"

"Who the hell else would call me at this ungodly hour on a weekend? Did it occur to you I might be tired from my hot date?"

"That's why I'm downstairs with coffee."

Oh Lord, she's not screwing around. She knows my weak spot: Coffee. *Now*.

I buzz her in and move the pile of books and papers on the table over to the counter, then check the fridge for anything breakfast-like—or even food-like. No dice; I have a bottle of ketchup, a foam container of leftover Thai takeout from last weekend, and a water pitcher that's currently as dry as the Sahara. How luxurious my life is.

I let Kari in and snatch my cup of coffee from her hand, taking a gulp. Double cream, double sugar. Perfection.

It's too hot, of course, and I immediately regret it when I burn my mouth, then immediately regret it *again* when I go back for more.

"Why did you call instead of buzzing?"

"I did, like five times."

Ugh. I'm gonna have to call the property management company and have them come to fix it, which is just about the last thing I feel like doing.

"And, I might add, I *called* five times as well. I was starting to think you were dead up here. Or had company."

I roll my eyes. "I did not have company. I'm exhausted, though."

"That sounds promising." She sets her coffee on the table and takes a seat facing me.

I lean against the counter rather than sit. "Thanks for the coffee."

"No problem," she says. "So, *are* you tired from your hot date?"

"Actually, I was home well before ten. I just couldn't sleep."

"You drink too much coffee," she says.

I nod, although it had much less to do with coffee than with thinking about that kiss at Jacks. "I had a lovely time but, as I predicted, there were no sparks." I take the lid off my coffee and blow on it to cool it. No sparks. Yeah, right.

"But did you have fun?" she asks.

"I had a lovely time," I repeat. "He's very charming and funny and smart, and we talked a lot about work and stuff."

Oops. I shouldn't have mentioned work. His work, after all, is what this visit is about—and a topic I actually want to avoid.

But it's too late now. "What about work?" she asks, her voice excited.

"Well, he wanted to know all about *Grow*," I say, spitting the last word out. Kari knows how I feel about this name; I've certainly made it clear more than once. More than twice really. Probably about six thousand times.

"And?"

"And so I told him all about it, and what I was working on. We didn't get into the stupid brochure, but—"

"*Jenna*," she half-yells, and bangs the table with the palm of her hand. "You know I don't want to hear about that right now! What did he say about *his* job?"

"To be honest, Kari, not a whole lot. I told you I wasn't going to grill him."

"Did he say anything about what his new storyline is going to be on *MC*?"

"He said a bunch of great stuff about the woman who plays his mom." That seems safe to pass along. "And they're pairing him with his stepsister. I forget the name." That might be less safe, but it's not like he told me to keep it to myself or anything.

"Cassie?" she prompts.

"Yeah, that's it. He said it was *scandalous*."

"I've seen worse," she says, but doesn't elaborate.

Just as well—the last thing I want is to get into a detailed discussion about some crazy soap opera plot I probably wouldn't be able to follow anyway.

"That was all he told me about that."

"You were with him all that time, and that's *all* he said about *MC*?"

"It was only a few hours. And, by the way, dinner was delicious, thanks for asking."

She throws her hands up. "I'm glad you had a nice dinner, but I sent you on a mission."

"Do you have to be so obsessive?"

"I prefer to think of it as *focused*. Now, this is an exciting tidbit, but it's not exactly going to set the internet on fire, you know."

"No, I don't know. I have no idea what sets your friends on fire." At this point, *I'd* like to set her friends on fire. Bunch of busybodies, ruining my perfectly nice date. *Evening*. Whatever.

"Did he say what his mom is going to do about it?"

Well, that's a weird question. "I don't know if he keeps his mom updated on his storylines."

"Not his *mom* mom! His soap opera mom. Lucille!" Kari has clearly had it with me. "You know, when he starts banging Cassie?"

"Oh. No, he didn't mention it. He really didn't say anything else." Well, he did drop that hint about leaving the last job because something stressed him out, but unless he decides to be more specific than that, I don't see how that can even be considered decent gossip.

Plus, there was something about the way he looked when he said it—something kind of defeated. I don't think I want to share it with anyone. He didn't tell me to keep that to myself, either … but I think I will anyway.

Her voice is exasperated now. "Surely he said *something*. You didn't just talk about yourself all night, did you?"

"Not *all* night. He was just kind of close-mouthed about work. We talked about our families and school and stuff like that. Just getting-to-know-you stuff."

Although now that I consider it, we talked about *my* family and *my* work. He didn't tell me much of anything, did he? He was born in North Carolina, moved to LA when he was nineteen … and that's all I've got. He plays it awfully close to the vest, Mitch does.

"Jenna," Kari says sternly, "you did a terrible job. One little tidbit about Cassie isn't going to amount to much as far as scoops go."

"Well, excuse me."

"When are you going to see him again? Did you set a date?"

"You make it sound like we're getting married," I say, and brood into my coffee.

"I should be so lucky. When's your next date?"

"We didn't make one. Like I said, there just wasn't any…." I hesitate. "Any spark."

Oh, I'm such a liar.

"I don't care about your spark! Call him and set up another date."

"I can't do that. That's so mercenary."

I finish off my coffee and wish I had more. Kari must see the coffee-related sadness in my eyes, because she holds hers out. I'm not too proud to take it, either.

"I don't see how it's any different from setting up the first date," she says. "Just this time you call him instead of vice versa."

I sigh. The thing is, I would love to see him again. And we did decide to be friends. It's not out of line for me to call him to get together—in fact, I'd *like* to call him to get together.

But do I want to do it as part of some scheme to get Kari her spoilers?

Not really. I sigh again.

"Quit sighing at me and call him," she barks.

"Stop being so bossy," I say. "I didn't agree to go out with him a million times."

"I told all my online friends that I met him and I'd be able to get good spoilers for them."

"I thought you and your friends didn't even like *Midnight Confessions*. You always made it sound like you just cared about *Doctors and Nurses*."

"Well, that's the best of them," she says. "But I watch the others, too. And now that Mitch has switched shows, a lot of people are paying more attention to *MC* than they used to. Myself included. And I told them I'd get them some spoilers."

"Hey, I told you that thing about his sister."

"Big deal. One measly spoiler. Everyone will be excited for about a day." She frowns. "I really want to outscoop Stace. She always scoops *DN* before anyone else, but if I can rely on you and Mitch, I can outscoop her for the New York soaps. Her New York source has been having a much harder time getting scripts out of the building lately."

"Someone smuggles scripts out of the building?"

She nods. "Yeah, I don't know who he is. Probably a janitor or something. He used to sell them on eBay but someone put a stop to that. So he just sells them direct now. He has an email list and people bid on them."

I'm incredulous. Completely boggled. "People *pay* for soap opera scripts? Real money?"

"They don't pay in rubles."

"Have you ever bought one of these scripts?" I demand. When she doesn't answer, it's all I can do not to shake her. "Kari, you can't afford that!"

Kari's a paralegal, and still pretty much entry-level. I wish she'd gone to law school, but she says she likes punching out at five o'clock and not having to think about the office again until the next day. That's a valid point, but it doesn't pay terribly well. And New York is pretty expensive.

"It's not much," she says defensively. "And I've only done it a couple of times. Usually it's Stace who gets them; she has tons of money."

"She can't think of a charity that could maybe use some extra cash?"

"It's her money." Kari sighs. "Damn it. She always knows everything first, and she's so *smug* about it."

"So you want better spoilers so you can outscoop some rich dilettante soap opera fan with more money than sense?"

"It's not that, it's just that she lords it over everyone like it makes her special."

"And you want to be special, too?"

She doesn't answer.

"Kari, you're special for a million reasons, and none of them have anything to do with Mitchell Cole or *Midnight Confessions* or anything even remotely related to them."

"I know that," she says. "But can't you just do this, for me?"

She looks so pitiful I don't know how to say no. And, anyway, I kind of *do* want to call him. "I'll call him on Monday."

"Monday? Why Monday?"

"Because calling him right now, before sane people have even gotten out of bed, sounds desperate and lame?"

"If you had a good date, why wouldn't you want to have another? It makes perfect sense to me."

"Well, I kind of have to figure out what to say, because it won't be a date." I stare fixedly at the coffee cup in my hands. "I kind of told him I couldn't date him anymore."

"You did *what*?" she shrieks. "Why on earth would you do that?"

"I just—" I can't very well tell her about the kissing. "I just didn't want to lead him on. I told you roughly seven million times that he's not my type."

"He's *everyone's* type."

"Not mine."

She snorts. "You like Kevin Bacon."

"He was Ren MacCormack! Stop doing that!"

"I'm just saying. You have eyes in your head. He's hot like fire. Like fire *on fire*."

I can't find it in me to protest as heartily as I might have done a week ago—as I *did* a week ago. I have to admit, when I'm not in a Drew-induced funk, Mitch looks pretty good.

Great, in fact.

But I'm not going to admit that to *Kari*. "Look, I said I'd call him. If he's cool with being friends, I'll get together with him again. But you're going to have to stop hoping for some grand romance."

"You're crazy," she says, and gets up to check out what's in my fridge.

"Quite possibly," I agree, nodding. "Do you want me to call him Monday, or what?"

"Stupid question." She slams the refrigerator door. "Unless we want to eat ketchup, we should probably go to Dot's and get some grub."

"It sounds so appetizing when you say it like that," I say, but I head for the bedroom to throw on some clothes.

I'm sure the grilling will recommence during our *grub*, but she's getting nothing out of me.

Especially not about the kissing.

## Chapter Ten

AS SOON AS I get to the office Monday morning, I dial Mitch's number, practicing my casual face in the reflection on my computer monitor. Cool as a cucumber, that's me.

He picks up on the first ring again. "Hello?"

God, that *voice*. So much for cucumbers. Now I'm red hot chili pepper all the way.

I have seriously got to talk to him about toning it down. This is getting to be a problem.

"It's Jenna."

"Oh, hi." He sounds happy to hear from me, so that's good. "What's up?"

"Oh, you know, not much. Work and stuff." Such a brilliant conversationalist. I'm sure I'm knocking his socks off.

"I've got about one minute before I have to be on set," he says, "and I really can't talk." He sounds a little regretful, though, which is gratifying. "Can I call you back? Or did you call for something specific?"

"Oh!" I guess I should have thought about this before actually dialing the phone. Instead, I wing it. "I just wanted to say I meant what I said. I'd like us to be friends."

And that's *all* I want.

"So you said."

"Well, I meant it," I say. "Like we could have lunch, and that kind of thing. I liked spending time with you."

That's the truth. It doesn't mean I have to date him. All the things I liked about him I can enjoy just as well if I'm his friend.

*Except the phenomenal kissing.* But I'm not thinking about that.

"I'd like that," he says. "I really enjoyed your company."

I'm much happier than the situation calls for, but I decide not to evaluate that right now.

"Would you like to have lunch later this week?" he asks.

I wince. "Okay, this is going to sound like I'm putting you off, but I swear I'm really not," I begin.

"I hardly think you would make a special point of calling me just to blow me off."

That's heartening, at least. "This is a horrid week at work. I have meetings every day that will make it impossible to go anywhere for lunch. In fact, Wednesday is the only day I don't have a meeting *during* lunch."

"That's too bad," he says. "Is your job usually like this?"

"No, definitely not. If it were, I'd quit. I'm not a fan of the cafeteria here," I joke. "I kind of *really* enjoy food."

"I know," he says.

"Well, if you know any lunch places that are as good as your dinner places, I'm in," I say. "As soon as I've got a little breathing room around here, I can meet you wherever."

"It's a deal. I really have to run," he says apologetically. "Why don't I call you at home later, and we can figure out when you might be able to get free."

"I'll look forward to it," I say, which is nothing but the absolute truth. The cowboy boots—and everything else—don't matter. It's different somehow if we're going to be just friends. You don't have to be embarrassed about your friends. In fact, I think everyone needs one or two really quirky pals. My new soap opera actor friend will fit right in with my weirdo soap opera fan friend.

It's a perfect arrangement.

And when Kari calls later that morning, I'm able to tell her with absolute honesty that Mitch and I touched base but didn't make any firm plans. Hopefully that will hold her for a while.

————

I half-expect that Mitch might not call after all—he wouldn't be the first guy to say *I'll call you* and not follow through. But the phone rings at nine o'clock, just as I'm settling in on the chaise with my well-worn copy of *Pride & Prejudice*.

"Hey!" he says, by way of greeting. "Glad I caught you. I called earlier and you weren't home."

"I stayed at work till seven-thirty," I say, dogearing my page and tossing the book on the coffee table. "And I'm sure as my deadline looms larger, I'll pull plenty of late nights. But let's not talk about my job, please. I just ate."

"What did you have?"

"My specialty: takeout. What'd you have?"

"Pizza. What a couple of culinary defectives."

"I can cook, I just prefer not to." I lean back against the arm of the chaise and tug the throw over my bare legs.

"I'm a damn good cook," he says, "but I don't usually bother with it for just me."

"Sure you are. Guys *say* they can cook, and then when push comes to shove they mean they can heat up a can of Spaghetti-Os."

"You wound me," he says dramatically. "I can certainly do better than a can of Spaghetti-Os. I'll show you sometime."

"When?"

"Soon."

"Okay, Betty Crocker, it's a deal. I'll bring the can opener."

"Ha ha," he says. "Very funny. This from the woman who just admitted she specializes in takeout."

"Touché."

"What kind?" he asks.

"What kind of what?"

"Takeout. What kind did you have?"

"Indian," I say. "Chicken tikka masala." It's literally the most boring, white-people food you can get in an Indian restaurant, but I like it.

"Speaking of food, we were going to make lunch plans," he reminds me.

"Yeah," I say. "About that—"

"No big deal. If you can't manage it, we'll get together when work slows down. I know my gig isn't the same, but it *does* go through those cycles of too much to do followed by nothing to do."

"I suppose," I say, considering this. "I suppose a job is a job is a job, right?"

"Yeah. Maybe there's an exception or two, but not many."

"Well, if you don't mind waiting, I can call you when my job isn't killing me," I say. "I suppose it will be a few weeks."

"*That's* no good," he says emphatically. "You'll have forgotten who I am by then."

"I don't think that's likely." As if. "You *do* make an impression."

"Must be my boyish good looks."

The deadpan delivery is absolutely perfect. I can't help but laugh, which I hate to do on the phone. I always worry that I sound stupid or that I'm too loud, or any number of other creative worries that I come up with on the spur of the moment.

"You should have been a comedian," I say.

"Like stand-up? No way. No money in it."

"Forgive me for being presumptuous, but you can't be breaking the bank at *Midnight Confessions*—or can you?"

"It's enough," he says simply. "And they *were* very glad to get me. I have all I need."

"So you're happy there?"

"I am. I could be doing something I like a lot less," he says, and even over the phone, I can tell he's grinning.

"You don't seem the sort to stick with something unpleasant." I poke around the edges of why he left his last job, wondering if he'll tell me anything I can tell Kari.

"Well, now," he says, slowly, "that depends on how you define *unpleasant*. In between roles, I've been known to go home and do roofing, or construction. Some people would call that unpleasant."

"Construction? Like building houses?"

"No, like building roads, and highways."

"And roofing? I assume you're not talking about a career in Rohypnol?"

This time he's the one laughing. I beam, very pleased with myself.

"No, definitely not. Shingles. Ripping them up, nailing them down."

"That sounds dangerous."

"I like it. I like being out in the sun, and I like working with my hands."

It's interesting thinking about someone working like that, using their strength and their body to build something. I mean, obviously, I know that things don't just build themselves. And we do have ironworkers and so forth in New York; I just don't know any of them. My circle of friends is made up pretty much exclusively of office types: a little pasty, not used to anything more physically demanding than walking down to the water cooler.

Come to think of it, I don't even do that anymore. Ryan brings me whatever I need. That's awful! I don't even go to the water cooler for myself?

"So, you still want to hear about my job?" he asks. "The indoors one."

I snuggle a little lower on the chaise, fighting a telltale heaviness in my eyelids. I'm having too much fun to go to sleep now. "Very much."

"What do you want to know?"

"I don't know. I don't know much about soaps."

"You and Kari couldn't be more different, could you?" he asks. "She already knows so much about everything that there wasn't much I could tell her. I think she was disappointed."

"Well, I won't be, because I'm a complete neophyte," I say. "I guess … just tell me how the day goes for you."

"On a normal day, I show up at eight, check for green sheets—those are last minute script changes. You want to look at those first thing, because sometimes there are a lot of them."

"They change things that far along?" I ask, incredulous.

"All the time."

"And you have to learn new lines? For that day?"

"All the time."

"That's no way to run a business!"

"Sure it is," he says. It's the verbal equivalent of a shrug.

"But it must be so hard."

"It's my job."

I think about it for a minute. I guess he's right, but I'm glad it's not *my* job, because it sounds like it would make me crazy. I like to know how things are going to happen.

It would be nice to be more like him. Laid back, easygoing, not worrying so much about it.

"It really doesn't bother you?" I ask.

"It really doesn't. All I've ever wanted was to be an actor; I'm not going to start pitching tantrums because I have too much new dialogue to learn."

"But isn't it hard?"

"A little," he says. "But what isn't? I think of it as a challenge."

"That's awesome."

"Nah." He sounds embarrassed. "It's just the only way to think. Anyone who's going to get upset about a thing like that should maybe find another job."

"I'm feeling like such a *baby* now," I say.

"What?"

"Maybe I should stop bitching about my job and just do it, you know? You make a lot of good points."

"Now wait a minute," he says. "I'm not talking about you. I'm talking about *me*. I doubt it's the same thing."

"Isn't it, though?" I ask.

"No, I really don't think it is. I'm talking about people who act, who audition to be on a soap opera, and then complain about the workload. Soap acting is *hard*. You have practically no time to learn lines, no time to rehearse, you shoot in one take unless someone screws up. People know this going in, so cry me a river if it's too much for you, right?"

"Yeah," I say, slowly, "but with me—"

"You told me yourself, your job isn't usually this crazy, right? So if you're a little overwhelmed when it took a turn for the crazier, how is that the same?"

"It's not?"

"Exactly." Then he laughs. "I guess I'm done lecturing."

"Good," I say. "So, after the green sheets?"

"Blocking in the morning. We run lines to be sure we haven't forgotten anything, and to make sure the new dialogue works. There's some 'You stand there, you stand there, turn this way, hold that look till we cut.' Then in the afternoon, makeup, then shooting. One take, like I said, unless something goes wrong—and, even then, it has to go *really* wrong."

"One take," I repeat. That's insane.

"Yeah," he says. "Today actually went great, no retakes on anything. I was out an hour early."

"What did you shoot?"

He hesitates. "You know, I'm not supposed to tell you that.

If you told Kari, it would be on the internet in a matter of seconds."

That shuts me up. I'd like to protest that I would never tell Kari, but of course that would be a flat-out lie. And for some reason lying to him isn't as easy as I thought it would be. "You shouldn't assume I'll tell her things just because she's my friend," I say.

There. That's not a lie. It's a *smokescreen*.

"Fair enough," he says. "You guys have been friends for a long time?"

"Since we were seven."

"How'd you meet her?"

"I ran over her with my bike." I haven't thought about that in years.

"Literally?"

"Yeah. Just her legs, though. She was lying in this little depression in the grass at the park, and I could barely see over the handlebars—and then—*wham*!"

"What did she say?"

"She said, 'Thanks a lot, I'm going to catch hell for getting dirt on these pants.' To which I replied, 'Hey, they were dirty before I showed up.'"

He laughs. "Your first fight."

"The first of many," I say. "She's the best friend I've ever had, but we *do* fight an awful lot. Two strong personalities."

"I'll say."

"I'm gonna pretend you didn't say that," I tell him. "Your turn to talk."

"What do you want to know?"

"Your first part," I say. "What was it?"

"Grade six. Charlie and the Chocolate Factory."

"Were you Charlie?"

"I was not," he says. "I was Augustus Gloop. Big orange inflatable life vest under my clothes to make me fat, with my little sixth-grade toothpick legs sticking out from underneath.

87

The chocolate river was a four-foot high piece of painted plywood, and when I fell in—which meant sort of diving around the side of it—I knocked it over."

I'm laughing out loud now, imagining it.

"It's not funny," he says. "It wasn't the highlight of my career, that's for sure."

"What was the highlight of your career?"

"I did an amazing indie film about four brothers coming to their father's funeral. Once the funeral is over they go back to the house they grew up in to divide up their dad's stuff, and they get wasted and end up fighting and having to face their past and the things that haunt them."

"It sounds interesting."

"It was really draining, and totally worth doing. I'd love to be in another movie like that." He's quiet for a moment. "But the gig I've got now is good."

I ask him some more questions about the movie, and then he tells me about the first movie he was in, a bit part that ended up on the cutting room floor. Then he asks me some more questions about my family and growing up, and I ask him about his family. We swap questions back and forth, and I lose track of time completely.

It's so odd to be the focus of this kind of attention; Drew and I were living together in what I thought was a real, serious relationship, and we didn't talk to each other like this. He didn't want to know this much about me after three years.

It occurs to me, in a very solid and real way that I haven't quite felt before, that Drew is a real asshole.

Mitch has known me for a week, and he wants to know absolutely everything; the story of how I met Kari isn't the only distant memory I find myself digging up.

Finally, when I feel like I'm really going to doze off if we keep talking, I check out the clock on the DVD player. It's ten minutes to midnight.

"Oh, my God, Mitch, I have to go," I say. "I have to be up at seven."

"So do I," he says. "We're idiots for staying up like this."

I feel a little hurt—I've loved our talk, and the time flew by. "Are you sorry we did?" I ask.

"Not a bit. I do idiotic things all the time—keeps me from getting boring."

"I highly doubt that you could *ever* be boring."

"I try," he says. "But no matter how un-boring I am, or this conversation is, we have to go to bed."

I shiver—literally shiver—at those words, because hearing them delivered in his warm, honey-smooth voice is …

Well, it's something, that's for sure.

"Call me tomorrow?" I ask recklessly.

"You serious?"

"Dead serious. I can't stay up this late again, but call me tomorrow night and I'll think of some other cool questions to ask you."

"All right." His voice takes on an interesting upbeat lilt, and I suspect that he's got one of those heart-stopping grins on his face. "I will."

"I can't wait," I say. "Good night."

"Night," he says, and hangs up.

I look at the phone for a second, more than a little surprised. Where did the time go?

Well, wherever it went, it was worth it. This is the first time in weeks I've gone this long without thinking about work. It feels great.

I head toward the bedroom, wearing a huge grin of my own.

## Chapter Eleven

MITCH DOESN'T CALL Tuesday night, which leaves me far more disappointed than I have any right to be. I try to shrug it off philosophically, and go to bed early to make up for the night before.

Wednesday brings good news: Web Development has finished the template for the *Grow* site, and it's really lovely—well, lovely except for the part where it still says *Grow* on it, but I'll work on that. Our color palette works especially well onscreen, and everyone in the department is walking around with big, self-satisfied smiles on their faces. I don't feel one bit bad about telling Ben that this is a direct result of my excellent overseeing.

For all I know, maybe it *is*. And if it's really just the vagaries of fate, why shouldn't someone get credit? Fate, after all, can't possibly get a raise out of this, while it's entirely conceivable that I might.

Add to that the fact that I arrived this morning to find a really snazzy-looking *Grow* mouse pad on my desk—that one was Melody's baby, her first solo project, and she hit it out of the park. It's all the right colors but she didn't put the name on it.

She knows me so well.

So I feel pretty damn good, despite my pile of message slips that never seems to get any smaller.

Ryan buzzes me. "Your lunch is here."

"My what?" Am I losing my mind? Did I order lunch and forget about it? Why can't I seem to keep any thought in my head these last couple of weeks?

"Your lunch. It's here."

I didn't order lunch. I'm sure of it. "It's a mistake, Ryan. Send it away."

"I don't think I can do that. You'd better come handle it yourself."

Well, that's odd. "Why can't you—Is this code? Are you being held at gunpoint or something?"

"Nope," he says, sounding decidedly cheerful for someone who might be in a hostage situation. "It's just something you need to handle."

When I venture out to investigate, he's putting his *Out to Lunch* sign on his desk. "See you in an hour," he says.

"What? Where are you going?" He always tells me in the morning when he's planning to go out at lunchtime. I mean, he doesn't have to, but he does. "And where's this delivery boy?"

Ryan looks pointedly over my shoulder, and I turn to follow his gaze.

Mitch is standing next to the door I just came through, resplendent once again in jeans and cowboy boots. No snaps today; he's wearing a long-sleeved green t-shirt that stretches over his broad chest in an alarmingly delicious way. He's also holding an enormous picnic basket.

"I guess I'm your delivery boy," he says, and when he says it in that unbelievable voice of his it sounds absolutely *filthy*.

I go a little weak in the knees. "Oh."

"See you in an hour," Ryan says again, and I hear the door shut behind him.

Mitch smiles, eye-crinkles and dimples out in full force. "Are you hungry?"

"Starving," I say.

I'm always telling him I'm starving, and that's not very ladylike. It's a good thing I'm not trying to impress him.

I show him into my office, and when he pulls a red-and-white checked blanket out of the picnic basket, I just laugh and move the guest chairs around to the other side of the desk.

He puts the basket on the now red-and-white checked floor and starts unpacking Saran-wrapped bundles of food: huge sandwiches, a platter of fresh veggies and dip, wedges of apple pie. And cream soda, which is a very interesting choice. In my experience, cream soda is one of those things that people either love or hate, and it's kind of risky to assume someone will like it and just show up with some.

As it happens, I love cream soda.

"Everything looks so good," I say, my mouth watering. We sit cross-legged on the blanket—thank God I'm in slacks—with the picnic basket between us. "How did you know this was exactly what I needed?"

"Anyone who's being overworked needs a lunch delivery, even when they don't know they need it." He hands me a sandwich and takes the other for himself. "I felt bad for not calling last night—my mom called and talked my ear off, and by the time she was done, if I called you, we were gonna be on the phone till midnight again—so I figured since I didn't have to tape today, I'd surprise you."

I don't respond for a moment while I savor the first bite of my sandwich—shaved ham, Genoa salami, provolone cheese. Exquisite. "It's a wonderful surprise," I tell him, and I mean it. Not just the food, of course, but that he would be so thoughtful. He really *is* a nice guy, and I'm glad he wants to be my friend. "I didn't know when I might be able to get away from this office again, and I really wanted to see you."

"You did?"

"Yeah, I—" I put down my sandwich. "Look, I don't want us to have to have a heavy conversation about this every time we get together, but I *do* want to tell you—to your face—that I owe you an apology for the other night."

"Okay," he says. And then he waits.

Apparently when I said "apology," he thought I meant an actual *apology*. I was hoping he would figure it's the thought that counts. Instead, it looks like I really am going to have to deliver the goods.

"I suppose … I suppose I was giving you mixed signals."

"You could say that."

"But it wasn't out of any malice or whatever. I just … you know, you're very good-looking—"

"I've been told," he says, with admirable restraint.

*I just bet.* "And I'm certainly not trying to say—"

"Is there an apology in here somewhere? Because so far all you're doing is making me want to shake you. Or kiss you again." Thankfully he says this with a big grin, so I don't need to faint. "You can't make a habit of kissing Mr. Wrong, you know."

"Don't call yourself that," I say, and lean across the picnic basket to swat his arm. "I'm just trying to say I hope you understand my reasons for acting the way I did."

"I don't," he says calmly. "But that's irrelevant. You feel how you feel. I really like talking to you and spending time with you, and I *am* a big boy; if this is how you want us to be, I'm fine with that." He takes a bite of his sandwich. "Good friends are harder to come by than girlfriends, anyway. Being turned down isn't going to kill me."

This is an interesting concept, since being turned down—even by someone I didn't like all that much—would crush me. "Of course. There are plenty of other fish in the sea," I say brightly.

"I don't date fish," he deadpans.

"Neither do I."

"No," he says, pointing at me with his sandwich. "You date jerky veterinarians."

"Point taken," I say, and even though I'm not even half done with my sandwich, I start on my pie. "My God, where did you buy this?"

"I know a little place," he says.

I have a feeling that no matter what neighborhood he was in, even though he's lived here for less than two months, he'd *know a little place*. He's that kind of guy.

"I might have to go online to let your legions of fans know that your true talents lie in being able to ferret out the most delicious food in any city."

"I don't have legions of fans."

"Well, you must have some, right?" I take another huge bite of pie. "Kari knew who you were right away."

"That's because Kari is a little…." He seems to be searching for the right word.

"Obsessed?" I offer.

"I was going to say *enthusiastic*."

"Same thing."

"Oh, no, it's not." He raises his eyebrows at me. "You don't know from obsessed, trust me."

"Do tell."

I've heard Kari's side of this stuff many times, but in all honestly I've always wondered about the other side. How do these guys feel about being the objects of so much attention?

"Oh, it's unbelievable. Has Kari told you about Fan Club Weekend?"

"Some of it, yeah."

"It's crazy." He moves the picnic basket to the side and leans back on his elbows, stretching his long legs out beside me and crossing them at the ankles.

We may be *just friends*, but that doesn't stop me from appreciating the view. God, he sure can fill out a pair of jeans. And that t-shirt is thin enough that I can see the muscle definition underneath—and just, wow. Chest, arms, abs—the guy's got it all.

"There's this huge room, right? And tables all along the walls. You get assigned a table, and you sit and you smile and you autograph things until your hand is going to fall off. Which is fine when people are genuinely happy to meet you and they're asking you interesting questions or telling you what stories they like you in—or even if they're shy and just get their autograph or picture and leave right away.

"But then there's always a group of them that think they *know* you—they hear rumors on the internet about this person who won't work with that person, or that person nixed this other person's storyline or whatever—and they give you hell for that. Or they tell you how awful you are, or how you shouldn't have taken advantage of that poor woman, or—" He breaks off. "Well, they say that to *me*. Obviously, there are some people whose characters aren't quite as … fluid in their morality."

"So, you're a bad guy." Funny, I never thought to ask Kari what kind of role he played.

"On *Doctors & Nurses* I was, yeah. Except that's the thing—I'm an actor. I don't have any interest in playing a *bad guy*. That might have been all anyone was *seeing*, but what I was *playing* was a flawed but well-intentioned person who loved deeply but had a hard time keeping his anger in check, and tended to act rashly. Where's the fun in playing someone one-dimensional?"

I shrug. "Aren't soap opera characters kind of one-dimensional by nature?"

"They don't have to be. With the right kind of writers, you can get fantastic material." He sighs. "*MC* has great writers right now. That really helped with my decision to make the move east."

"The other night, it sure sounded like you had another reason," I say.

He nods a little. "Listen, you really can't repeat this," he says.

"Deal."

"Let's just say the number one star of the show wasn't a lot of fun to work with. And with the kind of fan base he has, and given that he was a lifer—"

"A lifer?"

"Yeah. Someone that isn't going to make any kind of career outside of soaps for himself. There's nothing wrong with that if that's what you want to do, but my point is this guy is a lifer, so *he* wasn't going anywhere. The storyline … changed, and unless I wanted to spend the next few years being a cardboard villain, I had to go."

"But why?"

"Our characters were kind of facing off over a girl," he says slowly. "Played by an actress named Vickie Walsh. She's an absolutely fantastic actress, totally professional. Unlike some people."

"And?"

"And as far as the *who's gonna get the girl* question, I was winning."

"Oh."

"Fan mail was really high for us. It was kind of threatening, so he went to the head writer. In the end the show wasn't willing to risk rocking the boat, not on the off chance that Vickie and I could pull it off." He shrugs. "I think we could have. She didn't want to work with him anymore, and she was really selling our pairing. We were building a pretty big fan base of our own, which was nice. The fans called us Recon."

"Recon?"

"Yeah, the characters were named Rebecca and Connor. That's what internet fans do when they love a couple. They smash their names together into something cool. Or, if they don't like them, into something awful." He grins. "Pity the poor Jason and Liz fans."

I think about it for a moment, then giggle. "I wonder what the Blake and Cassie fans will call you?"

He smiles and shakes his head. "They're calling us Cake."

"How can they be calling you anything? You haven't even gotten together yet."

"We've been onscreen together, and sometimes that's all it takes," he says. "So, with Recon, the fans were loving us, which was ruffling someone's feathers."

"And?" I say again.

"And the writers kind of stacked the deck—had me do some pretty underhanded things in the interest of getting the girl—and she ended up riding off into the sunset with our hero." He takes a bite of his pie. "Vickie was disgusted, though you can't tell onscreen how miserable she is. Like I said, she's a total pro."

"And you?"

"I decided not to renew my contract, and Connor went to jail."

"Ouch."

"It's okay. The network didn't want to lose me, so they wrote this new part at *MC*, and that was that. I like the challenge of playing someone completely new, and it's not like I couldn't go back someday. At least they didn't kill Connor off." He takes a long drink of his cream soda and shrugs again.

It occurs to me that he must have been pretty popular if they wrote a whole new character specifically for him. But what do I know about soaps? I'll have to ask Kari if that's as impressive as I think it is.

*Kari.*

Oh, shit.

This is exactly the kind of thing Kari wants to hear about.

If I tell her, it'll be all over the internet in four seconds. And Mitch will know where it came from, and he'll be disappointed that I didn't keep my word. That matters to me. He's smart and funny and genuinely interesting, and he trusted me enough to tell me this. I can't stab him in the back like that.

I don't think Kari's going to be very happy with me.

"So, here I am, back on the east coast," he says, dragging me out of my horrified reverie. "I'm not looking forward to snow, I can tell you that. I'm closer to my family, so that's also a plus, but it was hard to leave. I'd been in LA for a long time."

I hadn't really thought about him being homesick. Now that I think about it, I wasn't really thinking about him at all, except to think that he's not my type—which is becoming harder and harder to say, because he kind of turns me on anyway. That's really self-centered—seeing him only as someone who has an impact on my life in one way or another, and forgetting to take into account that he's a person in his own right—and I kind of wish I never figured it out. Because now I feel like the biggest jerk ever.

"Am I boring you?" he says, sounding slightly testy.

I've been so busy castigating myself for being self-absorbed that I failed to notice he wasn't speaking anymore. Oh, sweet irony!

"No," I say firmly. "I'm so sorry. I was lost in thought, but it wasn't because I didn't want to listen to you." I want to have his full attention—this is important—so I set aside the remains of my pie and focus on him. "Listen. I might come across as really selfish sometimes, and maybe sometimes I am. But mostly I'm just flaky, and I don't mean to be insensitive. You are easily the nicest guy—the nicest *person*—that I've met in a while, and I've really loved the conversations we've had, and I'd like to know even more about you. So I'm sorry if I seem like I'm totally flaking out and don't care what you're saying. That is most decidedly not the case."

He looks at me for a long time; so long and so inscrutably that I'm a little afraid he might grab me and start kissing me again.

He smells so good—*looks* so good—that the idea doesn't

sound at all unappealing right now, and I push it away. That tangent is going to get me daydreaming again, and I don't want to look away from him until he knows I mean it. "Tell me more about your job. Sleeping with your stepsister, *scandalous*!"

"You really want to know?" he says.

"Yes," I say, stretching out on my stomach next to him and propping my chin in my hands. "Tell me everything."

And he does.

## Chapter Twelve

THERE WAS A TIME, not all that long ago, when Friday night was an opportunity to go out and get a couple of drinks, or go dancing, or both, or whatever. Those days—nights—are over. This Friday finds me collapsed on the chaise, still in my work clothes even though I've been home for an hour. It's all I can do to work the remote control. Frankly, I shouldn't have bothered; there's nothing good on.

When the phone rings and I pick it up to find that it's Mitch, even that voice doesn't zing me out of my stupor.

Well, maybe a little.

"Hey," he says. "Want to get a beer? Jacks?"

I really, *really* want to say yes. That's the unvarnished truth. But the thought of putting on decent clothes, going all the way down to 5th Street, and attempting to make even semi-decent conversation is too daunting.

"Oh, I'd love that, but I've got to take a pass."

"Are you sure? I'll buy you a drink."

"Tempting, but no. Work's been a living hell."

"You doing okay?"

"I'm good. Just tired and antisocial, you know? Is that all right?" Kari would understand, but Mitch and I haven't known each other long. Maybe *I just don't feel like it* isn't acceptable yet.

"Absolutely. Get some rest—and don't forget the movie tomorrow."

I barely stop myself from groaning. After our office-floor picnic, Mitch suggested we get together Saturday to see the movie we skipped after our date—after our *not*-date, rather. It seemed like a really good idea when I agreed to it, but at the moment I think I'd rather sit on this couch until it's time to go to work on Monday.

On the other hand, I know I'll have a good time. Surely I can recoup enough energy in the next twenty-four hours.

And honestly? I want to see him. Our picnic was awesome, and we talked on the phone again last night for more than two hours. This time we didn't talk about just me; he told me more about his parents (loving, supportive, and slightly befuddled by the acting thing), his first real acting job (a commercial for a big-deal local gym in LA, in exchange for a membership), and his most recent girlfriend (cheated on him).

*Oh, that blows,* I said, and he said *She wasn't the first,* which led into a long side conversation about infidelity and how both of us think it's an absolutely garbage thing to do. The kind of conversation you have with a boyfriend, really, except … you know. Just friends.

I can't believe how differently I feel about him; the fact that I can't remember the last time I just sat quietly and let someone talk about themselves doesn't reflect well on me, but it's the truth.

So yeah. I want to stay home forever, or at least for the weekend, but I'll go to the movies with my friend.

*Just friends,* I remind myself again. To Mitch, I say: "I won't forget."

"Awesome," he says, and hangs up. Damn soap opera people.

But the phone rings again immediately, and this time it's Kari.

"I was gonna go hang out at Jacks. You want to come?"

Well, isn't Jacks just the hottest spot these days!

"I'd love that," I say, again, "but it's been a lousy week at work and I'm beat. I think I'm just going to turn in early."

"Does this have anything to do with Mitch?" she asks.

"What?"

"You said you were going to call him on Monday and then nothing happened. Are you avoiding Jacks because he might be there?"

"No, not at all. I—"

"He's really very sweet."

Yeah, I know this. It's ridiculous, her talking him up when I already like him perfectly well. But I still haven't told her about our phone chats, or the picnic. I kind of wanted them to be just mine for a little while.

And I'm not looking forward to the lecture about how I didn't do a good enough job getting spoilers for her and her stupid online friends.

I've got plenty of spoilers, actually—big, juicy ones.

On Wednesday, Mitch told me that he'd start having scenes with his onscreen mom in the next few days, but that she wasn't even going to know he was her son for a while, and that the stepfather would find out first and offer him great scads of money to get out of town, which would eventually lead to a rift between the mother and the stepfather. But that part won't happen for a couple of months; first he has to get in his stepsister's pants so she can be angry and disgusted when she finds out who he is.

Last night he told me that the network signed him to a two-year contract, and that they're doing a location shoot next spring—somewhere tropical, though he doesn't know where yet. Word on the set was he and his stepsister would have to travel to the rainforest to recover an ancient family heirloom.

Something about stopping a curse, of all things. And while they're doing that, he finds out she's knocked up, and she finds out Lucille is his mother.

It's all very … soapy. Kari would love it, but of course I can't tell her. I do at least have to tell her about the picnic, though.

*Might as well get it over with*, I think. "Look, Kari—" My call waiting beeps. "Hang on, that's my other line."

I click over, taking a deep breath. Seems like everyone who might want to invite me to Jacks has already called; I wonder who this can be.

"Hello?"

"Jenna? It's Drew."

I nearly drop the phone.

"Drew, I've got Kari on the other line." Drew? Calling me? Why? "Hang on a sec."

I click back to Kari. Drew has always hated call waiting; if this had happened when we were together, he would have hung up on me. Well, that's not true, because I would have just let Kari wait until I was done talking to Drew or until she hung up, whichever came first.

But he's not my boyfriend anymore; he can wait ten seconds.

"Kari, it's Drew."

"What the hell does he want?"

"Well, I don't know. I suppose I'll have to ask him. I'll call you later, or tomorrow or whatever?"

"Sure thing," she says, and hangs up.

I click back to Drew. "Sorry about that," I say. Frankly, I'm surprised he didn't hang up.

"It's fine. I didn't mind waiting."

*Since when?*

"Are you busy right now?" he asks.

Where on earth is this going? "No, I'm just hanging out at home. Long week."

"Would you like to meet me for a drink?"

Okay, did not see that coming. What can he possibly want? He obviously wants *something*, and I have to admit that I'm really curious about what it is. I don't want to go out, but ... there's something odd about his voice? And a weird kind of deference in the way he's asking me to meet him.

If I don't go, I'll just sit here all night wondering.

"I ... I guess I could?"

Seriously, what can he possibly want?

"Why don't you come down here?"

Drew still lives on 3rd Street; it's a matter of pride for him that even though he's doing well enough to live pretty much anywhere, he stayed in the neighborhood where he has *roots*. Frankly, I think his huge rent-controlled apartment might have been a contributing factor as well, but he'd never admit it.

The thought of the train ride is daunting—why did I move uptown again? "Listen, as I think about it, I'm really tired and it's an awfully long way to go for a drink. You want to meet halfway?"

"Okay," he says, surprising me. He's never been big on compromise, and, except to go to work, he never goes above 14th Street. "Marty's?"

Marty's is the place Drew and I had our first date, actually, so that's a little weird. It's around the corner from the vet's office where we met. Two days after my friend had her dog put down, he got her number out of her file and called her for my number—which she gave him without a second thought. Not that I minded. When he finally tracked me down he asked me to meet him at Marty's for a drink when he got out of work. And the rest is, as they say, history.

Ancient history. So why is he calling me now?

"Marty's it is," I say. "Give me an hour."

———

Marty's hasn't changed at all. The jukebox is still turned up too high, and the crowd around the dartboard is nearly loud enough to drown it out anyway. Drew isn't there when I arrive, so I grab a seat at the bar and order a Cosmo.

I had a bit of a time figuring what to wear. What *do* you wear to meet with your ex-boyfriend who's engaged to someone else? I ended up going with jeans and a pink cable-knit sweater that makes me look a bit like a kindergarten teacher. I don't want to look like I was trying too hard.

Actually, I don't want to look like I was trying at *all*—because this is weird.

"Jenna," Drew says from behind me.

I jump a little, then turn around on my barstool. "Hey."

Drew orders a martini, and the bartender mixes one up. Drink in hand, Drew settles my tab as well as his and says, "Let's go sit at a table."

I pick up my drink and follow him. He chooses a table in the corner farthest from the door, where it's shadowy and just slightly quieter than the rest of the place.

"So," I say, taking a seat, "I was surprised to hear from you. What's going on?"

He looks a little embarrassed. "I should have kept in better touch with you—"

"Drew, I walked out on you. I didn't expect us to wind up best friends."

"Still, I should have called or something. I've missed talking to you." He takes a long swallow of his drink. "You always understood about work and stuff like that."

That's me: understanding as hell. Not good enough to marry, but no one can have it all, right?

"Is something wrong at work?" I ask. I don't ask *And if so, why aren't you talking to Trudi about it?*, but I think it.

"Well, yeah." He drains the martini and gestures for another. "I think my partners want me out."

"Out? Out of the practice?" This is a shock. Drew is an

excellent veterinarian. Not such a great people person, but fantastic at his job.

"They haven't really said anything outright," he says.

The bartender drops off Drew's drink, and he drinks about half of it at one go. I've never seen him drink like this. Of course, he's never had trouble at work before, either.

"They just keep dropping hints—how much would I want for them to buy me out, have I ever thought about a solo practice? They're not exactly subtle."

"But I can't imagine *why*," I say. "Drew, you're a great vet."

"Thank you," he says. "It means a lot that you would say that."

"It's true." I'm actually indignant on his behalf, which is also weird since I was thinking ill of him just the other day.

"Unfortunately, it was their practice for a long time before I came on board—if they want me to go, I probably should. But where would I go?"

"Oh, Drew," I say. "I'm so sorry this is happening."

"Thanks." He smiles weakly and finishes his drink.

I'm surprised when he signals for yet another. "You're welcome," I say.

He reaches across the table and lays his hand over mine. I tug a little but he doesn't let go, and I don't say anything. It's not a big deal, really.

"What do you think about going somewhere quieter?" he asks, and it occurs to me that he must be very, very drunk.

"What I think is that you've had enough to drink," I say. "Come on, let's walk it off." Greeley Square—which is really more of a triangle, so figure that out—is only a block or so away; we can circle that a few times and see if he sobers up. Then I can stuff him in a cab and wash my hands of this weirdness.

"Whatever you want," he says, but his agreeability is sort of undermined by the fact that he picks up his fresh martini and drinks the whole thing. He drops some bills on the table with a flourish, takes my hand and leads me outside.

It's gotten a little chilly out, and I'm grateful my sweater is warm—it's this really amazing soft wool, and wasn't expensive at all. I wish it wasn't pink, but you get what you get when you shop almost exclusively clearance—and if I'm going to walk a drunk around the park, I don't need to freeze to death while I do it.

"Where to?" he asks. "Your place?" And he slings his arm around my shoulder, pulling me close and giving me a look that I recognize perfectly well. It may have been over a year since I've seen it, but even with my lousy memory I could hardly forget it.

Whoa. Just a minute. This is heading someplace I don't want to go. There is one thing I absolutely *never* do, and that is cheat on anyone or get involved with anyone who is. As far as I'm concerned, there's nothing exciting about infidelity.

"Drew," I say, "I'm glad you felt you could talk to me about your work trouble, and I make a great sympathetic ear—but that's as far as it goes. You'll have to get whatever other kind of comfort you're looking for from your wife-to-be."

"I can't," he says. "We broke up."

"You what?" I say.

"We broke up," he says again.

I go sort of numb from shock. It's literally the last thing I expect, and I don't quite know how to process it.

This is what I've been wishing for, right? For a whole year.

So this time, when he pulls me close, I wrap my arms around his waist, and when he bends to kiss me, I let him.

"I'll get a cab," he says.

I hesitate. I … kind of don't want him to come to my place? He knows where it is—he had to forward my mail—but he's never been inside.

Plus, you know what? I want to see his place. If he's lying about the breakup, I'll be able to tell.

"Let's go to your place," I say.

So that's what we do. Drew flags down a cab and we sit quietly during the short trip downtown. The cab drops us off and I stand looking at the building for a moment. I can't believe I used to live here. It seems a lifetime ago.

It still feels strange, though, to see Drew unlocking the front door and then the inner door. I used to have those keys, after all. I left them on the dining room table when I moved out. I carried the last of my things out in a cheap duffel bag I bought at the surplus store, stepped out of this very elevator that we're getting into now, walked out, and never looked back.

At the time, I thought I might be making the biggest mistake of my life. In retrospect, I'm proud of myself. I didn't settle. I knew that if I couldn't have what I wanted, it was better to be alone than to accept less.

And look. It paid off, right?

So why don't I feel triumphant?

The apartment looks much the same as it did when I lived there. All the furniture is in the same place, no major redecorating to remind me that someone else lived here after me. Drew never really liked to have his stuff moved around; I see Gertrude didn't change that about him.

There's nothing to indicate that anyone but him lives here. I guess she really did move out.

He closes the door quietly behind me and I turn to see him staring at me, not saying anything. "Don't talk," he says. "I just want to look at you. It's been such a long time."

It *has* been a long time, hasn't it? I stand there, helplessly, looking around me, buffeted by memory after memory. The day I moved in, when we had sex on the balcony after dark. The first time we had his parents over for dinner here—no wonder they didn't like me, after what I did to that pork tenderloin. The day I got my promotion—things were already starting to go bad between us then, with little resentments piling up and never being discussed. But when I came home, Drew made dinner, and we danced to Etta James in the middle of the living room.

It was also the beginning of the end, as I recall. I was so sure after that night that a marriage proposal was right around the corner, that I'd found Mr. Right and we were finally headed in the direction I wanted.

And I waited, and waited—and *waited*—until I thought I would scream from frustration. Until finally I asked point blank if we were ever going to get married.

I don't want to think about this anymore, don't want to remember any of the hurtful things that were said—and, to be fair, I should admit that hurtful things were said on *both* sides.

Those things don't matter now. I'm home.

But it's funny—it doesn't feel like home.

Drew steps away from the door and takes me in his arms. He smells like Old Spice. It seems like I used to love that smell, like that smell used to represent everything I wanted in the world, but it's all so far away and academic now. I feel myself disassociating from the whole thing, distancing myself from all these complicated and unwelcome feelings.

"You are so beautiful," he says, and I'm in his arms, and his eyes are looking into mine like he's drowning and I'm a life preserver. Or maybe I'm the one who's drowning. "I've missed you so much."

"I've missed you, too," I say, and I suppose it's true. I remember that it *was* true, but everything is so out of synch now. I keep feeling like something is terribly wrong, and I can't put my finger on it.

I shouldn't be doing this. I know that I shouldn't be doing this, but I don't know why I feel that way. And that weird confusion stays with me even as Drew begins to kiss me again and walk me backwards to the bedroom, and through everything that comes after.

## Chapter Thirteen

IT'S ONLY LATER, when Drew's deep breathing fills the silence of his bedroom and I'm lying beside him, feeling empty and a little sad instead of happy and fulfilled, that I allow myself to think about what it was that he said to me that night, when I asked him *why*, after all the time we'd been together, he would say he never intended to marry me at all.

*"Because," he said. "There are girls you marry, and there are girls you just live with. You're not the first kind, Jenna."*

I bolt for the bathroom and throw up what little I've had to drink. I've been so careful not to think about that. It's quite possibly the most hurtful thing anyone has ever said—or could ever say—to me, after I worked so hard to overcome the strikes against me and be someone that a man like Drew could be proud of.

What kind of man—what kind of *person*—would say something like that?

I lie down on the bathroom floor for a minute, the tiles cold against my back. Then I get up. I root around in the cabinet to find an unopened toothbrush, then I brush my teeth, rinse, have a drink of water, and return to bed. Drew hasn't moved. I climb back under the covers and stare up at the ceiling.

He said that, sure—but if I make things right between us, there's no way those words can be true.

———

I sleep uneasily, and I'm almost grateful when *The Battle Hymn of the Republic* wakes me up. Drew stirs but doesn't wake. I grab a blanket from the foot of the bed to wind around myself and head for the living room, where I dig my phone out of my purse.

"Kari? What on earth are you doing calling me at"—I check the clock on the VCR—"eight o'clock on a Saturday?"

"Believe me, it's not my idea of a fun time, either. I'd much rather be curled up in bed." She yawns audibly. "But I'm having breakfast at Dot's in half an hour with Mitch and Luis. Wanna meet us?"

"I can't this morning," I say.

"I'm sure Mitch would love to see you," she says. "And if someone doesn't get you two crazy kids together, how am I ever going to get my scoops? He won't tell *me* anything."

"I really can't."

There's a long pause. "Are you avoiding him?" she asks.

Oh, this is ridiculous. It can't go on for another minute. "Kari, look—I can't talk about this right this second, but no, I am not avoiding him. In fact, totally the opposite. We've talked on the phone a few times and he brought me lunch at work earlier this week. He's very nice, but he's not spilling anything—"

"What do you mean, he brought you lunch?"

"He brought me lunch. At my office. Like, in a picnic basket." It was actually very sweet, and talking about it is making me feel a little weepy, which is ridiculous. Why on earth would I feel sad, thinking of that? Why would I feel this heavy ache in the center of my chest, thinking of that?

"And you've been gabbing on the phone."

"Well, yes." It occurs to me that she might be getting the wrong idea. "I mean, as friends. I told you, we agreed that we'd just be friends."

"Yes, I know what you agreed," she says testily. "I'm just trying to figure out why you're only now getting around to telling me about your lunchtime picnic. Mitch didn't mention it."

"It just … didn't come up." Wow, that's pretty weak, even for me.

"'It just didn't come up?'"

"Kari, listen to me. It made you cranky when I went to dinner with him and didn't squeeze any info out of him. I didn't want you to lecture me again about doing a bad job." I hear Drew stirring in the bedroom. "And I really—*really*—can't talk about this right now."

"Why are you being weird?" she demands. "Did you sleep with him?"

"No!" Drew is moving around in earnest now, and I can't have this conversation anymore. "Look, I can't talk right now. I'll call you when I get home, okay?"

She's quiet for a second, and then asks, "Where are you?"

"What?" I say, hedging. I don't want to tell her. She hates Drew.

"You weren't home. That's why I called your cell. Where are you?"

I sigh. I suppose she'll have to know eventually, if we're getting back together. "Oh, for God's sake, Kari, I'm at Drew's but I can't—"

"Jenna, he's getting married!"

"No, he's not, and frankly I'm offended you wouldn't have figured that out right away. You know how I feel about poaching." She should know me better than that by now. "They broke up. And he needs me. We're going to get back together."

"Really?" she asks. "Did he tell you that?"

"We haven't talked about it, exactly," I say. And it somehow doesn't seem as appealing as it used to.

"And I doubt you ever will," she says. She's mad, but there's a little sad in there, too. "He's using you; I can't believe you don't see that. Why would you want to get involved with him again when you finally got free?"

"That's not fair. You know how I feel about him."

"I know how you *felt* about him. And he was never any good for you, and he never treated you like you deserved."

"Kari—"

"And I can't believe you'd even give him the time of day when a great guy like Mitch is into you—"

"He's not into me!" I whisper furiously.

*Certainly not anymore, anyway.*

"He *was*; I know he was really interested in you. And you've blown it for some selfish jackass who'll just get you to take care of him and then treat you like shit—again."

"Look, I can't talk to you about this right now; I have to go. It's not because I don't want to talk, okay? But I have to go."

"Fine," she says, and hangs up. She sure didn't sound like it was fine. She sounded like she was super-pissed, which means I'll probably get the cold shoulder. Kari's not really one for protracted arguing; she'll choose radio silence every time. And I know she'll get over it, probably before the week is out.

But I could really use her *now*.

I put my phone back in my purse slowly, hoping none of that filtered into the bedroom.

Drew appears in the bedroom doorway, fully dressed. This puts me at a distinct disadvantage, undressed as I am. I wrap the blanket a little more tightly around me and stand up, trying to smile.

But I'm at an absolute loss. I don't know what to say to him, or what he expects of me. Or what I expect of him.

"Good morning," he says.

"Good morning," I say tentatively. "How did you sleep?"

"Like a baby." He doesn't ask how I slept.

"Feeling better about the issue at work?" I ask. It's a stupid question, really; nothing we did last night is going to do much to solve his work problem.

"Not really."

We stare at each other for a minute.

"I'm going to go get dressed," I say.

"I think that's a good idea." He turns and goes into the kitchen. I stand where I am for another minute, trying to figure out why I feel like I've just been slapped. Then I go back to the bedroom and start picking my clothes up off the floor. I can't believe I left this sweater on the floor all night.

I can't believe I'm going to have to get it dry-cleaned.

I can't believe I'm sitting here thinking about this sweater like it actually matters at all.

But if I stop thinking about the sweater, I'm going to think about last night, and I'm going to think about how cheap and lousy I feel, and I'm going to cry.

Oh, look: too late! I wipe the tears off my face, furious at myself. What the hell am I doing? No crying.

I pull on my clothes and grimace. Everything smells like Drew's bedroom carpet. I sit down on the bed and pull myself together. At least I've stopped crying.

"Jenna?" Drew says. I look up and he's in the bedroom doorway, looking at me.

I stand, and then I'm not quite sure what to do with myself. "I … um. I should probably go," I say.

"Okay," he says. "Do you want me to call you a cab?"

"No, I can do it."

We look at each other for a minute.

"So," I say. "I guess … I mean, that is…."

"Yes?" he asks—but the thing is, he doesn't look at all interested.

"I suppose I was just … wondering, I guess. About what we do now."

"Do?" he says, as though the idea of doing anything is so foreign he's not sure what I even mean. "About what?"

"About … about us."

"Us?" he echoes.

"Yeah."

There's another long silence, and I don't want to be the one to break it this time, so I let it stretch until he looks almost as uncomfortable as I am.

"What do you want me to say?" he finally asks.

"I don't have any particular ideas."

"Neither do I." How helpful.

"I guess we could start with 'Here's what I think we should do, Jenna,'" I say.

"That's not as simple as you make it sound," he says.

"Why not?" I ask.

"Because I don't know what we should do," he says. "Come sit down in the other room."

In the living room, he sits on the overstuffed chair by the television, and gestures for me to sit across from him, on the couch. I sit. I should want him to sit over here with me, but I don't.

"Here's the thing," he begins. "Last night was … was nice—"

"Nice?" I ask.

He nods. "But I didn't mean for things to go this way. It's just too early for me to deal with something like this."

"'Something like this?'"

He nods again. "I can't get into some heavy thing. My breakup with Trudi is still very fresh. I miss her terribly."

It's like a slap in the face.

I've got to get out of here, right now. I'll just take the train. Maybe I can still meet Kari—

No, wait. Mitch is with her. And I can't—I absolutely *cannot* —see him right now.

With no warning at all, I feel the tears gathering. *No*, I tell myself. *Not here, not now.* Drew has never seen me cry, not once in our whole relationship, and I'm certainly not going to start now. I'll call Kari and meet her after—

Oh my God, what if she tells Mitch what I did?

No, that's ridiculous. Kari would never do that, no matter how mad she is. We've had arguments before—and I can tell this one is going to be a doozy—but she would never. *Sisters before misters,* as they say.

But whether she spills the beans or not, *I* know what I did.

And I'm supposed to go to a movie with Mitch later today.

*Oh, God. I can't.*

I want to curl into a ball and pretend none of this is happening to me. Maybe if I'm very lucky I'll get run over by a train on the way home.

*Here's hoping.*

Meanwhile, Drew's still just standing there. Is he done talking? Is he waiting for me to say something?

Fuck him. He can grow old and die before I so much as give him the time of day.

Without another word, I get up to leave.

As I open the front door, Drew calls out from the living room. "I just need a little time, Jenna. I'll call you."

And after years of putting up with it, somehow I just don't have the energy to deal with his bullshit.

"Don't bother," I say, and slam the door behind me.

## Chapter Fourteen

MUCH TO MY DISMAY, I do not get run over by a train on the way home. The subway ride is totally uneventful, which gives me plenty of time to watch the instant replay of last night and beat myself up.

*What the hell was I thinking?*

But that's the problem: I don't know what I was thinking. I don't know what I think of anything right now. My reactions don't seem right to me, and it's hard to analyze what you're feeling when you're right in the thick of feeling it.

At home, I take the hottest shower I've ever taken.

One thing I do know: something in me has changed. I don't know what it is, exactly, or why it happened, but a month ago —hell, a week ago—I would have wanted to stay there at Drew's apartment. I would have tried to talk to him more about what happened, and I would have tried to coax him around to seeing it my way: *we belong together, this happening is a sign. Blah blah blah.*

But I don't feel those things. I feel empty, hollowed-out. I feel like there's something missing—and I don't mean that feeling after the breakup, where I felt like *Drew* was missing.

Something else.

The water starts to go lukewarm, so I get out and dry off. Wrapped in a towel, I lie down on my bed and stare at the ceiling, trying to pick my way through the stupid circular thoughts in my head.

Getting back together with Drew was everything I wanted. I know this to be true, so when did that change? What did he say, or do, that struck me wrong? What happened that I'm not able to put my finger on?

Once again I run through every minute that led to this morning, this time looking for some false note with him. Surely he said or did something, because it doesn't make sense that I should all of a sudden stop wanting him. And while I certainly can't accuse him of doing anything without my consent, the truth of the matter is that I didn't want to be there. I couldn't seem to get out of my own way and realize it at the time, but I sure see it now.

It should have been the joyous resolution of a year of waiting, but frankly it was awful.

I don't think Drew is the problem here.

I think I am.

———

I wake up with that terrible feeling of having napped too hard, and roll over to look at the clock.

Damn it! It's already four o'clock, and I slept the whole day away. I *hate* that.

I drag myself back to the bathroom and wash my face with some cool water, then peek in the kitchen cupboards. By some miracle, there's coffee. No cream, but whatever—this is medicinal. I brew up half a pot, and when it's done I bring a cup back to the bedroom with me. I stand there for a few minutes, sipping my sad, black coffee and looking at what's in my closet.

Not much, honestly. Mitch has already seen me in my D&G

top, and my hangover jeans, and my casual-but-not-really black dress. Maybe—

I freeze in the act of reaching for the Vera Wang. For one thing: to a movie? No. For another: What am I doing? Why do I care what I'm wearing to go to the movies with Mitch?

Well, I don't. I mean, I want to look nice—I always want to look nice—but that's it.

I push the dress aside and grab a white cashmere sweater off the shelf behind it. After the Vera Wang and the D&G top, it's probably the most beautiful thing I own. And honestly? It's just a little bit tight, which—

Which I completely don't care about, because I'm just going to the movies with Mitch.

I think about changing, decide this is fine. The part of my brain that's whirling around the question of why I'm dressing up right now quiets down when I put on jeans, but starts back up again when I pull out the black boots.

It's just that Mitch is so tall. It's nothing to do with making my ass look good.

I take the train down to SoHo and emerge from underground into the bustle of shoppers and tourists. The sun is about ready to touch the horizon, and I would swear there's a touch of winter in the air. Already? It's barely fall.

The building that houses the movie theater is only a block away from the subway entrance, and Mitch is waiting for me, leaning against the outside wall near the corner of the building. He's in jeans, because of course he is, and the snaps are back but I don't even care. He looks good, and I try to tell myself I don't notice—but I do. I *do* notice, and all my stupid circular thoughts from earlier come crashing back in like a tsunami.

*Oh, my God*, I think. *You screwed up so bad. Look at him. Look at him, you idiot.*

Some things are starting to clarify themselves in my head—

things about how I feel, and for whom, and what happened last night, and what can never happen now.

I push all of those thoughts away. I have to get through this. I put on my best poker face.

But I must not have a very good poker face, because when Mitch looks up and sees me coming his expression gets serious.

"Hey, are you all right?" he asks.

I shrug a little. "Yeah, I'm okay," I say, but there's a waver in my voice so it comes out sounding anything but okay. "I napped by accident. I'm not feeling 100 percent."

"Are you getting sick?" He reaches out and touches the back of his hand to my forehead, and I just about faint. Sexy, yet nurturing. Great. And of course he smells amazing. "Could be coming down with something that's making you tired."

"I ... I didn't sleep well," I say.

And then, without me even realizing it's about to happen, tears spring to my eyes.

*No. Oh, shit.*

I blink rapidly, then stand there in horrified silence as I feel them spill over and drip down my face.

Mitch blinks too, clearly surprised. "You seem to have sprung a leak," he says, softly.

I nod.

"Okay, this movie isn't happening," he says. "Let's go sit down."

Petrosino Square—which is also shaped like a triangle, actually, what is it with this city?—is on the opposite corner. Mitch takes my hand in his and steps onto the crosswalk.

I look at our joined hands as we cross the street. Such a small thing, but somehow everything—like it's the most natural thing in the world for him to shift immediately into protector mode, to want to know what's wrong, to try and fix it.

But the only thing I need protection from, apparently, is my own stupidity. And I don't think Mitch can fix this.

For lack of any better ideas, I let him lead me across the street, and then to a bench in the narrowest part of the park. He sits, and pulls me down next to him.

I take a few deep breaths and try my best to shut off the waterworks. I'm mostly successful, and when I look around no one seems to be paying attention anyway. There are a couple of women with strollers sitting on a bench, and a skateboarder—in absolute defiance of the rules—trying to ollie over a huge hump in the cracked pavement. He's almost good at it, but not quite. He hits the ground twice in a row, but keeps trying.

By this point the tears have stopped, so that's good. But nothing else is good right now. I'm embarrassed, and mortified, and a whole host of other synonyms. I'm also feeling a great deal of self-pity, which is stupid because I did this to myself. And I'm screwing up Mitch's chance to go see this movie.

Worst of all, he's going to ask me what's wrong. He's that sort of guy, right?

"You don't have to tell me what's wrong," he says. "But I hope you will."

It might be literally the only way he could have gotten me to talk, this asking-without-asking thing. I'd admire it as one hell of a tactic, except this is Mitch. It's not a tactic. It's just who he is.

If there is such a thing as *absolute good*, I think it's sitting here on this bench with me.

I don't know what to say, and I have to tell him *something*. I mean, I could say I don't want to talk about it, and we could just go to the movies, but he would know something was wrong. I know Mitch; that would eat at him.

I could make something up, maybe? But it wouldn't feel right to lie. Not to him.

"I slept with Drew." I just say it, right out loud like that. It sounds even worse out loud than it did in my head, and that's really saying something.

"I'm sorry?" he says, and he's looking at me like that was literally the last thing in the world he expected me to say. Which it probably was.

I lace my fingers together in my lap and stare straight ahead of me, not looking at him. At first it's hard to talk about it, but it actually feels better to have it out, so I keep talking until I've told the whole story.

Then I look at Mitch—and I don't even know what to think. I've never in my entire life seen anyone look that angry. He's staring straight ahead as well; anyone walking by would think that we find the traffic patterns on Lafayette Street absolutely fascinating.

He doesn't say anything, and I don't say anything, so that's pretty awkward. After maybe thirty seconds, which feels like thirty minutes, I finally ask, "Are you mad at me?"

It's a dumb question. Why would he be mad at me?

"Why would I be mad at you?" he says. He's got an excellent point—I ought to know, since I just made it myself—but he sure sounds angry.

"I don't know. I just—"

"I've got no right to be angry with you, Jenna." He turns his head to look at me, and his gaze is so intense that it makes me look down at my hands. "I was just surprised, that's all."

"Me, too," I say. "I guess … I guess I'm just mad at myself, and I'm projecting."

"Yeah, maybe," he says. His voice is a really odd kind of cold—restrained? I don't know the word, but I know that, for the first time, it doesn't make me feel shivery and delighted. I just feel sad. "So … well. That's what you've been wanting, right?"

"I … I certainly thought so."

"Okay."

"But now I'm not sure?"

"Okay."

"And I don't know, I feel really confused?" Understatement of the century there.

"That sucks."

"And I think maybe—"

He stands up, abruptly. "I just remembered I have to be somewhere."

I stare at him for a moment. That's completely ludicrous. He can't have to be somewhere; we were supposed to be watching a movie for the next two hours.

But I don't point that out. I'm sure he just wants to get away from me, and who could blame him? I'm sure he doesn't want to sit here while I whine about something that's really my own fault. I've been there. How many times have I listened to Kari complain about some guy and thought *Oh my God please make it stop*? And I'm sure she thinks the same of me; probably so does Mitch.

He's still standing there, like he's waiting for me to say something.

So I do. "Let's talk tomorrow? I'll call you?"

"Sure," he says, shortly. "But I'm doing some stuff. I might not be around."

"Oh, okay," I say. What does he want? What else can I say?

"Yeah, okay." He puts his hands in his pockets and rocks back on his heels a little bit, like he might be planning to say more, but he doesn't. Instead, he turns and strides out the side entrance to the park, cutting back towards the subway.

I'm going to the same subway if I'm going home—which I guess I am, because where else would I go? But it's obvious he wouldn't want my company, so I stay put on my bench and spend some quality time wallowing in remorse. Eventually, I drag myself to the subway, and home.

## Chapter Fifteen

ALTHOUGH IT SEEMS like it would be a lot less trouble to throw myself off the Empire State Building, I do manage to drag myself in to work Monday morning. Sure, I exploded my personal life into bits of shrapnel this weekend. Yes, I spent Sunday in a stupor in front of the TV.

Kari didn't call, and she didn't return any of my calls, so I guess we are officially fighting—which is a bummer, because I could really use a sympathetic ear right now. I didn't hear from Mitch, and he didn't answer my calls either, so it's a pretty sure bet he's washed his hands of me, too. There is no Chunky Monkey left in either of the two bodegas closest to my apartment.

But at least I've got work under control.

"You're late," Ryan says when I open the door.

I look at the clock. "No, I'm not."

"For the meeting."

"What meeting?"

"The meeting you're forty-five minutes late for," he says patiently. "When it became obvious that you weren't going to make it, Melody took all your reports and stuff, but I don't know how well she's covering for you."

I shake my head. "It's a mistake. We don't have a meeting today. It's tomorrow."

"Ben's off tomorrow, and he has to leave early today. He moved the meeting to this morning, before office hours. I sent you an email about it Wednesday." He points to the door behind me. "They're in the conference room across from Ben's office. Better get moving."

I stare at him for another few moments, unwilling to believe this. The meeting tomorrow—*today*—is a big deal, and Melody can't fill in for me, though I'm sure she's trying her hardest. How can I have missed such an important email?

But of course Wednesday was the day Mitch brought lunch. I was distracted, like I've been distracted so many other times lately. I've only got myself to blame.

I turn and sprint for the elevator.

———

"So, if the focus groups are right, then—" Ben cuts off what he's saying and glares at me over his glasses. "Good of you to join us, Jenna."

Ben's not the sort that wants a big flowery apology or a dramatic scene, so I opt for quiet and professional. "I'm sorry I'm late," I say, and slide into the empty seat beside Melody.

She has a stack of papers in front of her; she pushes them over to me and points to the focus group results Ben is discussing. That's enough to orient me, and by the time Ben finishes his sentence I'm up to speed.

"We're looking at this slightly off-center," I say. "The copy is focusing too much on long-term results and not enough on how very little is required to start. We can't continue to ask these kids to think about tomorrow instead of today."

"That makes sense," Ben says. He's every inch the professional, and he's not going to let my tardiness throw the meeting out of order. As long as I can jump right in and keep up, he'll do the same. "These are young people. Tomorrow is an eternity away." He turns to Aiyana. "You realize we're going to have to change the copy again."

"They don't need my help with that," Aiyana says, pointing with her chin across the table at the copywriters. They're all bunched up together in one corner of the table. Big surprise. "Not my department."

I wince.

"Everything is your department," Ben says coldly. "We all work together to create a final product, and everyone's work impacts everyone else's. If we rewrite copy, you're probably going to have to work out a new design."

"Oh, come on," she says. "Do you know how many changes we've already made? This is—"

Melody stands up and clears her throat. All eyes turn to her. She looks at me as if she's not quite sure why she just stood up and perhaps I could fill her in, but I'm as baffled as she is.

"Yes, Melody?" Ben says after a moment.

"Well, I was just thinking—I mean, what I mean is—" She looks lost for a moment, then moves to the giant mock-up of that damned brochure that sits on the easel at the foot of the table. "Can I write on this?" she asks.

Ben shrugs. "Go ahead. You can't make it any worse."

This gives rise to a lot of resentful looks around the table but no one disagrees with him. Obviously he's not feeling too friendly this morning.

"Look," Melody says, and uncaps a black Sharpie. "This part here, the part the focus groups don't think is as important —can't we sort of move it here?" She circles the bullet point in question and draws a line to a spot at the bottom of the right flap. "Congregate the longer-term details here, like fine print, only not fine."

"We can fit it there with a little tweaking," offers one of the copywriters. He's blond with a sleek goatee. I'll be damned if I can remember his name.

Melody leans in and draws more circles and arrows. Suddenly our brochure looks like it's covered in football plays. "Slide this chunk over here, put this here and maybe just bold it to punch up the emphasis? Then we've got a whole different perspective but we haven't lost anything. We've just emphasized the most effective points."

Everyone just stares at her, and when none of them have any response she forges on.

"We don't want to eliminate that stuff altogether, because I'll bet you that some of these kids are going to be running this by their parents, and the parents *are* going to be thinking long-term. We don't want to make it hard to find or, God forbid, get rid of it. We want it … not front-and-center. Front and right-of-center." She smiles a little. "Plus you might not have to change the design, or just change it a little."

Aiyana beams at her.

"You know what this means," Ben says.

Melody nods, and they say, in unison, "More focus groups."

Ben points at me. "Make it happen. I want parents of college-age children. Make sure you get a good cross-section education-wise. I want to know how the college-educated parents differ from the ones who aren't. And I want to know the investments they're making themselves, or if they're not making any." He pauses. "And I still want this off to the printer at the end of the week, regardless."

There are some muffled groans around the table, but I keep my game face on. "Shall we end, then?" I ask. "So I can go get this moving?"

"Yeah," he says, and the group breaks up. Everyone gathers their things and makes for the door.

I head out behind everyone else, but as I pass Ben's chair he reaches a hand out to stop me. "Bring her in on it," he says, nodding at Melody, who wanders out the door oblivious to his interest. "She's got good ideas."

"Bring her in how?" I say. "I mean, she's in everything anyway. I value her advice a lot."

"Now, so do I," he says. "Share the work, let her do as much as she feels she can. Like I said, she's got good ideas, and she did a great job filling in for you this morning. Speaking of which, Jenna—have you decided that our meetings aren't important to you?"

"I didn't get the email that you changed the day," I mumble.

"I hear that you're dropping the ball a lot," he says. "Is something going on that I need to know about?"

I shake my head, horrified not only that I've been messing up so much, but that *people are talking about it*. What am I supposed to say?

I guess I could tell him that I was distracted by my ex-boyfriend getting engaged to a girl that looks like a Victoria's Secret model, but that's all handled now because they broke up and, oh, by the way, I had ill-advised sex with him this weekend and he treated me like garbage.

I could tell him that my best friend isn't speaking to me because of the aforementioned sex-with-my-ex, and because I won't pass along spoiler information from her favorite soap opera.

I could tell him that the source of the aforementioned soap opera information is probably never going to call me again now that he knows what a moron I am, and that thought has absolutely wrecked me.

I'll be sure to fill him in, right after I stick hot pokers in my eyes and pull out all my fingernails.

"Nothing," I say. "I just missed the email somehow and Ryan never mentioned it."

"Ryan sent you the email," he said. "That's all the

mentioning he needed to do." The reprimand isn't as bad as it could be, but it stings nonetheless.

"Of course," I say.

"Don't let it happen again, Jenna."

I nod and scurry out the door. Back downstairs, I head for Melody's desk, where she's putting down her notes and things from the meeting.

"Hey," she says.

"Hey," I say. "Will you make copies of those for me?"

"My notes? Sure." She picks up her notebook. "You really didn't miss much. You know how long it takes to get everyone quieted down and on task."

"Still, I really appreciate you covering for me, Mel." I lean against her desk. "I know I've been off in space lately and it helps a lot to know someone around here is paying attention."

She blushes. "You've just got a lot going on, I guess?"

"Something like that. Listen, Ben was impressed, too. He notices these things."

"What things?"

"Things like knowing what's going on in your department, being prepared, stepping in when you're needed, taking initiative." I point my finger at her, cock my thumb, shoot. "Keep surprising Ben and you won't be sitting at this desk for much longer."

"There aren't a lot of other places to sit, Jenna," she says.

"Hey, you never know what might happen," I say. "I used to sit at this desk—actually, I sat at the next one over, but you get my point."

"I'm not sure I do."

"Ben likes to hire from within. He'll move you up the food chain before he brings in someone from outside. That's how I got my job."

"Last time I checked your job was unavailable," she says wryly.

I laugh. "Not the way I've been going lately." Hey, wait a

second. That isn't funny. I clear my throat awkwardly. "But, uh, seriously—keep it up, okay?"

"Okay."

"And come by my office after lunch. Ben asked me to use you more on this project, and you have great ideas. I'll look through my work and see where you can take some stuff on."

"Sure." She smiles brightly and walks off in the direction of the copy room.

I head back to my office, thinking idly about what I might have on the back burner because of *Grow*. There's always some damn thing getting neglected, it seems. Maybe I can find something on another project as well, something that will really showcase what she can do, look good on her resume.

And figuring all this out will stop me from thinking about the other thing. The thing I am most decidedly *not* thinking about at work—not after I just got the smackdown from my boss for not paying attention to my job.

Ryan looks up as I enter and asks, "How'd it go?"

"It went fine," I say. "Melody covered for me. She's going to be working more closely with me on this particular project from now on."

"What does that mean, exactly?" he asks, frowning.

"For starters, copy her on all emails that would normally come to me. That'll keep her in the loop."

"Okay," he says. "So how was your weekend?"

And then, out of nowhere, with no warning, something happens that is about as mortifying as anything could possibly be: I start to cry.

## Chapter Sixteen

THE TEARS ARE SO unexpected and excessive that even I'm surprised by them. I stand there helpless, trying to stop and failing at that as miserably as I've been failing at everything else.

I've never been one of those girls who can cry prettily—I'm one of those who whoops and sniffles and gets all blotchy and gross-looking. So poor Ryan is confronted with not only a hysterical female, but a horrifying one, as well.

Fortunately, I have excellent taste in assistants; Ryan is an extremely competent young man. In short order, he produces a box of tissues and a glass of cold water, and sits me down on the little loveseat in his office. We decided to buy it last year so that people waiting to see me would have a comfy place to sit. At the time, obviously, I had no idea it would come in handy for my as-yet-unimagined nervous breakdown.

"I'm so sorry," I say. "I don't know what's wrong with me. I just had a very bad weekend."

"It's really none of my business, of course," Ryan says, "but do you want to talk about it?"

"I slept with my ex."

Maybe I *should* have told Ben. I'm certainly telling everyone else.

The corners of Ryan's mouth turn down. "Ew."

"I know it was really stupid, you don't have to tell me I'm an idiot—"

He cuts me off. "Hey, I had no intention of telling you any such thing. You're not an idiot."

"Well, you looked—"

"I'm just surprised. I thought he was engaged."

I take a sip of water, then set the glass on the side table. "They broke up. I actually don't want to tell the whole story again; I'm sure you get the gist."

"And … did it not go well?"

"Honestly?" I put my head in my hands and blow out a lungful of air. "I don't even know how to answer that."

"'Well, Ryan, it was spectacular,'" he says. "Or 'Well, Ryan, I would have rather been doing laundry.' Like that."

I smile a little, and I'm grateful to him for causing it. "Well, Ryan, I would rather have been doing just about anything."

He nods. "Yeah, I thought as much. What with the crying and self-recrimination."

"It was just so *stupid*." I look over at him. "Listen, seriously: can I just be straight with you? Now that I've cried all over you and told you my most shameful secret to date?"

"Have at," he says.

He reaches for the trashcan beside the loveseat and holds it out; I drop my wad of tissues in there and press my fingers against my eyes. *No more.* I pick up my water again and take a long drink while he puts the wastebasket back in its spot.

"I didn't want to be there," I say, "and I don't even feel like I *was* there for most of it. My head was off somewhere else entirely."

He squints at me. "Do you think he—" He mimes pouring something into my glass of water.

"Oh, God no." I shake my head vehemently, and set the

glass back down. "He would never. No, I was just being a moron. I *wish* I could blame someone else."

"You're not a moron. You did something that a lot of people do, even people who are smart enough to know better. You're not the first person to fall into bed with an ex." He pats me awkwardly on the back. He doesn't seem any more comfortable than I am, but here we are. "It's only been a year, and he still had a hold on you."

"Not any more," I say, and I mean it. I really, truly mean it. I don't care if I never see him again. He's dead to me. "Lesson learned, never to be repeated."

"Well, since I'm an overprotective and, when necessary, violent friend, I could also offer to beat his ass if that was something you wanted. You can watch or whatever. It'll be great."

"That won't be necessary," I say, but the offer makes me feel immeasurably better.

"Hey, don't hurry to make a decision one way or the other," he says. "I never liked that guy anyway."

"Yeah, well," I say, taking a deep breath, "sad as I am to admit it, he didn't do anything this weekend that I didn't walk right into with my eyes open. Open but unseeing, of course. My specialty."

"It's the worst, isn't it?" he says, and he sounds really sympathetic.

"Being your own worst enemy?" I ask. "Yes."

"Been there, believe me."

I take a deep, shuddery breath. "Okay, back to work," I say. "Soldiering ever onward."

He nods. "Ever onward. But"—and here he looks thoughtful for a second—"you know what's funny?"

"Absolutely nothing about this situation?" I suggest.

"Well, yes, but also … the thing is, I thought you might be starting to move on. With Mitch."

*Oh, hell.* So much for ever onward. I collapse under a fresh wave of tears, and Ryan supplies a fresh round of tissues.

"I'm sorry," I say. "I'm so sorry. I don't cry. I never cry. I don't even know what's happening."

He holds the wastebasket out again; I drop in another wad of tissues. Deep breaths.

"I shouldn't have brought him up," Ryan says. "You were doing admirably well, all things considered."

"It's okay," I say, "but I really don't want to talk about Mitch. I can't even think about Mitch. I was supposed to see a movie with him Saturday, and I just … I just looked at him and —" Ah, well. In for a penny, in for a pound. "I looked at him and I knew Drew wasn't what I wanted anymore. I figured it out just a little too late."

"Damn," he says. "I'm sorry."

I pick up my water, take a sip. "He's upset with me about it, I could tell. I'm sure he thinks I was stupid, and I'm lucky I didn't get a big lecture from *him*—"

"Wait, what?" Ryan leans back, looks at me with his eyebrows raised. "Mitch knows about this?"

"Yeah." I fight off tears again—successfully this time. "I told him about it when we met up to go to the movie."

He's looking at me like I've taken complete leave of my senses. "You went on a date with Mitch and told him—"

"It wasn't a date."

"Yes, it was. Do you even *know* any guys?"

"What?" I can't follow him at all. "I know lots of guys."

"Well, you wouldn't know it by this," he says. "You don't do that to a guy."

"He agreed that we're just friends. He said that was *for the best*."

"I don't care what he said; you go out to the movies with a girl you like, and that's a date. And then she tells you about banging some other dude—"

"It wasn't a date. He doesn't like me that way anymore," I insist. "And I didn't *tell* him about it … well, I kind of did."

He just looks at me.

"Yeah, I guess I told him pretty much everything."

Ryan shakes his head. "I know I'm overstepping here, but you're an idiot."

I'm indignant. "You said I wasn't!"

"Not about that, about this." He takes my glass of water and sets it aside, then grabs me by the shoulders and looks directly into my eyes. "Listen to me, because this is important: I can guarantee, 100 percent, Mitch did not want you to tell him you had sex with your ex."

"Well, he asked what was wrong."

Ryan just shakes his head again. "Seriously, have you ever, even once, *met* a guy?"

"Stop saying that. I know guys."

"What did he do when you told him?"

"Well, he looked kind of ..." I trail off, thinking about Mitch's face: jaw clenched, eyes focused on Lafayette Street.

"Mad?" Ryan says.

"Furious," I say quietly.

"And then what happened?"

"He said he had somewhere to be," I say. "But I know he didn't."

"Of course he didn't."

"And then he looked like he wanted to say something, and then he left."

Ryan sighs. There's a lot of sympathy in that sigh, but then he says, "I can't believe you needed me to explain this to you."

"I just—" I stop, start again. "He asked. And I didn't stop to think how it might make him feel." I turn my hands, palms-up, as if to say *What was I supposed to do?* "I asked him if he was mad at me, and he said no, so what am I supposed to do now?"

"I don't think *mad* would even be the right word for what he is right now. He's crazy about you, Jenna."

"Don't say that," I wail, and he hands me some more

tissues, but I don't need them. I'm not even sad any more. I'm just angry. At Drew, for being selfish. At Mitch, for not telling me he was upset. At me, for being completely, totally, all-the-way the biggest dumbass on the entire island of Manhattan.

And probably the other four boroughs, too.

"It's just the truth," Ryan says. "He brought you a damn picnic."

"See, that was after we agreed just to be friends. It was a *just friends* picnic. He's fine with it."

Ryan snorts. "He is *not* fine with it. He is lying to you—and I will admit, possibly to himself—about this."

"Well, I'm not a mind-reader, am I?" I scowl at him. "I can only go by what he says, and if he said he was fine being friends, what am I supposed to do? Assume that every man I come in contact with wants to date me?"

"You can't tell me he's never acted interested, or put the moves on you."

I close my eyes and try not to think about it. I wish I could think about anything else. "He kissed me once."

"But you're just friends."

"I decided—*we* decided—after that happened. And there's been nothing since." I scowl. "He said it was fine. If it wasn't really, but he said it was? That part's not my fault."

Ryan nods a little. "Fair enough. But you're still dumb to have believed it."

"I know."

We sit in silence for a moment, then he says, "What did you mean when you said you realized Drew wasn't what you wanted?"

I shrug a little. It's too much, and I actually wish I hadn't said that part. Especially now that it's too late.

"Well, did you mean you gained some clarity and you want to be on your own for a while?" He lifts his eyebrows at me. "Or did you realize you don't want Drew anymore because you want something else?"

I wish Kari were here. She wouldn't have to ask—she would know—so I wouldn't have to say it out loud.

"I saw him there, waiting for me? And I thought—I mean, I made myself not think it, but for a second I thought about how we might have had a shot at something, and then … this business. I ruined it."

"So how do you feel about him?"

Tears threaten, a little, but blinking gets rid of them. "I think … I think I really like him." I nod. It feels right, when I say it. "I think I don't want to be just friends anymore. I'm not sure I ever really did. But now it's obviously way too late."

"Maybe," Ryan says. "Maybe not."

"He was pretty upset."

"Well, of course he was. But do you want him?"

"I think I do."

He raises his eyebrows at me again. "He's put up with a lot of shit from you. You're going to have to do better than that."

"Yes," I say. "I do."

"Well, then," he says, patting my knee. "You're going to have to do some serious chasing."

"I don't know how. Can you help me?"

And that, right there, is the most pathetic thing I've ever said in my whole life.

Fortunately, Ryan is nothing if not helpful. "Of course I can."

## Chapter Seventeen

MY FIRST ASSIGNMENT is to go into my office and call Mitch right away. *Not a moment to lose*, Ryan said, so here I am, hand shaking on the phone.

It rings three times, and I think I'm going to get voicemail again, but then he picks up.

"Hey." His voice is flat.

I've heard what feels like a thousand variations of that voice, but I've never heard this one, and I *hate* it. When Mitch talks to me, he's smiling. Even if it's on the phone, I know just by the sound of his voice that he's smiling.

He's not smiling now, and I miss it more than I could ever have imagined. There's an ache just behind my breastbone. I'm not sure I can go through with this.

But I have to. *He's put up with a lot of shit from you*, Ryan said, and he's right.

So I say, "Hey back. I was just calling to see how you're doing."

"I'm good," he says, shortly. "I'm between takes, though. I can't talk."

"No problem," I say. "I just wanted to hear your voice. Go break your legs or whatever, and I'll call you later."

"Sure," he says, and hangs up.

I set the phone down and look up at Ryan, who's watching from the doorway.

He shrugs. "I didn't say it was going to be easy."

———

The next three days are basically a mid-90s movie montage set to a Spin Doctors song. "Two Princes," probably.

I call Mitch on Monday evening, and he answers my questions in monosyllables, and after about ten minutes he says he has to go. *Okay.*

Tuesday morning, I confab with Ryan, who assures me that's normal, and I'm only just beginning. "It's going to be a long slog, Jenna," he says. "Don't get into this if you're not ready to do the work."

So I call Mitch again late Tuesday morning, and ask if he wants to get together for lunch. He's busy. How about dinner? Also busy.

I tell him I'll call him later. He says he might be busy and I say okay and we hang up.

Ryan shrugs. "Told you," he says, and sits down across from me to strategize some more.

We're not getting a lot of work done so far this week, but whatever.

Tuesday after work I call Mitch, and casually mention that I'm going down to Jacks that night and does he want to come? He makes some noncommittal noises, and I take that as a good sign. At least he didn't just say no.

But he doesn't show. I sit by myself all night, nursing a Guinness and turning down several propositions. I guess I don't usually go out to bars alone; I had no idea how sketchy it was.

Wednesday morning I feel a little hopeless, but Ryan gives me a pep talk.

"It's been two days, for God's sake. Stop whining and make some kind of grand gesture."

Okay, not so much a pep talk as a verbal beat-down. Close enough.

I ponder my grand gesture—and when the brainstorm comes, I'm amazed at my genius. I call a deli around the corner from the ABC studio and order lunch delivered, in a picnic basket. Basically the same thing we had at our picnic lunch, with a note that says *Picnics for two are more fun. Maybe next time?*

Ryan nods when I tell him. "*That's* what I'm talking about. Nice."

Just before quitting time on Wednesday, he pokes his head in.

"No calls," he says. "Cell?"

I shake my head. "No, but I know he got it because I called and they said they gave it directly to him, not the front desk."

"Well, call him now. Invite him out again."

My shoulders slump—this is very discouraging—but he's right, so I pick up the phone.

Mitch is notably less surly, though still not what I'd call friendly. "Thanks for lunch," he says. He doesn't mention the note, or even the picnic basket. Touchy subject, maybe.

Or he doesn't care.

I tell him I'm headed to Jacks again. "It was pretty slow last night," I say. "I ended up drinking all by myself and fending off douchebags."

"Luis would have kicked them out if you told him," he says, and it's the longest sentence he's said to me since he walked out of Petrosino Square.

"I'm a big girl," I say. "I can take care of myself. But if you want to come down and keep them off me, you're invited."

"Maybe," he says. "We'll see. I gotta go."

I hang up and Ryan raises his eyebrows at me. "That was inspired," he says.

"What?"

"Making him feel jealous," he says, "and like he has to protect you."

I stare at him for a couple of seconds.

He shakes his head. "You didn't do that on purpose, did you?"

"No," I say. "Is that what you think happened?"

"Someone has got to teach you how guys work sometime."

After work, I go home to change. I finally got around to my dry cleaning, so I can wear the floaty, flowery D&G tank again. It's chilly, but it will be warm in the bar, and I look seriously good in this top. And it's what I wore on our first date—our only date—so it makes me feel happy, something I sorely need. I don't seem to be making much headway.

Still, Ryan said it wouldn't be easy.

When I get to Jacks, I sit at the bar. Luis brings me a Guinness without being asked, bless him, and I sip at it and watch the minutes tick by on the clock over the bar.

One hundred thirty-seven of them have ticked by when Mitch slides onto the stool next to me. I smell him first, then the stool creaks. I turn to look at him—to drink him in, really, because no matter how much Ryan assured me I would wear him down, I wasn't entirely sure I would see him again.

Jeans and boots, that goes without saying. But he's also wearing the shirt he was wearing the first night I met him, and it strikes me that I've known him less than three weeks, but I already can't imagine what it would be like if he wasn't around.

My heart squeezes in my chest, like a fist, and I look at him while he very carefully looks at everything but me.

"Hey, stranger," I say.

"Hey."

He says nothing else. Luis drops off his drink; he takes a long swallow and stares at the bottles in back of the bar.

"How have you been?" I ask. "How's work?"

"The usual."

"Still up to shenanigans with the stepsister?"

He nods a little. "Yeah, that's good. Ratings for my first couple of weeks were high."

"Of course they were," I say. "Kari and her legion of online pals swarming over to watch, no doubt."

He doesn't reply, just turns his glass around and around on the bar.

"I'm glad you came down," I say. I feel like I should say something about protecting me from the constant propositioning—Ryan would probably tell me to, to nurture that territorial instinct—but I can't do it.

He shrugs. "Sure. So what's up? Two weeknights in a row."

"Nothing. Just didn't feel like sitting at home."

"Same," he says, nodding. "It's good to get out."

"Yeah, I'm trying to get out more." I don't have Ryan here to tell me what to do, and it's probably too soon, but I can't help it. "Would you … maybe want to go out for dinner or something this weekend?" I ask.

"This weekend's no good," he says.

My heart sinks—just sinks right down into my shoes. "Doesn't have to be the weekend," I say, and there's a plaintive note in my voice that I don't exactly like, but what am I supposed to do about it? I've never been good at hiding anything, and everything in me right now knows that I've messed this up so bad, and I don't really know how to fix it. "I just … I really miss you."

He takes another long swallow of his beer, then sets it back on the bar and stares at the glass for a few seconds. Then, without looking at me, he says: "What about lunch tomorrow?"

Talk about a hollow victory. Lunch won't work either, and I'm afraid if I say no he'll just stop trying.

"I would really, *really* love that," I say, "but I'm going to be swamped tomorrow."

"Okay."

"And I also kind of want to be around the office, for the sake of making a good impression. I've been screwing up really badly."

I hadn't intended to tell him that, actually. I was just trying to keep talking until I came up with a better plan.

He turns his head and looks at me, brows drawn together over those tawny eyes. "Screwing up how?"

Since he seems legitimately interested, and I consider that a small miracle, I give him a quick summary: losing things, being late, missing emails.

He's quiet for a moment after I finish, then: "Is your job at risk?"

"I don't know," I say, honestly. The very thought is terrifying. "I've never had anything like this happen before, so I don't know? I mean, I got a little verbal spanking from my boss earlier; is that all there is, or what? I just don't know. I'm never in trouble."

"Then what's going on?"

"I've been very distracted, I guess?" I drink some of my beer, and think about it. "I don't mess up at work. I don't lose things. I don't forget things. And I don't get lectures from my boss, because I don't do anything to deserve a lecture. But lately I just seem to be … falling apart."

"I don't know, Jenna," he says. "That sounds weird to me."

"How so?"

"Did your work suffer when you … after your breakup?"

I notice he avoids Drew's name. Fine by me, but I wish he hadn't come up at all, now that Mitch is finally talking to me again like a regular human being.

"I don't think so," I say. "I don't remember anything like this. And no one said anything at the time."

"That's something to think about," he says.

"Yeah," I say, but I don't know what part of it I'm supposed to be thinking about, and I really didn't even want to talk about work. I steer us back to earlier: "Hey, I just thought—what does your tomorrow after work look like? We could get dinner." Inspiration hits, and I pivot. "No, I'll make you dinner."

"Is it going to be Spaghetti-Os?"

That hits me right in the heart.

"No." I poke his bicep. Not a lot of give there; god, he's so sexy. "I'll make something nice—I don't get a chance to do that often. Then … we could watch a movie?"

There's a long pause. "A movie?"

"Yeah, I…." Ah, what the hell. "Remember you told me about that movie you really loved making? *Home*?"

"I remember."

"Well, I bought it. On eBay." I shrug a little. "Figured if you didn't mind watching yourself we could check it out."

He doesn't say anything, just looks at the bottles behind the bar again.

"I mean … I can watch it on my own, but it would be better with you there." Ryan said I should touch him if he seemed at all receptive—and he's talking to me. That's receptive, right? I reach out and touch the back of his wrist. "Please? If you don't come over I'll have to have a can of Spaghetti-Os."

There's another long pause. I wait it out.

Finally, he says, "Do you need me to pick anything up?"

My heart soars—I mean, seriously, if it literally flew out of my chest and around the bar a few times, I don't think I'd even be surprised. "I'll handle it," I say. "You just be there. Six-thirty."

He thinks about it. "That's pushing things. What about five-thirty?"

I'll have to duck out of work early, and I shouldn't. But this is important, and I'm not sure I can get away with another *no*.

"Five-thirty is great," I say, and give his knee a quick pat. *Nothing obtrusive*, Ryan said. I feel ridiculous, but okay.

"Sounds good," he says, then neither of us says anything for a minute.

On impulse, I stand up. I might not know as much as I should about guys, but I know about negotiations. I know how to take a small victory and get while the getting's good.

"I'd better head home," I say. "I'm pretty beat, and I've got back-to-back meetings all morning."

"Good luck," he says. "I'll see you tomorrow."

Perfect. I head out the door before he can second-guess himself. Outside, I flag down a cab. I'm going to have to go to the actual grocery store, which I don't do often, and I really don't want to be out too late. I was telling the truth about the back-to-back meetings.

But after work … well. I'll make a nice dinner and then, if I can drum up the nerve, maybe I'll see how Mitch feels about being a little bit more than friends.

And that thought makes me literally weak in the knees.

———

Thursday morning, I give Ryan the run-down and he high-fives me with both hands—high-tens me, I guess.

"That was a lot faster than I expected," he says, sitting in one of my guest chairs. "I thought you'd have to grovel for another week at least. He must have it bad for you."

"I don't know." I plop into my office chair, my stomach full of butterflies. "I hope so, but … I don't want to mess it up. What do I do?"

Wow, seriously pathetic.

"Oh, this part's easy," he says. "Feed him food. Stroke his ego." Then he flashes me a wicked grin. "Jump his bones."

And here come the weak knees again. But—

"Ryan, I slept with another guy like ten minutes ago."

"That's forever ago, in ex years."

"Ex years?"

"They're like dog years, but the difference is you're sad if a dog dies."

It does make me smile, so that's good. "I'm serious, though."

"So am I," he says. "And yeah, that's not ideal—and I'd be extra sure not to remind Mitch of that, or your date's going to go south pretty fast." He leans forward, puts on a serious face. "It was a severe lapse in judgment, and we are going to pretend it never happened. I'm giving you a pass on this one."

"Okay," I say, although I think he's not really the one who gets to decide that. "One last thing, though—I'm going to have to leave early."

"No problem," Ryan says.

"Well, could you—" I never do this, so it's weird. "I need you to cover for me. It'll only be an hour, but I don't want to spread it around that I'm goofing off at a crucial time."

Ryan shrugs. "Whatever. You work ten times harder than a lot of people around here who like to make out like the place would fall down without them."

I wonder fleetingly what's got him in such a snit, but mostly I'm too concerned with thinking about the upcoming evening. I'll have time to shower, put on some nice underwear. Just, you know, in case. Who knows what might happen?

The weak knees—and the butterflies in my stomach—have some ideas.

## Chapter Eighteen

I'M HOME BY FOUR-THIRTY. The message light is blinking, and I press Play, hear Drew's voice start to say my name, and hit Delete. Nope nope nope. Never again.

There's also a message from Kari, whose anger lasted exactly as long as I thought it would. "Hey, I'm sorry I was an asshole. Call me, okay? I have something awesome to tell you."

I pick up the phone to call her back, then put it down. I don't have time to get into a conversation with her right now. I'll call her tonight.

Or, you know … tomorrow. Depending.

I barely have enough time to shower and primp and dig out some cute underthings that actually match and haven't been through the washer a hundred times. I hesitate with my hand on the Vera Wang dress—it's so pretty, and I always talk myself out of wearing it.

But I'm not going to wear it around the house. That's just silly. It's a going-out dress.

So then I have to agonize over what I *am* going to wear. It has to be special. It can't be too fancy, because it's dinner and a movie in my apartment. It can't be too plain because he matters. It needs to be pretty, maybe even sexy, but not slutty. And I want it to be something he hasn't seen before.

I settle on a rust-colored peasant skirt and a beaded, scoop-neck tank in cream. The top is casual, but the scoop neck is low enough that I think it qualifies as special. I fasten on an ankle bracelet, hit the mascara and lip gloss, and call it good. I can only be who I am.

Mitch arrives promptly at five-thirty, carrying a bottle of wine and looking a little wary as he comes in. But he loosens up once I open the wine and settle him at the table with a glass. I move around the kitchen, pulling out pans I haven't used in ages, chopping and washing and mixing. I take it slow with the wine because I want my wits about me, and we make small talk about work—mine and his. I think, or maybe imagine, I can feel his eyes on me.

He wouldn't have come if he wasn't still kind of interested, right? I'm not out of time; even though I dithered about it there's still a shot for us.

"Here we go," I say, moving things from pans to plates. "If this doesn't melt in your mouth, I'm turning in my apron."

I only have a few recipes that are even close to being fancy, and this is the easiest of them. There's chicken and little bow-tie shaped pasta, and tomatoes and feta and black olives. The salty tang of the feta is like heaven, and the pasta catches all the sauce and holds it in its little crinkles.

Mitch laughs and digs in. "This is great," he says, after a couple of bites. "Almost as good as mother makes."

"You're a good son," I say, smiling. "Was it your mom who taught you how to cook?"

"Of course." He takes another bite. "She always said us boys had to learn how to take care of ourselves so we wouldn't starve to death if no woman would have us."

I laugh. "And why would she say that?"

"We were kind of hellions, always up to no good, always dirty, always noisy, always running in and out of the house and banging the screen door. She'd tell us no wife would ever want us, and we'd better learn to do our own laundry." He refills his wine glass and tops mine off. "She was teasing, of course. Nothing my mother ever said to any of us was said with anything but total love."

"My mom was pretty great that way, too," I say. "Though mostly all she says these days is 'When are you coming home to visit?'"

"They must miss you," he says.

"They do," I say. "They're really great."

"Sounds like sometimes it was rough, though? When you were a kid?"

I shrug. "Yeah, I guess."

"Hey," he says.

I look up and he's just looking at me across the table.

"Tell me about it," he says.

I open my mouth to say something distracting. What comes out instead is: "I never tell anyone how bad it was."

He nods, takes another bite of his food, and waits.

I take a deep breath, and before I can talk myself out of it, I start to talk.

"I already told you, my parents bought the absolute worst house in a fairly upscale town, so I could live somewhere with good public schools? That's a real feel-good story at its heart: poor people scrimping and saving to give their kid a better life, right? But there was nothing feel-good about it. It was the kind of grinding poverty that no one talks about except during election season. We were hungry a lot, and we were cold a lot."

He sets his fork down.

I take a long, nervous breath. Only Kari knows this stuff about me, because she was there. "So okay, good that I got a good education—and I did, I worked my ass off—but it was bad, too, because I wasn't like the other girls in my school, and we all knew it. They had more money, but it wasn't just that. It was what growing up with money had made them. They knew how to talk, and how to say the right things. They had better clothes, they lived in better neighborhoods, they were prettier—"

"I doubt it," he says.

I let that pass. It's like a flood now; I couldn't stop if I wanted to. "And as I got older, I saw the girls who were better than me dating a kind of guy who would never look at me twice. The kind of guy who was from a certain kind of family, a certain part of town. Mr. Right, you know? Just one more thing that I couldn't have—like the clothes, only more important. Even I knew that. I didn't go on dates. I didn't go to school dances. Kari was my only friend, and she took some flak for it, too."

He frowns, but doesn't say anything.

"And all I've ever wanted, my whole life, was to be good enough. To be the kind of person those girls from my neighborhood would admire and want to be like. So I decided that I would *become* that person, and that's what I did." I gesture to the view outside the living room window. "You know how much it costs to live in this neighborhood?"

"I can guess," he says.

"I pay it," I say. "Because the person I want to be—she would live in this neighborhood. Or a better one, if she could afford it, which I can't. I do *all* the right things, Mitch—I live in the right sort of neighborhood, I wear the right clothes, I date the right guys—and I know that if I ran into one of those girls from my high school, they would see through me in a heartbeat. They'd see that I'm a phony. I buy my clothes at discount because I can't afford to pay retail. I pay more than half my salary for rent."

"Whatever else you think about yourself," he says, "I won't

let you sit there and say you didn't make something of your life."

I shrug again. "I did, but … I don't know. It always feels like faking."

He's quiet for a long moment, then picks his fork up again and takes another bite. "I told you this before, but … seriously. You're really tough."

"Yeah, I guess." I don't talk about that stuff, and now I'm uncomfortable, and aware of his gaze, and a little embarrassed because that was all super-personal and he didn't ask to get dumped on like that. "Let's hear more about your family and less about mine. Tell me a story."

"Did I tell you about when I fell out of our treehouse directly *onto* my brother, and each of us wound up with a broken arm?" he asks. Unerring instincts, this one. This is the exact right sort of story to follow up a big heavy confession.

"No," I say, and for the next half an hour it's just like our phone calls, except that this way I get to look at him while he talks. He tells the story about the broken arms, and the trip to the hospital.

"Tell me another," I say when he's finished, but he shakes his head.

"Your turn," he says, standing and bringing our plates to the sink. "Tell me about your broken bones."

"I never had any," I say. I take my wine glass over to the chaise, hoping he'll follow me, and to my satisfaction he does. "I stepped on a rusty nail once and had to have a tetanus shot, but that's about it. I had a medically uneventful childhood."

"I wish I could say the same," he says, sitting on the other end of the chaise, turned sideways so he's looking at me. "I broke my arm, my pinky finger, and my knee in that one summer. I was always falling into or out of something."

"Clumsy?" I say.

"Not anymore," he says, and I wonder if it's wishful

thinking that makes his voice sound deeper and sort of suggestive.

"Well, then," I say. I'm trying to decide if that's a good cue to start a conversation about our relationship—our potential relationship, that is—and not sure where to begin. Another date? Is this a date? This feels like a date.

I would very much like this to be a date.

I'm probably still supposed to be the one doing the pursuing, so I figure I'll start there.

"You want to maybe do something this weekend?" I ask, purposely vague. *Any time, any place, any activity you like, buddy. I'm all yours.*

"I would, but I'm away this weekend."

"Oh," I say, disappointed. "Where are you going?"

"Fan Club Weekend in L.A." He smiles. "It's time to run the gauntlet again. I'm flying out really early tomorrow."

But … he can't go *now*. "You're not even on the show anymore."

"It's not like they killed me off." He sets his wine on the coffee table. "And I only just left, in TV time. People bought these tickets months ago, and I'm scheduled at a few other events. Plus, I'm still what they call a 'fan favorite.'"

"Oh, yeah?" I say. "What about your fans *here*?"

"Am I a fan favorite here, too?" he asks, and he's got that sexy, flirty growl in his voice that I haven't heard since our first date. Our only date? I still can't decide if this is a date.

Whatever the case, that voice is going to be the death of me.

"Yes, you are," I say, trying to be flirty right back.

But he seems oblivious to it. "Well, good."

"When do you come home?"

"Monday," he says. "Late, probably."

"I have Monday off," I tell him. "It's a bank holiday."

"Banks take a lot of holidays," he says.

I laugh a little. "That's actually really true."

He smiles at me, full force dimples and all. "You've earned it, though. You've been working your gorgeous ass off."

"Yeah," I say, but only because I'm too distracted to argue. *Gorgeous ass?*

"Let's put this movie on," he says.

Did he just say my *gorgeous ass*? I didn't think he was noticing anymore.

Maybe it's just a faint memory he has. Maybe it's just an expression, and he says it to everyone.

Maybe I really do still have a chance with him.

There's only one way to find out, I suppose. I put my wine glass down on the coffee table next to his.

And his cell rings.

Well, damn it. Someone's got lousy timing.

"One sec," he says, digging in his pocket for it. He does some impressive writhing around getting the phone out, and I admire every second of it. He really does know how to wear a pair of jeans, that's for sure.

He peeks at the display and says, "It's Kari. I should take this. She's probably calling about L.A. this weekend."

"L.A.?" I say, not understanding what Kari has to do with his trip to L.A.

"Yeah, I'm taking her to Fan Club Weekend," he says, as though it's the most natural thing in the world, and answers the phone. "Hey, what's up?" There's a long pause and then he laughs and says, "Yes, you can wear the same thing to two events … No, it won't be different people, but no one will care. Listen, I can't talk right now. Can I call you later?"

I listen to this one-sided conversation, still and cold all the way down to my toes. I could cry. I could just curl up into a ball on the chaise and cry for a week. Or maybe throw up. Who's got the lousy timing now?

He hangs up and looks at me, a little frown line appearing on his forehead. "Are you okay?"

"Yeah," I say dully. "I'm fine."

"You don't look fine. You're white as a sheet." He leans over and lays the back of his hand against my forehead.

I brush his hand away. He looks so worried, and he smells so good, and I can't—I mean, I completely *can't*—have this right now. I really am going to throw up, I think.

"I … I actually have a headache." I press my fingers to my temples. "I think I need to lie down."

"Do you want me to get you something?" he asks. "Some water?"

See? Nurturing. Lucky Kari.

"No, I'll be fine. Shouldn't you be going home to pack or something?"

"That won't take long," he says. "I'm pretty low-maintenance."

I just bet. And he manages, somehow, to be ten times more appealing than some guy who worked at it. This is the cruelest kind of fate; I should have jumped all over him when Kari first told me he was interested. Why was I so willfully blind?

"Still, you have to call Kari back, don't forget." There's a telltale prickling at the back of my eyes, but I will not cry. This is not a big deal. I've liked lots of guys I didn't have a shot with; the only difference here is that I *did* have a shot and blew it. In the end it comes to the same thing, right?

"I don't like leaving you with the mess, since you cooked," he says. "My mother taught me better manners than that."

"Oh, don't worry about it," I say, waving my hand to show how little I care. "I love to do dishes."

I absolutely do not love to do dishes.

"Okay," he says, slowly. "If you're sure?"

"Yes, very. Maybe I've had too much wine. I'm just going to lie here for a while."

"I'll see myself out," he says, which is just more of those good manners, because the door is right there. It's not like he has to find his way. "I'll call you Tuesday?"

"That would be great," I say, although that would be the opposite of great, and lean back against the mound of pillows.

He pulls the throw down over me, hands me the TV remote, and takes the wine glasses to the kitchen on his way out. When he's gone, I lie there looking at the ceiling until sleep comes for me.

## Chapter Nineteen

FRIDAY MORNING I'm sitting and staring blankly at my desk calendar when Ryan pokes his head in and says "Time's up."

"What?" I ask stupidly.

"You've been sitting there looking glum for an hour, and you still haven't told me how dinner went."

When I arrived, I simply swept past his desk, shaking my head. I knew there were things on my desk that couldn't wait another minute, and I did not want to get into a weepfest and drop any more balls. Things are already bad enough.

"Dinner was fine." I look up at him, try on a smile. I'm sure it looks ghastly.

"Wait a second," he says, and leaves. I continue to stare at the desk calendar, very carefully not thinking about Kari and Mitch on a plane, Kari and Mitch checking into a hotel, Kari and Mitch sitting together while legions of adoring fans drift by and look at her and think about how lucky she is.

Ryan comes back with the box of tissues just in time. That last thought breaks me, and for the second time this week, I get mascara all over the front of my admin.

"I'm so sorry," I say, between sobs. "Your poor sweater."

"Don't worry about the sweater," he says. "Worry about me, when I have to explain it to my girlfriend."

This makes me laugh through my tears, and I try to blot the mascara off his sweater, but I only succeed in spreading it around. I need to start buying more expensive mascara.

"Are you ready to talk about this yet?" he asks, sitting in one of the guest chairs. I take the other and stare vaguely at the wall behind him.

"I don't even know where to start," I say.

"Well, the beginning, I guess. How was dinner?"

"He's dating Kari," I say.

"Oh, so dinner was good."

"Like, everything was fine, everything seemed to be going great." I look at him. "I did everything you said."

"My advice is usually pretty solid, but—"

"No, your advice wasn't the problem." I rub the back of my neck, which feels like it will never be relaxed again. "It was just too late, is all. That's on me."

"But…." He seems to hunt for something to say, and settles on: "Are you sure?"

"Yeah, I'm sure."

I tell him about the phone call, and the weekend trip, and all of it. I manage not to cry again—because that whole thing is getting out of hand—and eventually I've spilled the whole story.

Ryan just looks at me for a moment, then shakes his head. "That *sucks*," he says.

"Tell me something I don't know."

"I just—Wow." He shakes his head again. "I did not see that coming."

"Me neither," I say. "And he's supposed to call me on Tuesday and … do what? Tell me what a great weekend he had?"

Ryan shrugs a little. "If you have some kind of *just friends* thing going on, then yeah, probably. Maybe you should think about breaking that off, kind of get the constant reminder out of your life."

"No," I say, and I mean it with all my heart. The idea of simply not seeing him again? I don't want to think about it. "We were friends before this stupid week, and I'll figure out how we can keep being that—just that. And anyway, if he's dating Kari, how exactly am I supposed to get him out of my life?"

He nods. "Yeah, I get that. But what are you going to do? Go to brunch with them every weekend and wish you were her? That's not gonna be a lot of fun."

"I'll figure it out," I say. "I don't know what, but I'll figure something out."

"Also … not to be insulting, but is spending time with him a great idea, when you feel how you do? I mean…." He raises his eyebrows. "Shit happens."

I have to look at him for a few seconds before I understand, and when it clicks I'm appalled. "Oh, my God. No, no way," I say. "First of all, I would never. Not ever."

"Okay."

"And even if I would—which I would *never*—he wouldn't." I think back to that early phone conversation. "He's been cheated on. He just … he absolutely wouldn't."

He looks skeptical. "People can surprise you."

"No," I say. "I know that as surely as I know the sun will come up tomorrow. He felt pretty strongly about it, and wasn't shy about saying so. That's … that's just not even a concern." I stand up and gesture at the door. "Now shoo, I've got work."

But when he's gone I sit in my chair with my head in my hands for what feels like a really long time. Finally, I grab my purse and jacket, tell Ryan I'm taking the rest of the day off, and go home. At least there I can change into sweatpants, and feel sorry for myself in comfort.

———

Saturday morning I sleep late. This takes superhuman effort, because I went to bed so early two nights running. I'm wide awake at seven o'clock, but I roll over, pull the covers over my head, and shut my eyes stubbornly until I drowse. I manage to pass a few more hours in this way, drifting in and out of a light sleep, feeling bad for myself.

I get up and eat, kick around until late afternoon, and then —God help me, I *know* better, I know no good can come of it— I decide maybe I'll have a look on the internet and see how the Fan Club thing is going.

I know I shouldn't do it but I can't help myself. I dig up my laptop, which I hardly ever even use, bring it over to the coffee table and Google *soap opera message boards*. The first couple of results don't yield much—some general posting about this being Fan Club Weekend, a couple of posts by people who've heard from friends who are attending. Most posts seem to be about the individual actor events. Nothing yet about Mitch, nothing about Kari.

Then I find SoapZone.com and hit what you could call pay dirt, only I don't think pay dirt is supposed to feel like a knife in the heart.

The very first post on the *Doctors and Nurses* board is from a poster named "JessB," and the subject line is "OMG YOU WILL NEVER GUESS WHO'S SITTING WITH MITCHELL COLE!"

Nice caps lock, JessB.

Almost unwillingly, I click on it.

*I just got a call from LizInAlabama, she's in line to see Mitchell Cole and you will NEVER guess who is sitting at his table with him. NYCParalegal! Liz has met her at other events, there's no question it's her. Liz said she's still about 20 people back in line and anyway it's not like she could grill NYCP right in front of him but NYCP looks out of her gourd with HAPPINESS. Has anyone heard from her directly? I'm dying to know what's going on!! She didn't even say she was going, did she??*

Most of the replies are surprised people wondering how on earth this turn of events has come about. Only one person seems to have any more information, a poster named "JakeBella4Ever," whose subject line is, *She was at MJ's event with him last night.* I click on it.

*MichaelBrendaFan called me last night right after Mark Jackman's event, said Mitchell Cole brought some girl and no one knew who she was. MC went up on stage with MJ to auction off a script signed by both of them and while he was gone MBF went over to chat with this girl, and that's when she told her she posts on SZ as NYCParalegal. I don't know her very well, but the name stuck in my head. Was going to ask about her this morning but I got distracted by the hot scoopage coming out of Nancy's event. (Go Brenda!)*

*Anyhoo, MBF said that NYCP said she'd known him for a few weeks, since right around the time he moved to Midnight Confessions, and that it had been a surprise to her that he invited her along, but no way was she going to say no. MBF pressed her as gently as she could to try to find out what's up with them, but all NYCP would say is that they'd "gotten close." That little tease! Then MC came back and wanted his chair (MBF said she about fell out of it when he spoke to her, that voice is even better in person than on screen), so she hightailed it back to her own table. She was with NancysMyGirl, who won that MC/MJ script, btw.*

*That's all I know.*

I read it through a second time, trying to get it all straight. Do these people speak entirely in acronyms or what?

*Gotten close,* eh? That's one way to put it. How discreet of her.

I refresh the page and there's a new post by JessB. "MORE ABOUT NYCP!"

*Liz called back, she hasn't talked to NYCP yet, but NYCP did see her in the line and wave. Liz said she was VERY chummy with MC, apparently she's been sharing lunch with him, not exactly the most romantic scene, I guess, but it's more than I'm doing sitting here in Pennsylvania too poor to go to FCW! LOL. And I guess it worked for Lady & the Tramp.*

Several people pipe up to swoon about this. I refresh again and there's another post from JessB. I'd say this girl needs a life, but who's the one hanging on her every word, right? Yeah.

This one is titled "MC / NYCP!"

*So Liz called again, I guess NYCP was working MC's line, saying he was sorry everything was taking so long, he takes a really long time talking to every fan—I love this guy!—and so NYCP came down the line passing out 8x10s and telling everyone how glad MC was that they were there. Liz waylaid her for a minute and asked her what was going on and she said NYCP just smiled and said "Nothing, really, just couldn't pass up a chance to go to FCW for free, right?" Then Liz said "Come on, you know what I want to know, girl," and NYCP said "I'll never tell," and laughed and went off to pass out more headshots.*

*HOLY CRAP RIGHT?*

Yeah, holy crap right? I go get myself a glass of water and drink it right there at the sink, trying to pull myself together. Then, like an idiot, I head back to the computer.

JessB's newest post is "MORE NYCP!" I'm tired of JessB and her caps lock key. I click on the post anyway.

*So Liz got up to the front of MC's line, she said his voice is "like buttah," and he was looking at NYCP like he might eat her up. Liz said "How come you never invited me to FCW, Mitch?" (Liz is hilarious!) and he said "You never asked, sweetheart." Suh-WOON! Anyway, he laughed about it, but neither of them was giving out any details and Liz is too supercool to act like a freak about it, so that's all I know. Has anyone else heard from anyone else about what's up with these two? It's so exciting!*

Oh, yeah, very exciting. I know I'm on the edge of my seat.

I linger over the board for a bit longer, refreshing, but the conversation turns to other things and not much more is said about Mitch, just repeats of what was already said about Kari and a few people posting about whatever little conversations they had with him while getting their picture signed.

He's universally adored by fans, that much I can see. Other actors are occasionally put down, said to be rushing fans, or pulling for one pairing when whoever is posting the information wants another pairing. One actor in particular seems universally reviled for "taking over" the show and "barging into every storyline." But no one has one bad word to say about Mitch.

I run a search on the whole *Doctors and Nurses* message board for his name and find that when he left *Doctors and Nurses*, almost everyone was sad to see him go. Quite a few posters said they'd start watching *Midnight Confessions* to see him. And all this, after he told me he wasn't playing one of the root-for guys.

Well, it should come as no surprise. He's a wonderful man.

And now he's Kari's man.

Sunday, I mope some more, read SoapZone some more. I feel bad for judging JessB so harshly; she's not always so heavy on the caps lock key. It was an exciting day, I guess.

SoapZone grows boring pretty quickly, though, since I don't have any idea what anyone is talking about.

I'm off work Monday, but it's not much of a holiday in this mood. It would be much better if I had anything to do or anyone to do it with. I stay away from SoapZone and try not to think about Mitch and Kari flying back together. I even watch *Midnight Confessions*, but I can't make sense of any of the storylines because every time Mitch is on screen I feel like crying. He seems to be doing a good job, but what do I know?

Eventually he ends up in a clinch with someone—I assume the stepsister—and I turn the TV off in disgust. There's no need for me to be watching *that*. I can get plenty of that in my own head, starring him and Kari.

My cell phone rings around dinner time; I ignore it. The house phone rings too, but whoever it is doesn't leave a message.

It's just as well. There's no one I want to talk to right now.

## Chapter Twenty

RYAN GREETS me with a grimace when I walk in the door Tuesday morning.

I eye him warily. "You know, it's getting so I don't even like to see you sometimes," I say. I don't mean it. Much. "What now?"

"Things kind of blew up here Friday afternoon," he says.

"Of course they did," I mutter. God forbid I take a day off; the place apparently will disintegrate if I keep that up. "What happened?"

"That report you said was on your computer?" He raises an eyebrow at me. "The focus group results analysis? It wasn't there. Ben was pissed."

"Of course it's there," I say, and head into my office, with him hot on my heels. The computer is on—I always leave it on—and I click on the folder labeled *Grow*. A list of files pops up and I scan it for the one I want. "It's called *Focus Group Results*, with the date."

"I'm telling you—"

"It's not here," I say. I re-sort the list a couple of times, alphabetically, then by date. It's not here. "I wonder if I renamed the file and forgot?"

"I opened every document," he says. "No luck."

"I'm sure I have it backed up somewhere, maybe not the final version but at least I won't have to write it from scratch," I say, mentally kicking my own ass for being so stupid. Distracted by my stupid laughable personal life, no doubt. I've got to get a handle on this absent-mindedness. This is no time to be a flake.

"No worries—after Ben had a little bit of a hissy fit out in the hallway, Melody told us she had a hard copy."

Oh, thank God. That report was the entire basis for the final design for the brochure. "I'm going to put that girl in for a raise," I say, feeling like I should go out and hug her.

"Well, while you're passing out raises, don't forget me," he says, and turns to leave.

"If you start pulling my fat out of the fire, I'll put you in for one, too," I call after him.

I shoot Melody an email thanking her for saving my butt again, then resolutely put my personal troubles out of my mind and get back to work.

Immediately after lunch, as I'm finishing up an email to Ben, Ryan buzzes me. "Mitch is on the phone," he says. "What do you want me to tell him?"

I press my fingers to my eyes and silently lament that I haven't been run over by a city bus.

"Jenna?"

"Put him through."

There's a click, then the voice. "Hey. Miss me?"

*So much*, I think, and very carefully say, "Oh, always," in the breeziest, most carefree tone I can fake. It actually comes out pretty good, I think. "How did the luncheon and stuff go?"

I know perfectly well how they went, since I've got pretty much every devastating detail I gleaned off the internet engraved in my brain, but I'm not going to tell him that.

"It was okay. Signed a lot of autographs. Posed for a lot of photos. Pretty much same as always."

"Did you get any lectures about being a bad guy?"

"Only a few. Most folks seemed bummed that I was gone, so that was nice. I really just wanted to get back, though."

I force it out: "Did Kari have fun?"

"Kari had a good time. The hotel rooms are pretty swank."

This only makes me think of him and Kari sharing a hotel room, which naturally leads me to think of him and Kari sharing a bed, which naturally leads to me wanting to toss myself out my office window. I take a moment to compose myself, refrain from actually jumping out the window—not exactly Herculean restraint—and close my eyes. This is actually worse than I thought, and I wouldn't have believed that possible.

"That's awesome," I say, aiming for a light and airy tone but only managing to sound kind of high-pitched and weird.

"But anyway, I'm back," he says. "And you seem to have recovered."

"Yes, thank you. I felt better the next day."

I most certainly did *not* feel better the next day.

"Good. I worried about you while I was gone. You want to get together?"

*Just friends, just friends, just friends.*

I force a huge smile on my face. I've read that if you're smiling on the phone, the person on the other end can hear a difference. I hope fake smiles work. "It's an absolutely shit week, actually. I expect I'll be at the office late for the next few days."

This is a straight-up lie, but I need a few days' breathing room. Just to get myself accustomed to … well, honestly, to the same thing I've been supposed to be accustomed to all along: *Just friends.*

"What's Friday like?"

"Um…" I think about it. "I have a half-day."

"Perfect," he says. "What do you think about finally getting a peek inside the hallowed halls of the ABC studio?"

"Meaning?"

"I have a late call on Friday, and I've only got two scenes to film. Why don't you meet me at the studio after lunch and watch me shoot? I'll probably only be on set a few hours."

Okay, this is a bridge too far. "Seems like Kari would be a better candidate for that," I say, still smiling my widest.

"She's already been," he says, "last week. She would have hounded me to death by now otherwise."

His tone is warm and affectionate; aren't they just the cutest thing? I remind myself that my window doesn't open, so I'm going to have to finish this phone call.

"I'm not sure," I say. "I'm not, like, a big fan."

"You don't have to be. It's still interesting, and I'll enjoy showing you around. Oh, and how about this: You said you don't know how to play pool? We can head to Jacks, beat the Friday crowd. I'll show you how to run a table. I'm going camping with Luis upstate this weekend, so it can't be a late night, but you deserve an afternoon off. And you might even have fun."

I don't tell him I took last Friday off. He might ask why, and what am I going to say? *Because every time I thought of you and Kari I wanted to go lie in traffic*?

Yeah, no.

What I *do* say, though I'm not positive I should, is: "I saw you on *Midnight Confessions* yesterday."

"Did you really?" He's got that warm grin in his voice.

"I had the day off. I couldn't follow much—"

"Oh, that's not good. These things are supposed to be written so you can jump right in, and catch on fast."

"You said the writing was good," I tease.

"It is," he says. "It can be both."

"I don't think the fault lay with the writing," I say, not wanting him to be insulted. "I was cleaning up the living room, and distracted. I saw you macking on some hot brunette though. Would that be the stepsister?"

"That would be the stepsister. She'll be there Friday. Come meet her."

This is just impossible. I open my mouth to say no … and stop, reconsidering. The thing is, his work *does* sound interesting; after the fuss Kari's made all this time, maybe I'd like to see what all the commotion is about. And it's a non-threatening way to spend time with him. He'll be busy doing other things and we won't have to be always having these uncomfortable conversations that remind me how badly I screwed everything up between us. No—the *possibility* of something between us.

And Ryan is right. I'm going to have to see him all the damn time. I can hardly stop being friends with Kari, and he'll be with her a lot. At least, if he was my boyfriend, I'd keep him around quite a lot.

Which he is not.

And that's the thing. A studio tour? A pool date with my best friend's guy? Kari loves me, and I'm sure Kari trusts me—she knows me well enough, how could she not?—but that really might be just a bit too much.

"Should we invite Kari?" I ask.

"She's at an *All the World* event on Long Island," he says. "But she was the one who suggested I take you to see the studio."

That's certainly not what I expected to hear. "She did?"

"She did. How about it?"

"You know what?" I say. "I *would* like that. That sounds like a fun way to end the week."

"Awesome," he says. "Do you know where the studio is?"

I can't help smiling. "I've spent more time stalking the front door of the ABC studio than I would admit to anyone but you. Because only you would understand it wasn't for my own shady ends."

He laughs. "Yeah, Kari is certainly something else," he says. His voice is warm and affectionate, and I want to die.

But I'm not going to die. I'm going to get a grip on myself and figure out exactly how I can make a place in my life for Mitch as a casual friend. It's too painful to imagine us being as close as we were, but I can manage something, if only for show.

I'm the one who made things turn out this way; it's my job to live with it as best I can.

"So do I just come up there and ask to be let in?"

"Be there at, say, twelve-thirty?" he says. "I'll take care of the rest."

"Okay. See you then."

He hangs up, and I bang my head ever-so-gently on the desk, just once. Then I hit *Send* on my email and turn to the next task in my inbox.

Hopefully by Friday I'll have figured out a way to deal with this.

———

When I get home, there's a message—my mom. Why haven't I called, am I ever going to come visit, and so on. I listen to the end, dutifully, and then delete it. I'll call her tomorrow, maybe.

There's also the message Kari left on Thursday. I listen to it again. *I have something awesome to tell you.*

I should call her back. Thursday was a while ago. Although, she was also in LA for four days, so it probably doesn't feel like it's been that long. I could get away with not calling her until tomorrow. Maybe even Thursday.

I just … the thing is, Kari and I share everything. I mean *everything*. And I think—no, I know—that if I go out for brunch or a drink or whatever with her, and she starts telling me about her trip to LA, and everything she did there? Yeah, no.

A day will come when I can listen to Kari talk about having sex with Mitch … but it is not this fucking day.

I'm gonna need some time and space before I wade into that. Maybe I'll call her tomorrow. I absolutely have to call her before I go out and play pool alone with her boyfriend—sanctioned or not, there's a BFF code—but there's no reason I can't do that tomorrow. Or Thursday.

Happy to have that settled, I open the refrigerator; I don't know why, because I haven't been shopping and it's not like elves would have come to fill the fridge while I was at work. As expected, there's nothing to eat.

I do have beer, though, so that's something.

I call for takeout and go down to prop the door open. The buzzer has officially given out, and everyone is just propping the door open all the time—something I will *not* mention to my mother when she calls. The property management company is supposed to send someone, but it might be a couple of weeks.

Which, honestly, no one is coming to see me anyway, so that's fine. I'll just hole up in here and be a hermit.

But I'll be a hermit who has beer and Thai food. There are worse things.

## Chapter Twenty-One

THE ABC STUDIO is not remotely what I expected—even though I can't quite figure out what it was that I expected.

For one thing, it's very no-frills. The front lobby is nicely appointed, with a security guard at the front desk, but once he clears me, and Mitch takes me through the doors into the studio proper, there's grime everywhere, and exposed wiring.

For another it's *tiny*, which makes sense, I suppose, given the cost of real estate in Manhattan. None of the sets seem to be actual full-size rooms; it's all just pieces of room. A corner here, a flat wall there. As a result, they've got something like 25 distinct "rooms" occurring in a space only about three times as big as my apartment. There's a bar set, which is really just one wall with a bar long enough for four stools. I assume this is where Luis works—or his character, rather—and Mitch confirms.

"But he's not on today," he says, leading me past that set and onto another one no more than three steps away.

"I saw you kissing your stepsister, right there," I say, pointing to an enormous marble fireplace mantle. "It looked like you were in, like, a big elaborate living room."

"It's all camera tricks," he says.

As a couple of burly guys move cameras into place, I see for myself. Everything is angled to hide the fact that walls top out at about six feet, and staircases don't go anywhere. Furniture is brought from somewhere to fill out the fireplace room—this is the Ratcliffe living room, I'm told. I recognize a couple of the other sets as well, from my abortive attempt to watch on Monday.

Mitch introduces me to the actress who plays Cassie, a gorgeous brunette named Martina with a thick New Jersey accent that she somehow slips completely out of while filming and then slips right back into when she's done. He also introduces me to the actress who plays his mother. Her name is Josephine, and she's gracious and charming, wisp-thin, and somehow imposing despite being no taller than five foot one.

I watch with interest as he films his two short scenes. In the first, he and Josephine (or Blake and Lucille, I guess) have an argument in the living room—something about controlling stock in Ratcliffe Enterprises. Apparently she still doesn't know that he's her son, and I wonder when that comes out. She's literally standing on a box for this scene, and still has to crane her neck to look up at him.

Later, in some sort of carriage house set, Blake tries once again to get into Cassie's pants, and she gives him a sound smack over it. They have some furious words—again with the freaking stock options, can't they find something sexier to fight about?—and then go in for another clinch. This time, apparently, he's destined to be successful; he topples back on some hay with her on top of him, she gives a breathy "The hell with it," and pulls his shirt open.

*Well, that's enough of that*, I think, and look at absolutely anything else.

Then someone yells "Cut!" and Mitch heads my way, bumps fists with the nearest cameraman and says, "And I'm out."

"I love filming with this guy," the cameraman says to no one in particular. "He just nails it every time."

"That was … interesting," I say, as Mitch reaches me. His shirt's still wide open, and I very, very carefully do *not* check out everything there is to check out. "What happens with Blake and Cassie now?"

He lifts his eyebrows at me. "About what you'd expect."

"And … how's that to film?"

He laughs. "Not at all what you'd expect. Tuesday will probably be a long day, because we'll spend some extra time blocking—but it's one take, remember?"

"Even the love scenes?"

"Maybe especially the love scenes," he says. "They're a pain in the ass. The set has to be cleared—anyone not in the scene or literally holding a camera is gone—and they black out the monitors. I actually wouldn't care at all, but Martina probably won't be in any more than her underwear."

Now it's my turn to lift my eyebrows.

He shakes his head. "It sounds a *lot* more fun than it is," he says. "I had no idea how hard this job would be when I took the part on *DN*."

I feel really proud of him and, hard on the heels of that, remember he's not mine to feel proud of. He gestures that I should precede him off set, so I do—right back out to the front lobby, even though he's still in full makeup.

"Don't you want to wash up?" I ask.

"Yeah, but I share a dressing room with two other guys," he says, "and they're both working today. Odds are about even whether they'd even have clothes on if I took you back there."

"You don't get your own dressing room?"

"Space, you might have noticed, is at a premium," he says. "The only person here with her own dressing room is Josephine, and she's been on the show twenty years."

"I hope I'm at my job in twenty years," I say.

"Why wouldn't you be?"

I shrug. "I told you, I've been screwing up a lot lately."

"You know," he says, and pauses for a long moment before he continues. "You might want to think about who benefits if it looks like you can't handle your job."

I laugh a little. "If I lost my job—which, perish the thought —they'd offer it to Aiyana."

"Okay?" he says.

"She'd turn it down," I say. "I'm not worried about her."

He shrugs. "You know your people better than I do, obviously. I'm gonna go change back into my own clothes, then if you don't mind we can head to my place so I can clean up?"

"Sure," I say.

"Cool. Then we'll try to get to Jacks before happy hour, or we'll never get a pool table."

———

His apartment is on Columbus Ave, only a few blocks from the studio, and it's just what I'd have expected if I'd stopped to think about it. It's small, the furniture looks lived-on and comfortable, and it smells fantastic. A huge arched window lets in the waning sunlight, making the whole place cheerful. "This is sweet," I say.

"Thanks," he says. "Grab a seat and I'll go wash up."

He heads through the only other door in the room and shuts it behind him. Bedroom, I presume, and tell my brain to just cut it out when it tries to linger over that. I'm not in it, nor am I *going* to be in it.

I hear water running, and take the opportunity to try out the couch, which is lumpy and comfortable all at once. There's a photo album on the coffee table, and I reach over and peek under the cover. The first picture is an 8 by 10 glossy photograph of Mitch. In it, he's wearing a tan suede coat, looking back over his shoulder and laughing at whoever's holding the camera.

I take the album in my lap and turn the pages one by one. They're all photos of Mitch, and to say he photographs well would be the understatement of the century. All the pictures are different—some black and white, some close-ups, some that seem to be candid, some posed. I linger over one of him straddling a chair in his cowboy boots and a gorgeous sweater the color of his eyes, thinking about every mistake I made on the road to this moment.

The last picture, though, is odd—different from everything else. I stare at it for a moment, trying to figure out why Mitch has a picture of some other guy in here. Then it slowly dawns on me that what I'm looking at is Mitch's eyes in a completely different face.

No, it's Mitch's face, too, if you know where to look—his jaw is unmistakable, and there's also something about the lower lip that gives it away.

But that's where the Mitch I know ends and some other guy begins. This guy is clean-shaven, with short spiky hair and the kind of serious, hollow-cheeked pout you'd expect from an underwear model. Not that he's in underwear. He's wearing jeans—just jeans, the better to show off an impressive six-pack —and his thumb is hooked in the waistband like he's just getting ready to give you a glimpse of what he's got in there.

This isn't Mitch. Yet it *is* him, without a doubt.

This is a guy nobody would call Mr. Wrong. But he's *all* wrong.

"That's a really old one," Mitch says from the doorway of his room. I jump a little and turn around, then wish I didn't. He's damp and shirtless—whatever else has changed, the abs are still model-worthy—and I'm not equipped to deal with either of those things right now.

*Just friends, just friends, just friends.*

When I told Ryan the plan for today—studio tour and pool date with my very good friend Mitch—he literally laughed at me. *Good luck with that*, he said.

I was indignant at the time, but he was so right. This is really hard.

Mitch moves across the room and sits down beside me, pulling the photo album so that it's half on his lap and half on mine. The hair framing his face is wet, and he smells clean and masculine, a very specific smell that is only him—and so good.

"It barely looks like you," I say.

"Yeah, I was young." He cocks his head as he looks at it. "Fresh off the bus in L.A. with a duffel bag and a manila envelope full of these, and just wanting to break into the business any way I could. I've never really liked it, though. It doesn't look like me."

"It is very different," I say.

"Do you like it?" he asks, looking at me intently.

I think about it for a moment before answering. "I don't dislike it."

"But?"

"I don't know; you're right, it doesn't look like you." I look back and forth between the picture of the man and the man himself a couple more times, then shake my head. How can one man look so different? "It's a very knock-'em-dead hot kind of picture, isn't it?"

"I think that was probably the intention," he says, nodding. "But I'm not really the knock-'em-dead type."

*Oh, I beg to differ.*

"Why don't you still look like this?" I ask, tapping the photo with my fingernail.

He shrugs. "Because that wasn't me." He flips back to the beginning, to the first picture of him in the suede jacket. "This is me—looser, more fun. Having a good time. This is the one I passed out at Fan Club Weekend. That other one, I look like every other guy in L.A. out on a casting call."

"You might have gotten more work, though."

He shrugs again. "I might have. But would it have been work I wanted? Eventually I figured out that getting jobs isn't worth being something I'm not."

"You could be a movie star, looking like that."

"Or I could do what I do now, and be me."

I know I'm staring at him but I can't seem to stop myself. He's so absolutely unlike anyone I've ever known, and in this moment I think he may be the most amazing, together, sensible person on earth. It's the most inspiring kind of honor —being completely true to himself the way he is.

It might be the sexiest thing about him.

*No, I still gotta go with the voice on that one.*

"What are you thinking?" he asks.

I say the first thing that pops into my head. "I was wondering how these photographers keep managing to find clothes the color of your eyes."

"Are they?" he asks, and flips through a few pages. "I guess they kind of are. Interesting."

"You know, for someone who wants to make a living being an actor, you're remarkably unaware of how you look."

"Acting isn't about looks," he says, "and I *do* make a living." He stands. "I'm going to go find a shirt."

*Good idea. Very good idea.*

And while he's finding something to wear, I sit on his comfortable couch surrounded by the smell of him and wonder what it would be like to not care one bit what anyone else thinks.

I think it sounds rather nice.

## Chapter Twenty-Two

JACKS IS LESS CROWDED than I'm used to, I suppose because we're here so early. With so few people, the jukebox seems louder—but it's playing Tom Waits, which always puts me in a good mood. There's a blond bartender I don't recognize; he nods at Mitch when we come in and is already drawing a Guinness by the time we get to the bar.

"How's it going, man?" he asks, tilting the glass at just the right angle. A Guinness well-poured is a truly beautiful thing.

"It's going. We'll want two of those."

"Sure thing."

We stand there for a minute, not speaking. The jukebox switches from Tom to Johnny Cash. Also fine with me.

The bartender sets the first glass on the bar in front of us. Mitch slides it in front of me. "Ladies first," he says, grinning.

I look around in mock confusion. "What lady?"

He laughs, and touches my upper arm so quickly I almost don't notice it. Almost. If it didn't go on tingling for a full thirty seconds, it would be safe to say I didn't notice it at all. "You're a class act all the way, darlin'," he says.

The bartender, again getting just the right angle on the glass, asks, "Who's your friend?"

*Just friends. Just friends. I can do this.*

"This is Jenna. Jenna, say hi to Kevin."

I do, and Mitch passes money across the bar in exchange for the second pint, and sets down another ten. "For the table," he says, and Kevin pops the cash register drawer and hands over a roll of quarters.

We take our drinks to the nearest pool table and Mitch holds up the roll of quarters. "You know where these go?"

I sigh. "Yes."

"This is the rack," he says, plucking the rack from the wall and tossing it on the table. "When the balls come out, you put them in here."

"I know what it's called, and what to do with it," I say. "I haven't been under a rock for the last thirty years, you know."

"Hey," he says, holding his hands up as if to fend me off, "you said *absolute beginner.* I'm just following your lead."

"I've *played,*" I say. "Just not often. And badly."

"That's about to change," he says, and leaves me to get started, heading over to the jukebox. I get the balls racked as best I can, hang the rack back up, and go over to pick out a pool cue. Since they all look pretty much the same to me, I pick them up one after another. I can't really tell if there's a difference in weight, and even if there is I don't know whether I want a heavy one or a light one.

"Don't use that one," Mitch says from right behind me, and I jump a little. He's standing just a little closer than is strictly necessary, in my opinion—close enough that I can feel his breath warming my neck. If I didn't know better—

But I do. So I remind myself again that we're just two good friends out for some beers and eight-ball.

"Why not?" I ask.

"It's crooked."

It looks straight enough to me, but I put it back and pick up another. Mitch reaches around me, takes it from my hand, and puts it back.

"What now?"

"Too light."

"So I want a heavy one?"

"Is it always all-or-nothing with you?" he asks absently. I assume he's distracted by trying to find me a pool cue, but I can't help wondering how he always manages to say these things that cut right to the heart of me and never seems to notice.

"I guess it is," I say.

"Well, try a little middle ground. You might like it." He hands me a pool cue and smiles. "You want this one."

"I do?"

"You do."

"I like the one I had," I say stubbornly, taking it back off the wall.

"You won't like it for long."

"Why?"

"We'll talk about why later."

"Why not now?"

"Because you won't understand until you've played with it a little."

"I'm sure I'd understand well enough."

He grins and grabs a cue for himself. "Trust me?"

I'm helpless when he smiles like that. I switch cues and position myself across the table from him.

Might be in everyone's best interest to keep the table between us.

The jukebox moves from Johnny to Springsteen, completing what we might call the gravelly-voiced, working-man trifecta.

*Let's Be Friends?* Really? A sexy song about trying to get in your friend's pants?

"Did you pick this?" I ask.

"I did."

I take a deep breath. Well, then. That's … weird?

Except I know it's not. He would never. So the only thing weird here is me, misinterpreting perfectly innocent music choices and making shit up in my head.

"You break," he says.

"Isn't that kind of advanced?"

"Advanced-beginner," he says, with a completely straight face, but I can see the smile at the corners of his eyes. "A girl who knows the lingo like you, and has such strong feelings about pool cues, will be a natural at it."

As it turns out—surprise!—I am not a natural at it. The balls barely move when I break.

"I guess I'm crummy at breaking," I venture.

"Not as crummy as you are at racking." He grabs the rack off the wall again and starts putting the balls back in. "You definitely suck at both, but I don't think anyone could have done much with that rack. Come here and I'll show you."

I move over to his side of the table, and he shows me how to do it right: alternating striped and solid balls and wedging them in tight, his hands quick and sure. I should stop thinking about his hands, but all I can seem to think about is the way he cupped my face in them, on our first date. Right before he kissed me.

Our *only* date. And he isn't going to be kissing me anymore.

*Because. We. Are. Just. Friends.*

I listen to Bruce crooning about how much he'd like to be friends—and he's full of it, he wants nothing of the kind—and watch Mitch's hands as he lines the rack up properly on the table, puts his fingers in to make sure the balls stay bunched up, and slips it off without moving any of them so much as a millimeter.

"Got it?" he asks.

I nod, and he sends me to the other side of the table to try breaking again. This time the balls at least move; about half of them break out from the triangle, though none of them go anywhere remotely near a pocket.

"Good enough," he says, and walks around the table once, slowly, then drops three striped balls in a row.

"You're supposed to be teaching me, not winning," I say.

"Same thing," he says, and takes another shot, this one directly into the center of the sad little cluster of balls left from my lousy break. They scatter to all four corners of the table, but none go in. He favors me with one of his wickedly sexy grins. "Your turn."

I walk around the table, like he did, trying to look like I'm sizing up all my potential shots. Really, what I'm trying to do is find one that's relatively straight so I have some chance at maybe not looking like a total waste of oxygen here. I'm not seeing any, though. "So," I say. "What shot would you recommend?"

He points. "The 5."

"Into what pocket?"

"Are we back to absolute beginner again?" he asks.

"It would appear so."

He leans over the table, tracing an invisible line from the cue ball to the 5. "You hit—here," he says.

"And?"

"And the ball banks off this side," he says, drawing more lines with his finger, "and goes in that corner."

"In theory," I say.

"It's an easy shot."

"Can't we do one in a straight line?"

"Jenna, do you see any straight lines?"

"*Absolute beginner* means straight lines."

He laughs, and moves the 5 ball so that it's directly between the cue ball and the corner pocket. "There."

"That's cheating," I protest weakly. It certainly does look like a much easier shot.

"It's not cheating. It's teaching."

I lean over and line up the two balls, and shoot. The 5 ball drops obligingly into the corner pocket, and the cue ball follows it like an obedient puppy.

*Well, crap.*

I look up and find Mitch has got the dimples and the eye-crinkles out again. Great.

"Still feel the same way about straight lines?"

"I didn't know that was going to happen."

"Would you like me to show you how to stop that from happening?"

I nod, and he comes around to my side of the table and takes the cue from my hand, turns it and balances it on his own hand for a second, then hands it back to me. "You're holding it too far forward," he says. "That's not why you scratched, but it's worth mentioning."

He leans down to fetch the cue ball, and sets it and the 7 up in the same shot I just botched. "Here," he says and moves behind me, crowding up close to show me how to hold the cue.

Oh shit, oh shit. I thought he was going to *show* me, not … whatever this is.

*Just friends.*

"Hold it back here, like this. I want the top half of your arm parallel to the floor. Now what you want is for the cue ball, when it hits, to roll back toward you, not continue on in the same direction. Right?"

He's so close behind me that I can feel the heat of his body. On the jukebox, Bruce gives way to Joe Cocker. *You Can Leave Your Hat On.* Seriously? One of the sexiest songs in the history of recorded music? Right *now*?

"Is this one yours, too?" I ask. How can he possibly be so oblivious?

"Yeah," he says, "pretty much the next hour is me. Now, lean—"

And then somehow I'm leaning over the pool table with

him draped completely over me, showing me how to line up what should be an easy shot—and I can barely hear a word he's saying. Something about geometry versus physics, and velocity, and "English." My ears are full of the sound of his incredible voice mingled with the rushing of my own blood, he's warm against my back and he smells *so* good, and on the jukebox Joe Cocker is suggesting quite strongly that I take off my dress—though he's totally down with it if I want to leave my hat on.

This *just friends* thing … it's not working out. And what's more, I was completely insane to ever imagine that it would. I will never doubt Ryan again.

"Jenna?" Mitch says. "Are you listening to me?" His mouth is so close to my ear that I can feel his breath, and every muscle in my body feels like it's pooling into molten lava. If I weren't trapped between him and the pool table, I'd be wobbling on unsteady knees.

I nod wordlessly because I don't trust my voice. Every nerve ending is screaming with the nearness of him, with the almost-painful urge to turn around and do something rash. If it was anyone other than Kari, I think, anyone at all, I might break a rule I thought was an immutable part of my morality.

He's pressed against me so tight that I can literally feel the buttons on his shirt through my blouse, his hair against the side of my neck. I don't think I've ever been *this* close to someone I wasn't currently—I mean, right that second—having sex with.

But for all that, there's something between us.

Twenty-three years of being closer to Kari than anyone else in the world. All the times she stuck up for me when we were kids. All the times she held my hair while I threw up from too much drinking in college. All the times she sat with me after the breakup with Drew, staying up all night and going to work feeling like a zombie because I needed her.

Dropping the cue on the table, I turn to face him. I'm still encircled by his arms, and he doesn't move for one very long moment. I put my hands against his chest and push; he takes a step back. It's not enough, but it's a start.

"I need … some fresh air."

He smiles at me—it doesn't quite reach his eyes—and takes another step back.

"I don't feel well," I say. "I think I should go home and get some rest."

There's a long pause, then he asks: "You okay to get yourself home?"

He doesn't put his hand on my forehead to see if I'm coming down with something. I think that's over for us.

I nod. "Yeah, I'm good. I'll take a cab."

"Cool," he says, "see you."

And he snags his empty glass off the edge of the pool table and heads for the bar.

I grab my purse and walk to the door slowly, wishing … I don't even know what I'm wishing. That I could be the kind of woman who could be his friend and let go of all that other stuff?

But I don't think I can.

I open the heavy outside door and turn back to look over my shoulder. Mitch is talking to Kevin, his back to me. Neither of them says anything as I step outside and let the door swing shut.

## Chapter Twenty-Three

WHEN I GET HOME, the answering machine light is blinking. It's not Mitch, obviously, and I don't really want to talk to anyone else, so I ignore it. But after two sitcoms and half a pint of Chunky Monkey, I'm ready to listen just to know that someone out there cared enough to leave me a message. With my luck, it will be a telemarketer.

Actually, my luck is worse. It's Drew. I almost delete it, but then I decide to see what he has to say for himself.

"Hi. It's, uh, Drew. I'm sorry I didn't catch you at home. I'd really like to talk to you. About ... you know, the other weekend." Oh, how well-spoken he is. "And I really want to see you. I was ... hoping you'd be free tonight. So ... call me, I guess."

*Never*, I think. *Never, ever again.*

I delete the message, and go back to the TV.

By eleven o'clock, there's pretty much nothing even remotely worth watching. I get ready for bed, and climb under the covers, but I'm not even tired.

Well, I guess I'm *tired* of listening to the same pitiful thoughts chasing each other around inside my skull, if that counts. I keep replaying the scene at Jacks over and over in my head—and every time, I come to the same conclusion, no matter how much I don't like it.

Trying not to think too hard about what I'm doing, I pick up my cell and dial Mitch's number. It rings twice and I almost hang up, realizing that if Kari answers I'm going to have no choice but to toss myself out my bedroom window—which *does* open. Although now that I think of it, there are decorative bars over it.

Foiled again.

Just as the phone rings for the third time, Mitch answers. "Hello?" His voice is thick and heavy with sleep—it's sexy as hell, of course.

"Mitch, it's me," I say hesitantly. "I'm sorry to wake you. I know you have an early morning."

"It's okay," he says. "Luis is driving."

"Still," I say. "I'm sorry. Maybe I shouldn't have called."

"But you did," he says. I can hear rustling in the background, and it occurs to me that he's in bed. My stomach does a slow, lazy flip at the thought of it.

"I did," I say.

"So?"

"So ... I have to tell you something." I say. "About earlier, and ... just about our friendship in general."

"What do you mean, 'about earlier'?"

"Why I took off so abruptly, and—"

"I don't know what's up with you, but I'm not into playing games." He sighs. "If you want me around, say so. If you don't, say that. But don't say one thing and do another. I don't have time for that."

"I'm not playing games," I say. "Mitch, I—I can't."

"Can't what?"

"Be your friend. I can't be friends with you, at all."

"Well," he says, after a moment. "I suppose that's up to you, but I guess I'm interested to hear why."

"It's ... it's just impossible." I take a deep breath. "There's a lot of stuff all mixed up in my head, and I need to get some clarity. I need to focus on what's important. I need to be who I am, and not be someone I don't recognize."

"Okay, but you do realize that didn't make any real sense?" There's more rustling as he moves around in bed. "I still haven't heard a reason. You don't owe me one, but I'd like one just the same."

"I'm afraid that's the best I can do," I say. "I have my reasons, and that's all I had to say. I'm sorry to call so late. I just wanted to catch you before … before you went away." *Before I lost my nerve.* "I hope I didn't … wake anyone up."

"You did," he says. "You woke me up. I got the impression you intended to? Or at least knew that you would."

"I mean anyone else."

"There's no one else here to wake up," he says.

"There's nobody there with you?"

"I'm leaving at oh-dark-thirty. Why would someone be here with me? What are you asking?"

"I was just … asking," I say. "I figured you might have someone there."

"There isn't anyone right now that would be here in bed with me."

"But I thought—" I find it really hard to just come right out and say Kari's name, so I pull back, make it more general. "I thought you were seeing someone."

"I *was* seeing someone," he says. "You, for about ten seconds. And I've been busy since."

"You're not dating anyone now? No one at all. Not even a little?"

There's a long pause, and then he says, "I am not."

But—

I mean, no one actually ever said he and Kari were dating. I just … I mean, they went away for the weekend. What was I supposed to think? I certainly don't go on weekend trips to the West Coast with guys I'm not sleeping with. I don't go on trips to the West Coast with guys I *am* sleeping with, either, but that's not the point.

If I did go on a trip like that, it would be a pretty fair indication we were banging, is all I'm saying.

"Are you sure?" My hands are shaking. This is so important.

His voice is impatient. "Yes, I'm sure. I think I would know."

"Promise me," I say.

"I'll be there in fifteen minutes," he says, and hangs up.

Shit.

I start to call him back and tell him I don't want him to come here, but hang up after three numbers. The thing is, I *do* want him to.

My teeth feel like they're coated in Ben & Jerry's, so I give them a quick brushing. Then I wash my face to make sure there's no stray makeup and close the bathroom door. I don't have time to pick up in there. I stop in my bedroom to dig out the bathrobe my mom gave me for my birthday—I never bother with it, but I can't very well greet him in my usual bedtime attire of a tank top and undies. I go downstairs, find the door already propped open. Great. It's only a matter of time before the hobos move in.

Then I sit silently in the dark kitchen, waiting for Mitch.

It's closer to twenty minutes when I hear the knock on my door. I open the door and he steps in; I close it and lean back against it, and look at him—the lines of his body, the planes of his face.

I notice sort of idly that he's in even more disarray than usual. I think his shirt is even buttoned—snapped—crooked. That's what I get for dragging him out of bed in the middle of the night.

But even as I'm thinking this, I'm also thinking of how beautiful his eyes are, how his voice makes me shiver.

"I'm glad you're here," I say.

He runs a hand through his hair. "What the hell is going on? Whatever this is, we have got to get it out and deal with it. You're making me fucking crazy."

He doesn't swear around me very often—he's got a weird chivalrous streak that way—so apparently he's not kidding. I don't want to make him crazy, but I don't know what to say, or even how to start. And he's standing so close to me that I can feel his body heat. It's scrambling my brain.

I can't stand it for another minute; this is making *me* crazy. I reach up, as I've wanted to do for so long, and run one hand down the line of his jaw. He's been unshaven for at least a couple of days now; this is *way* beyond five o'clock shadow. I feel it rasp against my hand, and he stands completely still; the only indication that he feels anything in particular is the increasing pace of his breathing.

There's something in the air between us—a tension, a just barely balanced moment when anything might happen.

It feels like a wave about to crash into foam. Like a dam about to break.

"I think I've been wanting to touch you like this from the moment I saw you," I murmur. "I just didn't know it."

He moves closer, trapping me against the apartment door, bracing his hands on either side of my head. I couldn't go anywhere if I wanted to. Which I don't.

"You've been wanting to touch me like how?" he asks, his eyes never leaving my face.

"Like I have the right to." I reach up and wrap my arms around his neck. "I thought there was someone else," I say. "But if there's not...."

I pull him down to kiss me.

He does nothing for a couple of seconds—which, not gonna lie, is alarming.

But then that dam breaks. That wave crashes. He sinks both hands into my hair, and takes my mouth.

*Oh, my.*

This is nothing like the other time he kissed me. Not even remotely. That kiss was almost a hello from his mouth to mine. This kiss doesn't have time to say hello; this kiss is fierce and hungry. I'm drowning in it, can't breathe. Can't stop.

His mouth leaves mine to travel down my neck, over my collarbone. His hand against the small of my back pulls me closer; I can feel what I'm doing to him, how hard he is, and I move my hips restlessly, trying to find a comfortable way to press myself against him.

He glides his hand down to cup my ass, and moves his other hand off the door to do the same. Then he lifts me, sliding me up, and wraps my legs around his waist. Through the thin cotton of my panties, I make contact with the heavy seam of his button-fly jeans, and the insistent—and impressive—bulge underneath. It's electric.

I tighten my legs around him and move to run my mouth along the same route my hand traveled earlier—his jaw is rough against my lips, but I don't mind. The taste of him on my tongue is just as I've imagined.

And yes, I *have* imagined it.

"You taste so good," I say, and I hardly recognize my own voice.

He makes a sound that's half groan and half sigh, and shifts me so that all of my weight is being supported by his hands, fitting me even more snugly against the front of his jeans. I moan against his neck and he pulls me away from the door, carrying me effortlessly into the living room and sinking onto the chaise with me underneath him.

His mouth never stops moving—it travels along my neck until he finds the sweet spot just behind my earlobe, and I gasp, tightening my fingers against the muscles of his back. He unties the sash of my robe with one hand while his other hand strokes my hip, my thigh. My bathrobe finally gives way, and he pulls his body away from mine just enough to look down at me.

I tangle my fingers in his hair, and I think *Finally*.

And then he lifts his head, looks up at me, and says, "No."

"No?"

He sits up, moves all the way to the other end of the chaise, runs his hand through his hair again. His eyes close; I see his jaw tense, then relax very slowly. Then he takes a long, deep breath, shakes his head a little, and looks at me, his eyes no longer clouded with desire.

A tiny, objective part of me is impressed by his control—but what the hell just happened here?

"Mitch—" I say, and he cuts me off.

"We're not doing this," he says. "We are not doing this, Jenna—and I have some things to say to you."

## Chapter Twenty-Four

I SIT UP, belt my robe around me. Mitch doesn't say anything, but when I open my mouth to speak, he holds up a hand.

"You want to be careful what you say to me right now," he says slowly. "I've been up and down too many times with you, and I don't like it."

"But—"

"Hear me out." He runs both hands through his hair this time. *No wonder it's always such a wreck*, I think, my heart swelling with tenderness. "You've been giving me this 'let's be friends' line almost from day one. And—"

"I—"

"I said hear me out."

I shut up. It's the least I can do. *Let him get it out*, I think. *Then we'll see what's what.*

He lets out a long breath, and starts again. "And I told you I was fine with that—and I would be—except that you've been looking at me like you could eat me up with a spoon for a long time. Since the night we were introduced, actually. And you just admitted that you *have* been feeling that way."

I nod.

"So one day we're out on a date, kissing at Jacks, and the

next day you want to be friends, and the next day you're looking at me like you're trying to take my clothes off with your mind. And I'm trying—I am honestly trying—to do whatever it is you want or need, because I *like* you. I want to hang out with you, and it has nothing to do with wanting to get in your pants or anything like that. You want to be friends? Cool. I'm a great friend.

"But it's just up and down on the rollercoaster with you, all the time. Every time you let your guard down with me, I find out something new about you, and my feelings for you get more complicated—and then you turn ice-cold, or push me away. And then you're right back to staring at me." His eyes catch and hold mine; his are steely. "My other friends don't look at me like that, Jenna."

I swallow convulsively, resist the urge to talk.

"And then somehow I'm sitting in some shitty half-assed park in SoHo, listening to you tell me you fucked your ex-boyfriend, and you want me to—what? Commiserate? Come over and watch *When Harry Met Sally*? Bring you Ben & Jerry's?" When I reach out to touch his arm, he shifts out of reach. "And I decide, okay, I'm out. I mean, come on. But then there you are, every time I turn around for three straight days. Calling, and inviting me down to the bar, and smiling and putting your hand on my knee. That's not even mixed signals, Jenna. That's just … signals."

I nod again.

"And you want to make me dinner. Okay, fine. I know I said I was done, but maybe … maybe what you did made you figure something out? Maybe—I don't know what. But I come here—against my better judgment—and we have dinner, and you sit there and you *look* at me. You look at me with your whole heart in your eyes, and I think *Okay, she's in this, look at how she looks at me*. You tell me all this personal stuff, and you bought my movie on eBay, and I'm like, *Yeah, she's in*." He blows out a frustrated breath. "And you were. I'm not stupid.

You *were*. But then you get sick—and I can see from the way you look that you're *really* sick, not the make-believe kind you like to use to get away from me—and I think, well, damn. But it's no big. We've got time.

"But when I come back it's like…. Whatever that was I thought I saw? It's gone. You're cool on the phone. You don't want to see me right away. Whatever I might have thought before I left, you are definitely not in anymore. And I think, did I imagine that? Maybe I just saw what I wanted to see. So okay, let's try this *just friends* thing again. Back on the fucking roller coaster."

Listening to him recount the story of us from the other perspective is kind of sickening. I'm not that person. I certainly never *meant* to be that person.

"And then you act … how you acted at Jacks earlier. You want to be around me, but you keep your distance. You look at me when you don't know I can see you looking, and there's something in your eyes again—that thing I saw the first night I met you. I can't walk away from that broken look in your eyes. I've been *trying*, and I don't know why, but I just can't."

That makes my heart beat even faster, and it was already pretty much beating out of my chest. I open my mouth to say something—I don't even know what—but he stands up abruptly and starts pacing the five steps in front of the chaise.

"And then you call me up in the middle of the night and tell me we can't be fucking friends anymore? You need clarity. You need to *focus*, whatever the hell that means. But by the way, you want to know if I'm seeing anyone.

"And I come over here even though I figure by the time I get here you'll be all closed off again and I'll leave just as confused as ever—but instead I get here and you want—" He comes to a stop in front of me and takes another of those deep breaths. "And no way am I going there with you. It's not that I don't want you. I've wanted you since that very first night, when I saw you for the first time. Christ, you were so *sad*. So sad. And I saw that you were struggling, and you were vulnerable, but you were trying to be brave … and I *knew*, I knew from that first second that nothing would be easy with you, Jenna, but I wanted you. And you wanted me too, even though you kept telling me—and yourself—that you didn't. I saw how you looked at me. I figured you'd come around. So I was patient. I've been patient until I had a hard time looking at myself in the mirror.

"And I just can't anymore. I'm done. It's like you're carrying my balls around in one of your little designer purses, and I'm done with it. I'm not going to bring you picnics, and take you to the movies, and watch you out of the corner of my eye looking at me like you're *hungry*, and then pushing me away. I'm not just going to keep coming back, hoping you'll be over your ex, or willing to tell me whatever the hell is going on in your head, or maybe—crazy thought—ready to actually take a stab at seeing if there's something going on between us. I can't do it."

"Okay," I say.

"I'm dead serious. Whatever it is about you that's under my skin, I'll find a way to scratch it out. I'm not doing this again." He sits heavily next to me, looks straight ahead. "And I'm not doing … *this*. No way."

I weigh my options, try to decide what to tell him, how much to tell him. And I realize it has to be all of it. Even the parts that make me sound crazy, which I guess I kind of am.

"You're right about almost all of it," I say. "I *was* looking at you like I was hungry—because I was. At Jacks tonight … I didn't leave because I was playing games with you, or because I went cold. I had to leave because I didn't want to betray Kari. Because I would never hurt her that way."

He just blinks at me, like he literally can't even understand where the conversation just went. "What does Kari have to do with any of this?"

"I just thought … you know. Maybe. I didn't know, I thought—well, you might be … something."

His brows draw together and he just looks at me for a moment. Probably trying to figure out what the hell I'm talking about. I mean, honestly, that was gibberish.

Then the light dawns. "You mean you thought—Kari and *me*?"

I nod.

"Is that why you asked me earlier if I was in bed with someone?"

I nod again.

He shakes his head. "Kari and I are friends. Just friends. And not the way *you* do it—I mean really just friends."

"I know," I say. "I know now—because you wouldn't lie to me. But I thought … when you took her to Fan Club Weekend—"

"No, it wasn't like that. Luis and I were talking about it, that morning at breakfast, after you—" He clenches his jaw, and chooses not to finish the sentence, which is just fine with me. "And she was kind of down about how she'd never gone, and I thought it would cheer her up and be a fun time for her. She stayed with friends at the event hotel, and I crashed with one of the other actors at his place."

"I get that. But that's not what I saw at the time."

"Why didn't you just ask me?"

"Because I was sure I already knew."

He sighs. "I'm glad that you're so sure now, but what happens the next time you get some crazy idea in your head?"

"You'll talk me out of it?"

He lifts his eyebrows at me.

"Okay, okay." I scrub my hands over my face. "I'm sorry," I say. "You're right. I should have asked you. If I ever doubt you again, about anything, I'll ask you, okay? But right now? I'm telling you that this"—I gesture with one finger, from me to him and back again—"I want to figure out what this is. I want you to help me figure out what this is."

"If you want someone to help you figure out how you feel about me, you might want to think about asking someone other than me. I have a lot invested in the answer."

"You do?"

"I do," he says. "Since the beginning."

"Why?"

He shrugs a little. "Because you were hurting, and trying so hard to act like it was no big deal. Because you're smart, and strong, and you're forgiving even when people aren't great to you, and you tell awesome stories and you make me laugh and … I don't know. I honest to God don't know. You hit me like a bolt of lightning. Maybe sometimes there's no reason. Maybe the reason is just *because*. Because I do."

He runs both hands through his hair again. It's a complete disaster, and I've never liked it so much as I do right now. I reach out and smooth it down a little, and this time he doesn't pull away from me.

"I just … I need to know where you're at, Jenna. I can't do this anymore. This is it; you're in, or you're out."

I let out a breath that I feel like I've been holding for two weeks. "I'm in."

He's quiet for a moment, then: "Are you sure?"

"One thousand percent," I say. "I'm in. I've been in, I just didn't know it." I lean forward and put my hands on his knees. "Look at me."

He does, and his eyes are amber in the dim light of my living room.

"I'm in this, okay? Everything that's gone wrong, every stupid misunderstanding—they're all on me. They were all me, trying to tick off all the boxes on that checklist you threw in my face at Angela's. I don't care about *any* of that anymore. I will not mess this up again. I won't keep secrets, and I won't doubt you." I kiss him, softly. "I'm all in."

There's a long moment where I'm not sure what he'll do. Then he lets out a long, slow breath, and rests his forehead against mine. "I thought you would drive me completely out of my mind, Jenna."

"I know, and I'm sorry. This is our reset button, okay? We start over, right now." I stroke his shoulders, rub the back of his neck. "You can stop waiting for the other shoe to drop."

And I see it. I can literally *see* the weight of uncertainty fall off his shoulders, feel them relax under my hands. Has he been carrying that this whole time?

"So now what?" he asks. "I've got my trip with Luis—"

"Go," I say. "You should go on your trip. We have time. But…."

"But?"

I sit up, and untie the knot in the belt of my bathrobe. "You said Luis is driving tomorrow?"

"That's right." His eyes are on my hands as I pull the robe open and let it drop off my shoulders.

"So you can sleep on the way up?"

"I can," he says.

"Good." I reach out and start to unbutton his shirt, and at last I understand how wonderful these snaps are. One hard pull, and the whole thing is open. I trail my fingertips down his chest and over his stomach. "Because you're not getting any sleep tonight."

## Chapter Twenty-Five

CAREFULLY, almost in slow motion, he leans over and touches his lips to mine. He takes my face in his hands, kisses me softly, like he did in the bar that first time. Back before I jerked him around, back before he had to always have his guard up.

I wrap my arms around his neck and kiss him back, shivering as his hands move up under my shirt. His fingers trace my backbone, stroke the soft skin of my waist. I grasp the hem of my t-shirt and pull it up over my head, and he leans back and just looks at me for what seems a very long time, his hands resting on my waist.

Then he stands, and swings me up into his arms, and carries me to the bedroom. It's ridiculous, and like something out of a movie—or a soap opera—but if I'm being totally honest, I love it. He lowers me to the bed and immediately his mouth is everywhere: my collarbone, my neck, my stomach, my breasts. I close my eyes against the rush of sensation and pull him up to kiss my mouth again, then slide a hand down to open the button of his jeans. I reach inside and wrap my hand around him as best I can—seriously, I wasn't kidding when I said impressive earlier—then stroke the smooth skin as he groans and toes off his boots.

I help him strip off his jeans and briefs, one hand still stroking him, the other pushing at his pants until they're in a pile on my floor. He shrugs out of his shirt, and I trail the fingers of my free hand over his shoulders, his chest, the hard ridges of his abs. He shivers and fists a hand in my hair, kissing me fiercely as his other hand slides between my legs and palms me through my panties, there where I'm so exquisitely sensitive for him.

I drop my head back and moan; he cups a breast in each hand, laving his tongue across first one nipple, then the other, then moves down between my legs. The throbbing at my core grows almost unbearable as he slides my panties down my legs, following their path with his mouth—thigh, knee, calf, ankle.

And then we're both naked, skin sliding on skin. He takes his time with me. His hands are everywhere, his mouth only a heartbeat behind—and not just the obvious places. He lingers at my neck, the curve of my hip, the small of my back. He turns me this way and that, finding every sensitive patch of skin and exploiting it without mercy. His fingers slip in and out of me, stroking all the sweetest spots, leaving me gasping.

Finally, he clamps his mouth over my hot, wet center, and I cry out his name as a stunning orgasm washes over me like a tidal wave. Swamped, I just lie there for a minute, catching my breath. Then I prop myself up on my elbows, look at him kneeling between my legs.

His size is a little daunting—but I've got a real can-do attitude, and I believe in *quid pro quo*. I sit up, bend forward, and take him in my mouth. He hisses in a breath and runs his hands over my hair, so gently I almost don't feel them.

But I do feel them, and the restraint of it is so hot I could combust.

So I show him, with my hands and my mouth, that I can give as well as take, that his pleasure matters to me as much as my own.

"Come here," he says, and pulls me up so we're kneeling together, our faces so close that our breath mingles. His hands smooth my hair back from my face, then pull me in for a long, searching kiss.

When he pulls away and his eyes meet mine, every possibility hovers in the space between us. But there was only ever one place we were going to end up, I think.

So I reach over to the drawer of the bedside table for a condom—and he looks at it, lifts his eyes to mine.

I bite my lip. "That's not going to be very comfortable, is it?"

"I didn't want to be the one to say it," he says. "I will if I have to … but hang on."

The universe must have decided to smile on us for a change, because when he fishes his wallet out of his pants, there's one in there.

*Glory hallelujah*, I think, closing my eyes and sending a heartfelt thank you to anyone who might be listening. *It's about time something went right around here.*

His mouth captures mine again, and he kisses me like he's drowning.

Then he moves over me, sliding his hands up my legs and spreading them wide for him. He presses his length into me slowly, opening me up, then tilting my hips so that he can go deeper still. It doesn't hurt, exactly, but I know I'm going to be feeling it even when we're done.

I buck up against him, eager for more. Eager for all of him.

He stops for a moment, holds my hips still. "Give me a second, here," he says. "I can't believe how hot and tight you are. Just … give me a minute."

And he leans over, kisses me deeply, slips his hand between us. His touch is sure and certain; his fingers stroke me to a fever pitch, and I feel another orgasm building. I tangle my fingers in his hair, kissing him fiercely. He pulls back and his eyes lock on mine; I wrap my legs around his waist and squeeze, pulling him into me.

He makes a noise low in his throat that jolts right through the center of me, and I'm nearly there again, my breath coming in gasps against his neck.

Then we are rocking together, his voice in my ear telling me how good I feel, how much he's wanted me. I press up to meet him with every movement, wrap my legs around his and stretch against him.

"Jenna," he says, lingering over my name.

"What?"

"Hold on," he says and then, holding me tightly, rolls over so I'm on top with him still seated deep inside me. I sit up and look down at him, then look down at the spot where we're joined together.

His gaze follows mine, and he hisses in another breath.

"*Fuck*," he says. Just that, then again: "Oh, fuck." He closes his eyes and lays his head back on the pillow. His hands are on my hips, showing me what he wants.

So that's what I give him. There's real power in this—in bringing a strong, clever man to helpless incoherence—and I revel in it, climbing higher and higher. A hard, hot need clenches low in my belly—like a knot, or a fist. It tightens when he moves his hands between us again, strokes me again.

I look down at him and his eyes are open now, locked on mine. He's looking at me like I'm every answer to every question—and I'm gone, up over the edge, calling his name as he pulls my hips down, hard, and follows me over.

When the aftershocks subside, I collapse on top of him and lay my head on his chest.

He doesn't say anything, just pulls me up to kiss him again, his mouth toying with mine almost lazily, all tension gone. His other hand strokes my hip, my waist.

I put my head back on his chest and listen to his heart beating, strong and steady. It's so nice, lying here. Feeling the sweat cooling on my skin, his hands on me. I might just stay here for a couple of years.

"Bathroom," he says, and slides out from under me. He's back in just few minutes, and when he climbs back into bed I curl against his side.

"Do you want to go to sleep?" I ask.

"I thought you weren't going to let me."

"That was before I found out you're not a normal guy." I poke his ribs. "Looks like it's *one and done* for us."

"Yeah," he says. "I could make do if I had to, but it's not ideal. I'll buy every box at every Duane Read in Manhattan when I get back on Monday."

"Well, that should hold us till maybe Thursday," I say.

He grins at me—dimples, crinkles, the whole nine—and I think Monday can't get here fast enough.

"I like the way you think." He closes his eyes and I admire the way his long lashes lie against his cheek. "I assume that's an alarm clock over there on your side?"

"Yeah."

"Set it for five, please."

I wince but I set it, then I make a quick trip to the bathroom. When I come back he's pulled up the sheet and blankets from the foot of the bed to make a cozy nest for us.

I slide in and he slips an arm around my waist, pulling me tight against him. His chest is warm against my back, he somehow still smells fantastic, and my heart feels so full I think it might burst.

"Mitch?" I say.

"Yeah?"

"I'm sorry I was such a pain in your ass."

"Me, too," he says, and kisses my shoulder, "but you're worth it. Now go to sleep."

So I do.

## Chapter Twenty-Six

I WAKE at ten o'clock Saturday morning with a faint ache between my legs and the covers tucked securely around me. Stupendously well-endowed *and* nurturing. Luckiest girl in the universe, right here.

When I go out to the kitchen, there's a note propped against the coffee maker:

*You look beautiful when you sleep. Hope your dreams were sweet.*

*I won't be home until really late Monday. Don't wait up. I'll see you Tuesday.*

*Mitch*

I stare at the note for a long time, tracing the pattern of his name, thinking about … everything, all at once.

The first time I saw him. The first time he called me and we talked half the night. Dinner at Angela's. The picnic.

Watching him work. Playing pool at Jacks.

The way my heart soared when I realized he could be mine, that there was still a chance for us.

The way he touched me last night, the way he took his time and savored me.

*One and done.* Not that I'm complaining, but….

"Every Duane Read in Manhattan," I whisper, and stand there smiling in my kitchen, holding his note and wishing it was Tuesday already.

Then I pick up the phone and do what I should have done a week ago: Call Kari.

————

Dot's is crowded, but our usual table is free. I grab a seat and wait for Kari to arrive, which she does only a couple of minutes after me. She sits down across from me just as Dot is pouring coffee for us, and since she's standing right there, we order our food.

Kari waits until Dot leaves, then folds her arms over her chest and says, "All right, spill. What the hell is going on?"

"Okay, listen," I say. "We can never fight again, ever, because you won't believe the crazy shit I got into when we weren't talking."

"Is this about the weird message you left for me? About Mitch?"

"Yes, but … I think I'd better start at the beginning."

I run through it quickly: Petrosino Square ("Oh, Jenna, you didn't!"), the Spin Doctors montage, the Fan Club Weekend phone call. Soapzone—and she laughs herself half to death at that part. My resolve to be *just friends*, for real this time.

The studio. Wet, shirtless Mitch at his apartment. Jacks.

"Okay," she says, forking up a bite of scrambled eggs, "so you're ogling my boyfriend with his shirt off, and then you think, *Hmmm, let's go play pool, that sounds like a great idea*?"

"Well, that's not exactly how it was, but close enough."

"Regular pool, or sexy pool?"

"Well … I thought it was regular pool, but it turned out to be pretty sexy."

"You trollop." She takes another bite of her eggs. "I don't

know how the hell you thought any of this was going to work."

"I really did think I could pull it off. I was trying so hard to do the right thing. Why do you think I called you?"

"Yeah, I thought you were nuts when I got your message. You're all 'I hope it's okay with you if I hang out with Mitch tomorrow?' and I'm over here like *Uh, sure? Have fun?*"

"Why didn't you call me back?" I spread a little jam on my toast, take a bite. "I was in agony at Jacks, trying not to jump all over him. At which I succeeded, by the way, even with Joe Cocker on the jukebox. That's how much I love you."

"Yeah, well, good job on that. I'm gratified to know it. But can I just say…." She pops a grape in her mouth, chews it thoughtfully. "I love you like a sister. I'd give you a kidney, Jenna. But if I did have a boyfriend, and you spent the whole day at his work with him and then went out to play sexy pool? You'd be dead, and I'd be in jail."

"Kari!"

"I'm serious. When they came to arrest me, I'd be wearing a cute little wrap I made from your back skin, and eating candy out of a bowl I made from your skull."

"Duly noted."

"Good." She eats another grape. "I didn't call you back that night because I got home late, and then I meant to call you at work yesterday, but we had an issue with a case file going missing it almost made me late for an event on Long Island. By the time it was all cleared up, I didn't really have time to call you, and anyway you were already off to the studio." She points her fork across the table at me. "You know, and then off to play sexy pool with *my boyfriend*."

I throw one of my grapes at her. "It wasn't like that, you jackass. I totally thought—admittedly because I'm not very bright—that we could be friends, and play pool, and drink beer, and I was like *I have totally got this*."

She snorts. "You absolutely did *not* have this."

"I sure didn't. It was awful. I had to bail quick, fast, and in a hurry—because holy shit, Kari. He's unspeakably hot."

"Yeah, I've got eyes," she says. "So much for your iron self-control."

"Well, yeah, but the thing is? I knew it would be okay because even if I couldn't control myself—which for the record I *did*, by removing myself from the situation—I knew he would never cheat on you."

She shrugs. "Who knows, with sexy pool? Things can get out of hand."

"Not in a million years. I'd have stabbed myself in the eye with that pool cue first." I polish off a piece of bacon. "That's no lie, Kari. I would never. And, if we hypothesize for a moment that I'm not one hundred percent trustworthy—which I totally am—I knew he would be. He has this crazy *thing* about cheating."

"That doesn't sound particularly crazy to me."

"Well, no, I mean … cheating is terrible. You know my feelings on that. Although, if it had been anyone other than you, while we were playing sexy pool…." I filch another piece of bacon off Kari's plate. I'm *starving*. "But he's got, like, a big thing about it. Previous girlfriend issues."

"That part's good, then. But how do you go from busting out of Jacks all sad and alone, to calling me this morning with 'I've got something to tell you'?"

"I called him," I say. "I couldn't sleep, and by midnight I couldn't stand it any more. So I called him."

"You called my boyfriend at midnight after a sexually-charged game of pool?"

"Stop calling him your boyfriend!" I laugh. "You're making me feel guilty and I didn't even do anything wrong."

"Except call my *boyfriend*"—she lingers over the word—"at midnight and invite him over for sexytimes."

"I did *not* invite him over for sexytimes, or for anything at all. I called and told him we couldn't be friends anymore."

She straight-up laughs at me. "You're ridiculous."

"You're not wrong."

"And what did he say to that?"

"After some hemming and hawing on my part, and him telling me he wasn't seeing anyone right now—which, since you are someone, meant I was wrong about you two—he got frustrated and stormed over to give me a piece of his mind."

"A piece of his *mind*." She waggles her eyebrows at me. "I just bet."

"No, seriously, though. He gave me chapter-and-verse about what a crazy bitch I am—without using those exact words, which is admirable on his part—and said I was either in or out, and he wasn't putting up with my shit anymore."

"Sounds like a well-deserved reaming." She grins, wickedly. "Followed, I assume, by a well-deserved reaming."

This is too much, and I laugh helplessly, almost choking. "Yes," I say, when I catch my breath. "Yes on both counts."

"Well, you can't just leave it at that," she says. "I'm gonna need a whole lot more information on this."

"You aren't going to put this on the internet somewhere, are you?"

"Hell, no," she says. "But as your best friend—and someone who is currently not getting any—I demand all the gory details."

I look around, make sure no one's close enough to hear. "Oh my god, Kari. He's hung like a rhino."

"Well, good for you," she says, and it's clear she means it. My BFF really rocks.

"And he just … I mean. Wow."

"That good?"

"That spectacular. I mean, that other part's good and all, but if it's all you bring to the table…."

"Boring," she says.

"Boring," I agree. "But he had a few tricks up his sleeve. And he's just … wow."

"You're eloquent this morning."

"Yeah, it's hard to explain. It's not like we did anything revolutionary—though we did manage to hit all the major milestones. He's just really exceptional at ... everything." I push my plate away. "And, of course, there's the voice."

"Okay," she says, and stacks her plate on top of mine. "*Now* I'm jealous."

And we laugh as Dot stomps over to clear our plates.

———

Saturday night, when I go to bed, I can smell him on my sheets, and it makes me smile. If I wrap my arms around the pillow he used, can anyone really blame me?

Sunday, I pick up the house. I scrub the shower tiles—who knows, we might have shower sex—and throw away all the leftovers growing interesting new life forms in my fridge. Later, I go to the grocery store and stock up on stuff we might want if we hole up in here this week and spend our evenings doing what I hope we'll spend our evenings doing.

And when I go to bed, I can still smell him, faintly, and I fall asleep with a smile on my face.

## Chapter Twenty-Seven

MONDAY MORNING, I fill Ryan in—with a bit less detail than I shared with Kari—and he high-tens me again.

"I knew that wasn't right," he says. "When you said he was with Kari. I saw how that guy looked at you. No way was he with someone else a week later."

"Yeah, well. It looked bad," I say. "But it's all good now, and I need to buckle down and focus. This last few weeks I haven't been bringing my A game, and that's not cool. Hold my calls, okay?"

He agrees, so I'm surprised when, barely an hour later, the door opens and I look up to see Ryan in the doorway. His face is pale, and I set down the file I was flipping through.

"What's up? Are you okay?"

"I just got off the phone with Leonora, and she says Ben wants you up there. Now."

"But I'm right in the middle of—"

"You've got to go upstairs, Jenna," he says. "Something is very wrong."

"But what?" I ask, mystified. Nothing has gone even slightly wrong since that missing report, and even that turned out fine in the end. Plus, that was over a week ago.

"I have no idea, but I want you to understand that I am not remotely joking when I tell you I have never heard him so angry. I could hear him yelling while Leanora was on the phone with me." He looks away and says, "He said he'd fire me, too, if you weren't up there in fifteen minutes."

My stomach turns upside down. "What do you mean, fire you, *too*?" I say.

He doesn't answer me.

"Ryan!"

"You heard me," he says quietly. "Please go figure out what's wrong with him. My rent is ridiculous."

Without another word, I stand and bolt past him, toward the elevator.

———

I can hear Ben bellowing as soon as I step off the elevator on his floor. This is in part because it's not a very big floor; there are only four offices and the conference room up here. One of the perks of being upper management, I suppose. That, and threatening to fire perfectly adequate employees for no reason at all, as well as their hardworking administrative assistants.

Ben's hardworking administrative assistant, Leanora—who probably works a lot harder than Ryan, honestly—grimaces at me as I open the door. Ben's shouting from the inner office becomes clearer. "I don't *care*," he bellows. "Change it back *now*."

"What's he so pissed off about?" I whisper.

"You screwed up bad," she says. "What were you thinking?"

"I don't even know what I did—" I begin, but then Ben bellows again and I scurry over to tap on the door to his office, and open it gingerly.

His face is a livid red, and just as I close the door behind me he slams down the phone. I guess he isn't done being mad at it, because he picks it up and then slams it down again. Or maybe he was just thinking of calling someone else and changed his mind. Or maybe he's just trying to intimidate me. Or maybe this is all a mistake and he's found the person he's *really* mad at, and that's who he was yelling at—

He interrupts my frenzied thoughts, his voice quieter but no less deadly. "What. the. *hell*. were. you. thinking?" He lays each word down like a brick.

"I don't know?" I say.

"Well, you'd better think of something, and fast. I'm about ten seconds away from telling you to find another job. The only reason—*the only reason*—you still have a job is that Leonora, of all people, insists you must have made an honest mistake."

That comes as a bit of a surprise. I had no idea he valued her opinion so much. For that matter, I had no idea she held any particular opinion, good or bad, of me.

"Ben," I say, feeling small and terrified. I love my job. "I don't want to tick you off worse, but I have no idea what you're talking about."

He glares at me. "I'm talking about the design changes. You've just cost me tens of thousands of dollars and a lot of very valuable manpower at a time when we have neither of those things to spare. And as far as anyone can tell, you've done it on nothing more than a whim."

I latch on to the only thing in his little speech that makes any sense. "What design changes?"

"The ones you decided to implement without consulting anyone, *including* Creative." His face goes even redder, which I kind of wouldn't have thought possible, and his voice keeps getting louder. "The ones that went into production and arrived this morning at all of our branches, in the form of hundreds of boxes of brochures and posters and other collaterals. The ones that look like they were designed by a colorblind three year old."

I'm speechless. I have literally no idea what he's talking about, to the point where I'm starting to think he's having a break with reality. Very quietly, trying not to make him any angrier, I say, "I don't mean to be obtuse, I swear, but I have no idea what on earth is going on here. I haven't made *any* design changes in *anything* since we agreed on the palettes and layouts. This was all decided over a week ago."

"It was," he agrees. "And then after the design decisions were finalized, *you* sent the design team an email—circumventing Aiyana, by the way, which in itself is a firing offense—and told them to redesign and use a new palette. And if you'd pulled it off, I suppose we were all supposed to think you were a genius, but unfortunately you've confused your marketing expertise with creativity. Your changes, quite frankly, look like *shit*."

He picks up something off his desk and throws it on the floor at my feet. It's a trifold brochure like the one we designed for Grow, only in garish shades of orange and yellow and green. Perhaps it's supposed to look postmodern. I reach down to pick it up and to my horror I realize it *is* a brochure for Grow—it says that right across the top: "*Grow* with us at Home Bank." I scan the copy quickly. It's the copy we agreed on. Everything is just as it was supposed to be for the Grow brochures but all the color choices have been turned on their heads—and Ben is right, it looks like it was designed by a colorblind child. Possibly one who was on drugs.

I look up at him, speechless. "What the hell—" I begin, but he cuts me off.

"Is this deliberate sabotage instead of a stupid design mistake?" he asks hotly. "Because you lost the debate about what to name the program?"

I shake my head vehemently. "Ben, I would never do this. It's not just that this isn't my job—I'm not qualified to do this. This is Aiyana's job."

"You're technically Aiyana's superior," he points out. "Maybe you think you know her job better than she does?"

"I don't think anything of the kind," I say, shaking my head again. At this rate I'm going to shake my brains out, which will be a blessed relief, as they're obviously not doing me a lick of good.

Maybe they would, if I used them.

Mitch's voice echoes in my head. *You might want to think about who benefits if it looks like you can't handle your job.*

It's like a bolt of lightning.

"Ben, someone else did this. On purpose. To sabotage me."

"That's a very serious accusation." His glare is steely, but at least he doesn't dismiss me out of hand.

"I know it is," I say. "I haven't wanted to believe it myself. But it's true. It's all part of the same thing—since when do I make decisions that affect the whole company without asking? Since when do I lose reports, or collateral material, or forget about important meetings?"

"My understanding is that you've got a lot going on," he says. "Personally."

"I do," I tell him earnestly. "But what difference does that make? I went through a bad breakup last year, and you never saw that in my work, did you?"

"Not that I'm aware of," he says.

"I didn't do anything wrong, Ben, and I haven't been forgetting things. I don't understand how it's being done, but it's all very clear if you look at it the right way."

"I don't think I'm entirely sure who it is you're accusing, Jenna."

"Someone told me recently that I should think about who benefits if it looks like I can't handle my job."

"If I were looking for someone to replace you in your position," he says, and I kind of want to throw up, "my first instinct would be to offer it to Aiyana."

"That's what I said," I tell him.

"But Aiyana would most likely turn it down."

"That's *also* what I said."

"Which leaves…."

I nod. "Yes."

"You're making a very serious accusation here."

"I know. Will you have Leanora ask Ryan to come up? I think he'll have some insight." I say a quick prayer that this was why Ryan was being snarky.

He makes the request, and Ryan joins us so swiftly I suspect he might have even taken the stairs.

Ben takes the lead, filling Ryan in on the email I supposedly sent that basically equated to everyone in the entire building, right down to the night janitor, wiping their asses with big handfuls of hundred-dollar bills.

Ryan doesn't even look at me before speaking. "No way would Jenna do that, sir. Not ever. She has a lot of respect for chain of command, and for Creative in particular."

"Why do you say so?" Ben wants to know.

"I've often heard her say you couldn't pay her enough to do what they do."

"It's true. I have said that. I don't have a creative bone in my body—though, even in spite of that, if I *had* secretly designed that brochure it wouldn't look as bad as it does."

"Can I see it?" Ryan asks, and Ben pushes one across the desk to him. Ryan glances at it and winces. "Oh, that *is* bad. This is a bank, not a Taco Loco."

Ben nods curtly. "And I've got an email here, originating from Jenna's email address, that clearly lays out *that* palette as the 'most recent and final change' to the brochure." His eyes flick to me again. "No one can log into your internal email from anywhere other than your desk, Jenna."

"When was it sent, sir?" Ryan asks.

God bless him; I haven't even thought to ask that.

Ben shuffles some papers and comes up with a printout of the email. "Thursday before last," he says. "At four-thirty."

I close my eyes and think back, counting days, then open them and look at Ryan.

He's grinning at me, fiercely. "Is it?" he asks me.

"It is." The worry rolls off me like the rock from the tomb of Lazarus. To Ben, I say, "I left early that day, at four. It's in my time tracker."

He tilts his head and looks at me. "I wasn't aware you left."

I nod and wince a little. "I didn't exactly tell anyone. I asked Ryan to keep it quiet unless someone asked directly."

"But you put it in your time tracker."

"I left early to get ready for a date," I say. "It was personal time."

Ben actually smiles, just a little. "You left a measly hour early, and you made sure to note that for HR?"

"It was personal time," I repeat. "We're supposed to mark personal time."

"I have to say, HR should consider using this example in that little training they do about why you shouldn't fudge your hours even a little bit. Marking that personal time just saved your job, Jenna."

The relief is so huge and overwhelming that I sag a little where I'm standing. Ryan catches my arm at the elbow and steers me into a chair. He's *so* getting a raise.

"Now what?" I ask, weakly.

"Now we have to figure out who did this."

"We know who did it," I say.

"Knowing and proving are not the same thing," he reminds me.

And Ryan, bless him again, chimes in. "It was Melody."

"What makes you say that?" Ben asks.

"She was in Jenna's office that afternoon." To me, he says, "I told her you went to the cafeteria and she said she would just go leave you some stuff to look at. I was going to mention it the next day but you went home sick, and then the next time

I saw you we were talking about the missing report, and I forgot."

"That report went missing at the same time," I said. "She could easily have deleted the report *and* sent that email, right from my desk, that day. She didn't know I'd have an excuse."

"She was in your office the morning I sent you the email about the meeting being moved," Ryan says. "The meeting that you almost missed, about the brochure."

"That was a Monday," I say.

"Yeah, the meeting was on a Monday, but the email I sent you was the Wednesday before, remember? And I looked for it after you said you never got it, to make sure I definitely sent it. It was the morning of the day you had the—" He hesitates, very clearly decides *what the hell*, and forges onward. "The day you had the picnic in your office."

Ben raises an eyebrow, but doesn't say anything.

"That's right!" I exclaim. "There was a mouse pad on my desk when I got to work. I thought she just wanted to show me how well they came out."

"They didn't come out well enough to qualify her for your job," Ben says.

The quiet fury in his voice is fully as terrifying as the red face and raised voice earlier. More so, in fact. I'm awfully glad it's not directed at me.

"What are you going to do?" I ask. "She's not going to want to admit it."

"She'll admit it to me," he says, very calmly. "And then I'm going to fire her on the spot and have her escorted from the building."

"Oh," I say. "What will happen to her?"

"Maybe the Taco Loco is hiring," Ryan says.

Ben's lips twitch, but he holds it together. "It's no concern of mine what happens to her once she's gone. My only question is, do you want to be there? As her supervisor, you're entitled to be there."

I shake my head mutely. I want no part of it. I tried to help her; I tried to give her a chance. The whole time she was stabbing me in the back, I was handing her knife after knife. I don't want to look at her ever again.

"Can I be there?" Ryan says eagerly. "I'll watch her pack up, make sure she doesn't steal anything."

"We have security for that, Ryan," Ben says, and waves us both out. "Go back downstairs. Not one word to her."

So we do as he says, and go back to Ryan's office, and when the security guys pass by on their way to Melody's cube, I just look away and shut the door.

# Chapter Twenty-Eight

I SPEND the rest of the day going through all Melody's paper files and her computer, to see what else she might have been up to. Ryan hangs out with me while I do it, though it seems like that's mostly so he can crow about how he knew all along that she was up to no good.

I think, but don't say, that he could have told *me*, if he was so sure. You know, before I almost got fired?

But I wouldn't have listened to him, so I hold my tongue and just keep opening documents and archiving anything that could be important. I haven't found anything nefarious, but who knows what she might have done that won't make itself evident for days—or even weeks? She was playing a long game.

It's almost seven o'clock by the time I shut the computer down. "Can you see that this goes in one of our cabinets or closets, clearly labeled?" I ask Ryan. "Just in case I missed something and we have to dig it out down the road?"

"Sure thing," he says.

I stand, and pat him on the shoulder. "Thanks for everything. You saved my ass."

"Good," he says. "We can talk about my raise tomorrow."

I laugh, which feels damn good after this hellish day, and head to my office. I have a report to file, and a couple of emails to follow up on.

I finally wrap that up, and head out. I stop at a store close to work, pick up some wine for tomorrow night, and hail a cab to get home. I'm not remotely up for packing into a subway car at rush hour. Not that rush hour traffic is all that great either, but at least I'm alone in the back seat.

I pay the cabbie and let myself in. Mrs. Corinthos is in the vestibule, collecting her mail, and I skirt around her walker, mumbling a greeting and heading for the elevator. But her words stop me cold.

"There's a man up there waiting for you," she says. "Is it safe?"

"Waiting for me?" I say, turning back.

"Yeah. Youngish. Black coat."

Mitch? Home early?

But when I step off the elevator, it's not Mitch.

It's Drew.

He's sitting in the hall outside my apartment door, leaning back against it with his head hanging down. If I didn't know better, I'd say he was drunk.

Then I get within three feet, catch a whiff of him, and realize he *is* drunk. Or he took a bath in booze. Which, given the way he was sucking them down last time I saw him, isn't out of the realm of possibility, I suppose.

I crouch down and shake him. "Drew!"

He opens bleary eyes. "There she is," he says. "You don't ever call me back."

His head rolls forward again and I realize he's absolutely shitfaced, blackout drunk. When we were together, this would happen maybe once a year, but I haven't seen him like this in a while. Not even after Marty's, and all those martinis.

"Oh, for God's sake," I say to no one in particular.

I stand and unlock the door, then grab his shirt so I can

open it without him falling back into my apartment and braining himself on the linoleum. I lay him down, half-in and half-out of the apartment, set down my stuff, and come back to "help" him inside. It's not exactly ideal, but I can't have Mrs. Corinthos asking me about some drunk passed out literally in my doorway.

I haul him inside; he rouses enough to help a little, and with some stumbling, staggering, and one memorable moment when he reaches out to steady himself and gets a handful of my ass, we make our way to the chaise. He collapses onto it, and looks up at me blearily.

"Why are you here?" I ask. I'm too tired to be polite.

"I wanted … to talk … to you," he says, in the careful cadence of someone who is very, very drunk, and formulating a sentence a few words at a time.

"About what?"

"My partners … voted me out."

I'm human enough that I feel bad for him. He's coming to me for some kind of comfort, and I don't have any energy at all for him.

"But why?" I ask

"Too much … drinking."

"I'm sorry," I say, although it's clearly his own fault. "That sucks."

"'sokay," he says. "I'll start a new clinic."

I lift an eyebrow at that. As far as I can tell, he's one step from being a wino in the street. And he's gonna start a vet clinic? Sure.

"Here," I say, "sit up a sec." I pull out most of the throw pillows and toss them on the floor, then get one situated under his head and pull the throw over him. "Sleep it off, man. We'll talk about your imaginary vet clinic in the morning."

But he's already passed out cold, and doesn't hear me.

Shaking my head, I go into the bedroom and shut the door.

After a second, I push the little lock thingy in. I don't want any visitors in the wee hours.

My sheets don't smell like Mitch anymore, which is sad, but he's coming home tomorrow, and that's the opposite of sad. I don't know how I'm going to sleep, when it feels a lot like Christmas Eve right now.

And, thinking that, I'm out like a light.

————

The next thing I know, there's an insistent knocking sound. I know my alarm clock doesn't make a noise like that, but I smack at the buttons anyway. I open one eye. It's ten minutes to six. Who the hell is here at this hour?

I hear shuffling in the next room, and Drew calls out, "I'm coming already, quiet down."

Oh, no. Oh, *shit*. This can't be happening.

I bolt out of bed and fling open the bedroom door just in time to see Drew—wearing nothing but boxers—swing open the apartment door, revealing Mitch on the other side.

"Can I help you?" Drew says, and Mitch doesn't answer. He doesn't say anything at all—but both of his hands ball into fists, and again I think *Oh shit.*

I step out of my room, acutely aware that I'm only wearing my t-shirt and panties, and feeling very defenseless. Mitch looks over, and his eyes narrow.

Now Drew is looking at me too, as if to say, *Who the hell is this guy?* And I don't know what to say to either of them, but all I can think is that I'd better get between them before somebody's bleeding.

I mean, let's get real here. It's gonna be Drew.

I move across the floor, and when I step between them I can practically feel the air vibrating.

This is bad. This is really bad.

And then Drew makes it a thousand times worse. He shifts

so that we're standing side-by-side, and puts his hand on the small of my back. The body language could not be more clear —he and I, united against the interloper. For one crucial moment, I'm paralyzed.

Drew is first to speak, because of course he is. "Who—"

"You're gonna want to take your hand off her right now," Mitch says, "unless you don't particularly want to keep it."

Drew blinks but drops his hand back down to hang at his side.

"Whatever you two do on your own time is one thing, but if I ever see your hands on her again, you won't have any."

Holy shit. That would be really hot if everything weren't so awful.

Okay, think. Get Drew out, talk Mitch down. Have a good laugh about how ridiculous this scene is.

"Drew," I say. "You have to go."

"I'm not sure—"

I grab him by the wrist and drag him over to the chaise—I can't leave him over by the door with Mitch—and shove his shirt and shoes at him.

"Jenna, I don't think—"

"You need to go. Now." His pants are under the coffee table, and I pull them out and add them to the pile in his arms. "Go."

"I'm not dressed."

"Dress in the hall." I grab his wrist again and start dragging him back toward the door. "You need to get out of here. Seriously."

"Who *is* this guy?"

"Drew. Just *go*."

I push him past Mitch and out the door, and shut it behind him, then rest my forehead against it for a moment. This is literally the worst possible thing that could happen. How is this my life?

But no. Mitch knows better, after Friday.

Then he speaks, and his voice could cut glass. "What the fuck is this?"

I turn and look at him. I thought he looked angry that day in Petrosino Square, but I guess I didn't know how bad it could get. He's practically incandescent with rage.

"Mitch—"

"You told me you were done with him," he says. "After what happened last time, you said you were done. I would never have ... stayed here, with you, if I didn't believe he was out of the picture."

"I know—"

"You said—" He breaks off, breathes deep. His eyes flick over me from head to toe. "I guess it doesn't matter what you said."

"This isn't—"

"What exactly was the plan, Jenna? Meet me in some park somewhere and tell me you did it again? Or just not tell me, and carry on like it didn't happen?"

Oh, for God's sake. Is this what it's like for him, when I act like a crazy person, and assume things, and make a bunch of decisions about things—about *us*—with my shitty, made-up information? "I thought you were—"

"I got back a couple of hours ago. What if I had shown up then? What would I have walked in on? But I figured *No, I'll let her get her sleep. I'll see her after work.*" He runs his hands through his hair, and his eyes are wild. "But then I wanted to see you. I just wanted to be here. With you."

"Stop it," I say. I get that this is his *thing*; this is his big red-button issue. And I know that it looks bad. But he has to calm the hell down and let me talk. I reach out and lay my hand on his arm. "You have to listen to me."

He shakes me off. "I don't," he says. "I don't have to listen to you. I come over here to surprise you, because I don't want to be away from you for one more minute, and here's fucking *Drew*? In his fucking *underwear*? And you're standing there telling me I have to listen to you, when you've got another man's sweat drying on your skin? *Fuck* you."

"No, that's—"

"Lose my number, Jenna," he says, icy cold. "We're done."

It feels like a punch in the stomach. I literally forget how to breathe for a few seconds, and while I'm trying to remember he brushes past me and slams out the door.

# Chapter Twenty-Nine

I MANAGE to make it to the chaise before I have a complete breakdown, but once I'm there I cry for a full half an hour straight. I try to call Mitch three times, but he doesn't pick up.

Finally, when the sobs subside, I drag myself off the chaise, splash my face with some cold water, and call Kari. What else can I do?

She answers the phone brightly, chirping "Hello" in my ear in a tone so completely the opposite of what I'm feeling that I start to cry again. I manage to identify myself through my tears and she asks, "Are you at home?"

I mumble assent, crying too hard to do any better.

"I'll be right there," she says, and hangs up.

I manage to stop the tears long enough to call work. I tell Ryan I'm sick, and I'm sure I sound it because I'm all stuffed up and hoarse. He's disappointed, because apparently he brought in cake and ice cream to celebrate Melody's firing. He says he'll save me a piece.

When I hang up, I go downstairs to prop the door open. It's already open, and I come back up, cursing the stupid slow repairmen who haven't fixed the buzzer yet. If the damn buzzer was working, the damn door wouldn't be open half the time, and Mitch would have never made it upstairs like that. For that matter, neither would Drew.

I call Mitch's cell again. It goes to voicemail. Again.

*Lose my number, Jenna. We're done.*

That brings on a fresh wave of tears. When Kari knocks fifteen minutes later I answer the door in all my glory: red eyes and a runny nose, my hair limp around my face. There's a wad of damp tissues in one hand, the entire box of tissues in the other. Glorious me.

"Oh, my God," she says. "What is going *on*?"

"Mitch left me," I say, and pull a new tissue out of the box.

She looks at me like I've lost what little was left of my mind. "What do you mean Mitch *left* you?"

"He left," I say. I'm speaking English; what exactly doesn't she understand here? "He left me, he hates me. He's never coming back."

I shuffle back to the living room and collapse onto the chaise. I'm going to have to burn it. My sheets, too. And that note he left. And—

"What is going on?" Kari sits down beside me and takes the box of tissues. "I'm missing work for this. You have to talk. Stop crying."

"I can't stop crying," I say, through tears.

"You don't cry," she reminds me.

I throw my hands up, gesture at my face, my tissues, my everything. "I guess I do now," I say. "I cried on *Ryan*."

"Come on, sit up, talk to me."

I think briefly about disobeying, maybe lapsing into another crying fit, but I'd rather have a sympathetic ear. So I take a few deep breaths, straighten up, and look her dead in the eye so she gets that I'm one hundred percent serious.

"I think I'm in love with Mitch," I say.

"Jenna, that's *wonderful*," she says. "He's obviously crazy about you, too."

"Don't say that," I wail. "That doesn't matter anymore. Everything is ruined."

"Oh, come on—don't be melodramatic." She smiles. "What can possibly have gone wrong when he hasn't even been around for the last three days."

"He thinks I slept with Drew."

"You *did* sleep with Drew. Which you already told him a couple of weeks ago."

"No, not that." I'm telling everything the wrong way. "He thinks I slept with Drew last night."

"Why on earth would he think that?"

"Because he showed up here this morning and Drew answered the door."

She says nothing for a moment, then asks, "Did you sleep with him?"

"Who?"

"*Drew*!"

"No," I say, shaking my head so violently it makes me a little nauseated.

"Okay, good." She pats my cheek. "I didn't think so."

"It doesn't matter, though. He's gone." I put my face in my hands. "It looked really bad, Kari."

"I imagine it did," she says. "I guess if I were him, I'd certainly wonder why were you having a sleepover with your ex."

"He showed up drunk, and passed out. I let him sleep it off in here," I say, indicating the living room. "I didn't know Mitch would show up and think—"

"How bad was it?" she asks. "Scale of one to ten."

"Fifty. Drew answered the door in his underwear."

She winces. "Ouch. What did Mitch say?"

"Oh, God, so many things." I look at her helplessly. "He said he was going to break Drew's hands."

She arches her eyebrows. "Oh, really?"

"Yeah, and then he said we were … done."

My voice hitches on the last word, and she rubs my back a little.

"Okay, excuse me if this is a stupid question, but … why didn't you just tell him you didn't sleep with Drew?"

I tell her what happened—throwing Drew out, everything Mitch said, the way I could literally not get a word in edgewise—and by the time I'm done she just looks incredulous.

"It's a soap opera," she says. "This is literally a soap opera plot. I mean, maybe even one I've seen before—"

"This is my life," I say, "and I don't know how to fix it."

"Call him!" She hands me my cell phone.

I set it back on the table. "There's no point."

"Why don't you let him decide if there's any point?" She hands me the phone again. "Call him."

"I've *been* calling him. He said we're done. He meant it."

She waves this off. "They always mean it when they say it."

"No, I'm serious. I told you—he already gave me a choice. In or out, no more playing with his feelings. He's not coming back for another round of that—especially not after *this*."

"For God's sake, Jenna—give me that. I'll do it myself." She punches in his number angrily, then waits. Then she hangs up. "Voice mail. You should leave him one."

"You don't understand how mad he is." I jump up and grab her purse from the kitchen table, rummaging in it until I find her phone. "Here. Call him from your phone. Don't tell him you're with me. See what happens."

"This is ridiculous."

"Do it."

She shakes her head, but she dials the number. I can hear it ring, twice, then Mitch answers.

"Oops, sorry!" Kari says brightly, but her eyes on me are sad. "Meant to call Jenna. I'll talk to you later, okay?"

She hangs up and pulls me back down beside her, and I rest my head on her shoulder.

"See?" I say.

"Okay, so he's mad. He'll get over it."

"He won't."

"He *will*. I promise you. Give him a little time, and he'll come back around, no matter what he said. Doesn't he always?"

That hits me—really hits me, right in the heart. I sit up straight and look at her. She's absolutely right. "Yeah. He always does. Even though it makes him feel like shit."

"Then he will this time," she says.

"I don't think he will, but … you know what? That doesn't matter." I toss my wad of tissues on the coffee table. "He's come back every time I've fucked up or pushed him away … except that one time."

"Which one time?"

"When I slept with Drew. I had to chase him after that. Ryan told me what to do."

"Ryan?"

"Guys know stuff—about other guys, and like, how they think." I stand up. "And you know what? Even then, he had to be the one to come to me. I mean, I called him and called him, and I made it clear what I wanted … but in the end, he had to come to me."

"Okay, but what—"

"I don't have Ryan, so I'm going to have to wing it. I have to go to him, right now."

She looks up at me. "He'll be at the studio."

"Then I'll go to the studio." I walk into my room and start pawing through my closet.

Kari follows me. "And do what? Pull him out of work and tell him you're not banging Drew again? I mean, it can wait. Why would he listen at work any better than he'd listen anywhere else? Wait till he gets home."

"And what? Go over there and ring the doorbell and he

doesn't let me in?" I shake my head. "That's not going to work."

"Of course he'd let you in. And that way at least you'd be alone. You can't do this at his *job*."

"We don't need to be alone," I say. "He needs me to come after him. He needs me to stop expecting him to always be the one who tries again."

I push my black sheath aside, and there it is. The Vera Wang dress. The one that no occasion has ever been special enough for.

I pull it off the hanger and lay it on the bed, then start stripping off my bathrobe, my t-shirt.

"Jenna," she says, and her voice is tentative now. "I'm trying to be positive, and I really do think he'll get over this, but ... what if you get there and he doesn't want you? Do you want that to play out in front of the cast of *Midnight Confessions*?"

I pull the dress over my head and thread my arms through the forty million criss-crossing shoulder straps. The dress settles around me like a cloud, all billowy layers of white with a delicate floral print. "I have nothing to lose." I put a hand on each of her shoulders and stare directly into her eyes. "*Nothing*. If it's already over, then I'll embarrass myself a little. And Kari? He's so worth it. But if there's a chance I can fix this ... it has to be this way." I turn around, present her with my back. "Zip me."

## Chapter Thirty

TWENTY MINUTES later I'm standing in front of the ABC Studios building on 66th, mustering the very small reserves of courage inside me. A breeze has picked up, and I listen to the flags above me rustle as my dress blows around my legs.

"I can do this," I say, to no one. To myself.

Then I breathe in through my nose, hard, exhale through my mouth, and push open the doors.

The security guard is the same one that was on duty last time I was here; with any luck he'll recognize me and figure I belong. He does seem to think I look familiar, but I can also tell he's not quite placing me. I approach the desk, rooting in my memory—not good even at the best of times, certainly not good now—for his name.

"Can I help you?" he says.

"Yes," I say, giving him what I hope is an engaging and sincere smile. "You're … Al, right?"

He nods, narrows his eyes at me. "And you are?"

"Jenna—remember I was here with Mitch last week? Mitchell Cole?"

He nods, smiling back at me now. "Oh, yeah, of course. Let me just let him know you're here—"

"No!" I say, startling him with his hand halfway to the phone. "I mean, I—I want to surprise him."

*Yeah, surprise him with a visit from the last person he wants to see right now. How's that sound, Al?*

He's shaking his head. "Sorry, ma'am, I can't let you in unless he comes out to get you. Can't have just anyone traipsing around back there."

"No, no, of course not," I agree, nodding. "It's just—it's a little surprise, you know?" Again, I pull out my most winning smile.

He remains unimpressed, and picks up the phone.

"Maybe I could just sort of peek around the corner and flag him down?" I say.

He shakes his head and starts to punch in numbers.

This is it. I can stand there while Mitch tells him to send me away, or I can *do* something for once in my life, instead of waiting for it to be done for me.

I dart around the corner of the desk and leg it for the set. Al calls after me—"Hey!"—and I keep moving, figuring it will take him a minute to stand and be after me. But my figuring doesn't account for the fact that he's trained security personnel, and within thirty seconds he's hot on my heels, so close I can hear him breathing, as I swing around a corner into the Ratcliffe living room and run smack into Mitch.

He staggers back a couple of steps, I rebound backwards in the other direction, and Al catches my arm and starts pulling me backwards.

Mitch is silent, still. Is it just shock at seeing me, or is he really going to let security escort me off the set?

There are about half a dozen people milling around, but no one is in makeup. Blocking, then. At least I didn't interrupt shooting. Martina is standing in the carriage house set in jeans and a t-shirt, holding a handful of green sheets and just watching the bizarre scene unfolding in front of her.

Oh, shit, it's love scene day.

But I can't spare a thought for that. I look at Mitch, who just looks back at me, still not speaking, still not moving.

I pull against Al's grip on me; he shifts so that he's holding both arms now. This is really going to happen. He's really going to haul me out of here.

"Mitch," I say, trying to put everything, the entirety of what I feel and what I want, in my voice. Willing him to hear me. "Please."

He runs a hand through his hair, looks away from me, then back. "You can let her go."

I sag with relief. It's actually kind of a good thing that Al doesn't immediately obey, because for a moment or two he's the only thing holding me up.

After a couple of seconds, Mitch repeats himself. "You can let her go."

Al does. "I tried to stop her out front—I never thought—"

"It's fine," Mitch says, never taking his eyes off my face. "She … difficult."

I feel like I should object or defend myself—but he's not wrong. I *am* difficult. So I don't say anything.

Al backs away slowly, then shrugs and leaves, returning to the front to stand once again between the cast of *Midnight Confessions* and the unwashed masses. Hopefully with more success than he had with me.

"Mitch," I say again. "I have to talk to you."

"I see that," he says, but his voice is still as cold as it was in my apartment. "Let's go somewhere private."

He starts to turn away and I stop him with my hand on his arm.

"No," I say.

He just looks at me.

"No," I say again. "I don't want to go anywhere private. I don't have anything to say to you that I can't say in front of the whole world." And no matter how much I envisioned this triumphant moment on the way over here, no matter how brilliantly I imagined myself telling him how I feel about him, now that the time is here I can't seem to formulate one sensible word.

All I have is the truth, which might not be enough.

He sighs. "Come on, Jenna. Let's go to my dressing room."

"I don't want to go to your dressing room," I tell him. "I want to talk right here."

"In front of half the cast?" he says.

"I don't care about that. I just want to stop this before it gets any more out of control, before we let another dumb misunderstanding come between us."

"What misunderstanding would that be?"

"How about that time you jumped to conclusions, and assumed the worst of me because of some crazy thing you invented in your own mind?" I ask. "Isn't that my job?"

"Jenna—"

"So if we're switching roles, here I am," I say. "You've put up with all my craziness, and everything I dragged you through, and you've always come back to try to work it out. It's my turn."

"Jenna—"

"And I have to make you listen to me, because what you walked in on this—"

He moves forward and grabs my wrist. "No," he says quietly. "Not here."

I drop my voice as well. "I need to tell you—"

"Not here," he says again, and turns and pulls me behind him as he strides to a door at the other end of the set.

I try to twist free but I'd probably have to break my own wrist to do it; he's not hurting me but neither is he letting me go. There's a hallway, then another door, then another hallway, then one last door with three names on a placard beside it. One of them is his.

Inside, the room is spare: a couple of chairs, a small sink and counter. Slightly grimy, dude stuff everywhere, plain walls. I step across the room—it takes all of five steps—and put my back against the wall opposite the door. He's not dragging me anywhere again. Especially since the only other place I can think of him dragging me is right out of here.

And I'm not going. Not without a fight.

He locks the door behind him and stands against it, looking at me with furious eyes. "Are you out of your mind?"

I shake my head. "I just wanted—"

"What part of you could possibly think that I want to stand there in front of my coworkers and listen to you make excuses for sleeping with Drew—"

"I didn't!"

He's obviously never going to let me get a word in edgewise, so I just steamroll over him.

He's trying to be quiet; I'm not, so I win.

"I know it looks bad, I know how it looks," I say, "but look at me. I'm here. I'm here because you're wrong, you're so wrong, and I can't let you go one more minute thinking—"

He crosses the room and traps me against the wall with a hand braced on either side of my head. He smells so good I could weep. "Do I look stupid? I saw what I saw." His eyes are locked on mine, and there's a storm brewing in them. He's furious, but there's genuine suffering layered under the fury. The air between us is charged with everything that's happened —all the misunderstandings and missed chances, all the mistakes we made.

Well, mostly the mistakes *I* made. There would be more trust between us if I hadn't been so *stupid* for ninety percent of the time we've known each other. One night, no matter how amazing, doesn't cancel that.

But I'm not leaving here until he believes me, so that's just going to have to be that.

"No," I say. "You're not stupid, I know what you saw." I reach up, take his face in my hands—this face that's changed my life completely in four short weeks. I speak softly, to ward off the storm, but firmly, so he knows I mean it. Every bit of what I feel for him has to be in this. Nothing held back. No fear that I might look dumb, no worry that putting myself on the line is too dangerous. "But you need to listen to me now, okay? I know I've been crazy. I know I've hurt you. And I know that what you saw this morning—"

He turns his head away.

I wait a moment, then gently turn it back, make him meet my eyes again. "I didn't sleep with Drew. I know how it looked. I know that it couldn't possibly have looked worse, but I didn't. I swear I didn't. He showed up at my door drunk as hell, and passed out in my living room, and I left him there instead of tossing him out the window—which I very much wish I had done, actually, all things considered. That's *it*. That's all of it. I promise, I swear to you, I wouldn't—I couldn't. Okay? I could never, not after you. Not after us. And I'm going to keep telling you until you believe it."

"He put his hands on you," he says, and his voice actually cracks. "Right in front of me. Like he had a right to."

"He doesn't have that right, and he never will again. If you'd waited five seconds before threatening him with bodily injury, I would have taken care of it myself." I let myself smile, just a little, because wouldn't that have been fun? "I only want one person to put his hands on me."

The storm breaks. He closes in all the way, pinning me against the wall and sliding an arm around my waist, a hand into my hair. His mouth comes down on mine, and his kiss is rough and dangerous, nothing like how he's kissed me before.

It's a claiming, and I know that; it seems that all Ryan's tutoring on the mysterious and territorial ways of the red-blooded American male has actually made an impact on me. Mitch is telling me—telling himself—that I'm his. Which is exactly what I want, anyway, so I slide my arms around his neck and kiss him back, hard, because that's what he needs.

He pulls back and drops his forehead against mine. "It

broke me," he says, his voice uneven. "I felt something inside me break."

"I know. I saw." I kiss him, softly. "I'll fix it. Let me fix it. I —" I falter, stumble over it. It's scary. But I take his face in my hands again, keep my eyes on his so there can be no doubt. "I love you. I love you so much I can't think straight. I don't even know when it happened, but I'm crazy, head-over-heels in old-fashioned love with you. When you walked out this morning, and I actually thought about what the rest of my life would look like without you in it? I wanted to be dead. I have never felt like this with anyone in my whole life, and I can't even imagine ever feeling this way about anyone ever again."

He doesn't move, doesn't blink. For a couple of seconds, he doesn't even breathe.

"Jenna," he says. Just my name.

"I love you," I say again, "and there's not going to be anyone else for me, not anymore. So unless you plan to let me grow old and die alone, and be eaten by my fourteen cats, you have to let me make this okay."

I was hoping for a smile, but instead he wraps both arms around me and buries his face in my hair. His "I love you" is muffled, but that doesn't matter.

"Good," I say. "You'd better." I rub the back of his neck, his shoulders. "After I came all this way, and in my best dress, you'd better love me."

He lifts his head; the storm is gone from his eyes. "I think I've loved you since I saw your face at Jacks that first night. Literally from that moment."

"I think I fell in love with your voice that night," I say, "but the rest of it took some time to catch up. I'm going to have to love you harder to make up for it."

My hands are shaking a little as I reach out and start unbuttoning his shirt. I almost lost him. I don't know what I would have done if I'd lost him.

And I've got to do something with all this adrenaline.

He slides his hands down my sides, rests them on my hips. "Is this really your best dress?" he asks. "I've never seen it."

I nod, opening the last button and sliding my hands inside his shirt. His skin is warm against my palms. "I've been saving it for a special occasion."

"I'll be careful with it, then," he says. His voice is low, rumbly—the exact sort of growl that frazzles my nerve endings—and his fingers brush the skin of my back as he slides the zipper down slowly. "You should wear it more often."

"I will," I say. And I pull it over my head and let it drop to the floor.

THE END

*(but definitely turn the page)*

# Wait, that's it?

I've taken a little flack for the ending of this book. ("What ending?!" you cry, and you are not alone.)

Some books lend themselves to a Happy-Ever-After—a proposal (maybe in public, maybe in bed), a ring, a baby … maybe all three—and I know that readers love them.

But some stories need a Happy-For-Now. When the conflict of the story is simply even getting *into* the relationship, as it is here with stupid Jenna and the ever-patient Mitch, sometimes the end really is just the part where they settle in to actually being together.

That's great and all, but if you're the sort that likes to see how it all turned out, what do you do now? As it happens, I've got some good news for you.

First, I'm at work on a separate, novella-length epilogue that takes place a couple of years after this book ends. I know where and how Mitch and Jenna find their HEA, and I'm about ready to give it to you.

Second—and maybe even better—I'm hard at work on a follow-up story about Kari (which people have been asking for literally since this book was released). Kari waited a long time for her perfect man, and I hope that you guys will agree he was worth the wait. That book should be out late this year (2018) or early next, and it's called *Mr. Right*. (Because of course it is. Did you honestly think it could be called anything else?) I should have a cover soon, and I think it's going to be a doozy; my new cover artist is a-ma-zing. I'll be sure to do a big splashy cover reveal for it.

"Tammi!" you're shouting (I hope). "How do I get access to these amazing things?!"

Well, good news. All you have to do is go to my website (tammilabrecque.com) and sign up for my newsletter. I'll send the bonus epilogue to the list as soon as it's ready, and I'll let you know when *Mr. Right* is available to purchase. It will be on all retailers, so go ahead and sign up no matter what store you buy from.

And keep reading if you'd like to see the updated Author's Note for *Mr. Wrong*. The original version got a Goodreads reviewer to leave me a three-star review instead of a one-star review, and I think that means it's a pretty great read!

———

# Author's Note

This is the story of how it took me 12 years to write *Mr. Wrong*.

It's a long one. Settle in.

I'll be honest: I don't know where to even start talking about this book. It's currently my favorite thing I've written, by far. I love the stupid, self-sabotaging dumbass at the center of it, and I love Mitch for sticking around until she got her shit together.

But this book was *hell* to create.

I first started writing it, on a borrowed laptop with a glitchy screen, for National Novel Writing Month (NaNoWriMo) in November of 2005. Yes, you're counting correctly—over a dozen years ago.

In 2005, I was a huge *General Hospital* fan, and very involved in the online soap fandom; SoapZone was my second home, and I made friends there that are still friends to this day. (If any of them are reading this, they're going to nail me on the bit of stolen Jax/Brenda dialogue. That's what us professional author types call an *homage*, guys.)

And yes, we did drive to big conventions (and small ones) to get autographs and pictures, and we did pay a guy who smuggled scripts out of the studio, and we did know an awful lot of backstage gossip. (Some of it might even have been true.)

We all had favorite couples, and favorite characters, and favorite actors, and banded together in groups united in our love for (or hatred of) any of those things. We made entire websites devoted to specific couples, and the actors that played them. And some of us gravitated to the ones who didn't get quite as much attention.

And there was one actor in particular—not even a contract actor, just an occasional appearance—with a voice that made female hormones sit up and take notice, and a lazy sexy drawl that could make a strong woman weak. That voice is where Mitch was born.

(This actor also had a predilection for plaid shirts with snaps. No way was that not going in there. The section where the snaps first make their appearance is virtually unchanged from the first draft.)

It was right around this time that I first heard of NaNoWriMo, and I thought, "Hell, why not?" I'd been writing since childhood, had even been published back in the 90s. I could do this.

So I gave *GH* a fake name, and the other ABC soaps, too, and I stuck Kari in there as an amalgam of me and my friends, and I said *what-if*? Not what if a soap fan fell in love with a soap actor—which is why Kari couldn't be the main character —but what if someone else did? Someone who would think he wasn't anything special and then discover he was everything. And so that was Jenna. And I stuck them in a story together, and gave her a bunch of terrible reasons not to like Mitch. (In the very earliest version, it was because he had a mustache. I wasn't always the towering talent I am today. *\*snicker\**)

I "won" NaNo that year—meaning that I got to 50,000 words, which is the goal of the challenge. The problem was, I didn't finish the book.

I had quite a lot of a book. I had the ending, very much as it is today. I had the beginning; in fact, that first line hasn't changed—not so much as a single letter or punctuation mark —since I first wrote it on November 18th, 2005.

(Oh, yeah, I left out that part. I started NaNo that year (my first year) working on a completely different book, and couldn't get anywhere with it. So I scrapped it on the 18th and started over, and I *still* managed to write 50,000 words of this book before the month was over. Go me!)

But what I didn't have was an awful lot of the middle. It was a mishmash of half-written dialogue, notes to myself, scene summaries, and then the occasional actual chapter, like signposts along the road telling me "This way to Mitch and Jenna's happy ending."

And what I *really* didn't have was real people who had real thoughts and feelings, and did things for reasons that made sense. I had some cardboard cutouts going through the motions.

It wasn't good enough.

So I put the book away, and I wrote something different for NaNo the next year, and something different the year after that, and so on. And every once in a while I'd drag out this manuscript and move some words around or add a scene. And in this way, over the course of nearly a decade, I cobbled together 70,000 words—and the story still sucked like a black hole.

And then, in the waning days of 2014, fresh out of a job and with a single short story published on the largest self-publishing platform, I did something crazy: I listed *Midnight Confessions* (which had been its name for many years at that point, though I can't remember what I called it initially) as a preorder, to be released in late March. That was 90 whole days away. Surely I could whip it into shape and put some … I don't know, *something*, in the middle and voila!

Then I opened the file, remembered what a disaster the whole thing was, and how it had been pieced together over ten very long and erratic years, and went straight into a panic attack.

When I recovered, I went to work. I had a deadline, and missing it would be catastrophic. (Retailers do *not* like it when you let customers down.) I thought most of the story worked, but some whole sections had to go. I had to change Jenna's profession because I no longer had access to the person on whom I had based her, who had a very specialized and unique job. I tried to update it to 2014, but at that point it had been 20 years since I lived in Manhattan, and I knew I was getting everything wrong. (Frankly, I probably got some of the 2004 details wrong too, but hopefully not too badly.) And, most important, soaps were no longer what they had been. The New York-based ABC soaps had all been cancelled, which made my plot literally impossible. The soap opera stuff was literally the backbone of the plot; it was more important to get that right than it was to know exactly what the bar scene on the Lower East Side was like in the mid-oughts, so I decided I knew enough to fake that part, and that the story was very much a product of its time. I left it in 2004 (TiVo! *Landline* phones!) and moved on.

It took me every single one of those 90 days to get the book ready. I wrote the studio tour scene literally the day I had to turn in my preorder, with only a few hours to spare, hoping I wasn't introducing any contradictions with anything I'd written a decade before. (*Spoiler: I was.*) And then I had to let it go. I had done the best I could in the short time I had given myself, and it was going to have to be good enough.

And it did *okay*, and got mostly good reviews, but I never got enough eyes on it to really go anywhere. I put a total of four covers on it over the 18 months it was published; none of them helped. I switched it into all kinds of other categories in the store; that didn't help either. The fact was, the book *wasn't* good enough, and I knew it.

And that was incredibly sad, because I loved the story, and

had such tender feelings for its origins and what it had meant to me.

Meanwhile, I'd started doing freelance editing for other authors, and was doing a lot more of that than I was writing. My books stopped selling at all, and I abandoned a series in the middle, which is a Very Bad Thing. Out of desperation more than anything, I began writing a totally ridiculous, over-the-top, smutty billionaire serial under a pen name. I fell absolutely in love with what I had initially called my "billionaire nonsense," and writing that story was the most fun I'd ever had with my clothes on; after very little time, the pen name was outselling my other books by quite a large margin. Which was great, but what about my Tammi books?

But what was done was done. My two standalone books were water under the bridge, and much as I loved them, I felt I had to look at them as failed experiments on my way to figuring out how to write a decent book. (The other book I'm talking about here was another NaNoWriMo novel, I screwed it up even worse than this one, and I'll be republishing that, too—once I figure out how to fix it.)

And then a friend said, "Why don't you do a quick revision and republish them under your pen name, now that you understand the market better?"

Well, hell. Why didn't *I* think of that?

So I unpublished them, got a new cover made for *Midnight Confessions* (now called *Mr. Wrong*, because that's obviously much better), and set a preorder for July 2017—three months away (because one thing you can say about me is that I never, ever learn).

Then I opened the file, and once again went straight into a panic attack.

The book, which I hadn't reread since it was published, was a *disaster*. No wonder it had never found readers. Jenna was flaky and unlikeable—and, even worse, she was unrelatable. There didn't seem to be much reason for the things she did, or the horrifically cavalier way she played with Mitch's feelings. I couldn't stand her.

And Mitch. Well. My fellow romance author (and, at the time, dear friend) Claire read the first half and asked me, quite bluntly: "Why does Mitch have a giant vagina?"

I laughed myself almost to death, and then when I was done I looked at the story with fresh eyes. She was right; the dude was a *doormat*. He never stuck up for himself, he never got mad at Jenna for being not just a flake but downright cruel, and when he found out about her night with Drew he called her up to offer a sympathetic ear. *I wrote that.* Hell, if I'd had him come over with some Ben & Jerry's and some tissues it wouldn't have been all that out of character, and I could have cut Kari out of the story. He and Jenna could have put their hair up in hot rollers and watched a chick flick. It was *awful*.

So I put together a short playlist of songs that told me what I *really* wanted this story to be about, what these characters were feeling that I hadn't gotten down on the page properly. (You can find that playlist at tammilabrecque.com/mr-wrong, if you're so inclined.) I dug in, tore the story apart, and put it back together using all the tricks I had learned over the eighteen months of editing that were now under my belt. I gave Jenna a better backstory, and some believable and understandable motivations. I made it obvious right from the beginning that Mitch kept coming around because she kept making it clear that she wanted him there, even if she was too damn stupid to figure it out. And I let Mitch stick up for himself, go toe-to-toe with her, and call her on her shit.

I had to replot the whole thing and write new scenes. I cut about 8,000 words, and then wrote 10,000 new ones. I had to write new lines in every scene that remained, and create whole new scenes to push the story in the direction it needed to go. Not a single word of the scene in Petrosino Square existed two weeks before I republished, and almost none of the scene where Mitch tells Jenna to lose his number. (Oh my God, how I cried when I wrote that scene—that line about another man's sweat? Kill me, right?) I combined a bunch of repetitious scenes, and went through every chapter with a fine-toothed comb. At last! The book it was always supposed to be! I wrote the first version of this Author's Note, then sat back and waited for the accolades from my beta readers.

*They fucking hated it.*

They both absolutely hated Jenna. *Hated* her. Were thrilled when Mitch left her, because it was exactly what she deserved. They pointed out all the places where I was asking people to believe impossible things and root for unlikable people. And the part where I just repeated a major conflict because hey, two is better than one, right? And the fact that the ending didn't ring at all true because frankly, at that point, there was literally no reason for Mitch to believe Jenna loved him.

I looked at the scenes they hated (which was, like, most of them) … and they were right. I had given Jenna a bunch of motivations that made sense in my head, and then I didn't put them on the page. I had made some huge plot errors, not the least of which was *more* repetitious back and forth. I thought I had Mitch stand up to Jenna (and I did), but they both insisted he *still* had more patience than any mortal man could possess.

So, back to the drawing board. I had patched this book together like Frankenstein's monster, and the seams were showing. There was no way I could do yet more patching; it all had to go.

Oh, and by the way? I'd already told everyone it would be out in a few days (which was not going to happen). And, even if I were comfortable missing *that* deadline, I only had ten days to work on it, because I was leaving the country. (Yeah, I set my preorder up to go live three days after I came back from an overseas vacation, because—in case you haven't caught on to this yet—I am really not very smart at all.)

I wrote a new outline, started the playlist back up. And I opened the broken book on one screen, a clean file on another, and started typing. I rewrote the whole thing from scratch, layering in all that Jenna was, all that she felt, all her motivations. We had to know her why, and she had to walk the walk. I had to figure out exactly where a real man's breaking point would be and bring Mitch right to the edge without pushing him over, and I had to cut an entire plot arc because it was utterly, completely unbelievable. (In my defense, when I first plotted this book, I was watching a *lot* of soap operas. "Believable" isn't really the criteria over there.)

A second round of beta reading. Better … but not quite there. The first two chapters were a total snoozefest. How had I not seen that?

Another round of edits. More consultation with my second-round betas. Some minor (thank God) tweaks.

And finally—*finally*—it was good enough. (I hoped.)

Again, it got some good reviews, people seemed to like it, but it didn't really resonate with my new set of readers. I didn't understand. Why didn't they like it? It was, if I said so myself, *really good now*.

And it was; I truly believe that. But what I failed to take into account was the the readers who'd met me under my new pen name expected something *very* different from me. *Mr. Wrong*, heartfelt and a little sweet, only slightly steamy, and (in my opinion at least) pretty funny, didn't dovetail *at all* with my billionaire nonsense, which was over-the-top but not at all tongue-in-cheek, written in a completely different voice, and—this part actually really matters—*super* filthy.

Both types of books were great, and I loved writing both of them. But readers that liked one generally didn't like the other. I was confusing them, and it was easier for them to just find another author—one who didn't jump all over and write such different books.

I realized, after some wailing and gnashing of teeth, that I needed to split my pen name into two pen names, so that readers of any particular book could know what to expect from books written by the same author. (This is Publishing 101, and the fact that I had been consulting and advising people of exactly this fact for years, without ever internalizing it to my own situation, is more than a bit embarrassing.)

And, of course, the only thing that made any sense to me was to bring this book of my heart back into the fold, so to speak—to publish it under my own name again. Yes, it was getting a little ridiculous to be shuffling it around in this way, but … whatever. I couldn't give up on this book. I love this book. So I pulled it from publication, got another (another! My god!) new cover, and here I am, putting it back out into the world—for the last time. Of that much, I am certain. I've done everything I can.

So that's what you've got in your hands now. I think that this story is a million times better than it was in its first incarnation, and I think you would agree if you saw it (which you never will because no way, man). I think that the frightened, vulnerable woman at its heart is someone we can all relate to (even as we want very much to throw her out her office window—too bad it doesn't open), and I think Mitch's quiet patience is admirable, but his eventual refusal to be jerked around anymore is believable and real.

I kept the voice, though, and the snaps. Because of course I did.

I have never done anything as difficult as writing and publishing this book—but I kept at it because I love it. I hope you loved it, too.

I owe an enormous debt to Claire Kingsley, who not only helped me get rid of Mitch's vagina, but also asked me *the* pivotal question in what I thought would be the last couple days of revision; it didn't fix the book but it brought it within reach of being fixable. Also I have to thank Katie Sullivan from the bottom of my heart for reading chapters hot off the keyboard and making incredibly insightful comments and suggestions. Nikki Quinn and Claire (again) slogged their way through a beta read of a book they hated and then spent literally *hours* answering my questions about how to fix it—and then read most of it *again* in bits and pieces as I made my way through, trying to repair it. It was one of the most generous things anyone has ever done for me, and I learned a ton from their critiques. And Ginger Forsyth and Nicki Ann Holt did the final beta read, showed me all the spots where I had still not quite hit the mark, and had an enormous impact on the first two chapters. If this book actually *is* any good at all, it's thanks to them.

One last thing, and I'm sorry to end with sadness, but this is important: While I was in the first major rewrite stage, in June of 2017, a very dear friend from those long-ago soap opera fandom days passed away unexpectedly. She was a champion for this book in its first incarnation, loved it despite its imperfections, and knew without having to ask exactly which characters were standing in for which real-life actors. She had only recently embarked on what was clearly going to be *her* happy-ever-after. Her light shone bright on everyone she loved, and she had one of the biggest hearts I've ever known. I'm better for having had her in my life, and the world is poorer without her. This new, better book is dedicated to her. Love you, JessB.

Tammi
9/10/2018

# About the Author

Tammi Labrecque lives in Bangor, Maine with two kids, three cats, and dozens of fictional characters that keep her awake nights.

She writes under a few pen names across several genres, including romance, fantasy, urban fantasy, mystery, LitRPG, and horror.

Under her own name, you can find her editing at larksandkatydids.com or teaching at newsletterninja.net.

*Connect with her at:*
FB: AuthorTammiLabrecque
Twitter: @tammilily
tammilabrecque.com

Gabriel ne pouvait s'empêcher d'embrasser Clara.

Il ne pouvait s'empêcher de la caresser.

Il ne pouvait s'empêcher de s'adonner aux sensations qui se répandaient dans son torse.

*Merde.*

Il n'avait jamais vécu une telle chose. Son corps était si tendu qu'il avait l'impression qu'il allait exploser sans même être en elle. Cela n'avait aucun sens et pourtant, pour la première fois de son existence, il choisit de ne pas chercher de recours pratique.

Au lieu de cela, il s'autorisa à *ressentir*...

Sexy.

Trop sexy... Bordel !

Il arracha la serviette du corps de Clara et avala son glapissement de surprise. Il maintint sa main dans ses cheveux, la retenant contre lui tandis que sa bouche la dévorait.

Le sexe n'avait jamais eu d'intérêt pour lui.

Pourtant, il mourrait s'il y mettait fin maintenant.

Tous les principes et apprentissages passés submergeaient son esprit, tentant de le ramener à un semblant de rationalité. Mais tout ce qu'il pouvait voir, c'était Clara. Ses seins nus pressés contre lui. Sa fine gorge où coulait le sang de la blessure qu'il avait créée. Sa respiration rapide et ses lèvres pulpeuses.

Il l'embrassa à nouveau, plus fort cette fois, la dominant de sa langue et gémissant sous l'effet des sons délicieux qu'elle produisait en retour.

Les décennies de sa vie paraissaient dérisoires face à cette passion, cette sensation, ce violent besoin de baiser.

C'était ce qui lui avait manqué lors de ses rencontres précédentes, ce désir ardent qui le faisait plonger dans une nouvelle réalité existentielle.

Il n'y avait aucune logique ici.

Aucun raisonnement.

Aucun édit.

Seulement du désir.

www.ingramcontent.com/pod-product-compliance
Lightning Source LLC
Chambersburg PA
CBHW031713170626
46808CB00005B/1727